This Large Print Book carries the Seal of Approval of N.A.V.H.

Waiting for Daybreak

Kathryn CUSHMAN

CENTER POINT PUBLISHING
THORNDIKE, MAINE

Library of Congress Cataloging-in-Publication Data

Cushman, Kathryn.
  Waiting for daybreak / Kathryn Cushman.
    p. cm.
  ISBN 978-1-60285-407-9 (lib. bdg. : alk. paper)
  1. Pharmacists--Fiction. 2. Competition (Psychology)--Fiction.
  3. Middle-aged women--Fiction. 4. Large type books. I. Title.

PS3603.U825W35 2009
813'.6--dc22

2008047223

to **Carl Parrish**—
A fabulous father and
a totally cool pharmacist

Paige Woodward sat in the Christmas Eve service, staring at the giant cross that hung above the pulpit of her parents' church and silently pleading with God. *We've been praying our hearts out, this whole church has been praying their hearts out.* She turned to survey the packed house. *Look at all of them. Mom has been a faithful servant to You all her life. Why are You letting this happen again?*

Her eyes began to sting, and she knew she needed to stay in control—by appearances at least. She needed to pretend to be strong, and in control, and full of faith, even if she was none of those things.

The congregation stood to sing "O Holy Night." Paige could hear the words coming from her mouth, so she knew she must be singing, but the beauty of the melody, the magnitude of the words, were completely lost on her. Each member held the candle they'd been given, and as the flame passed from person to person, the dark sanctuary filled with warm light. It had always been the most meaningful part of the service to Paige. Tonight, she merely went through the motions.

She looked again at the cross. *You know, if You heal her, it will show everyone Your power. The Bible says "ask and you shall receive." If she doesn't deserve Your anointing, who does?*

The cross hung silent and dark on the wall. As she'd expected, no answer came. The service ended; the candles were extinguished, leaving nothing behind but a wisp of smoke and the smell of what had once been.

Her family filed out of the sanctuary, speaking subdued greetings to friends, murmuring the ever cheerful "Merry Christmas," knowing that this year, it simply didn't apply to them. As soon as they walked out the door, nothing more was spoken. The three of them linked hands and walked through the parking lot in quiet solidarity.

Back at her parents' home, they seated themselves in front of the Christmas tree and turned on Christmas carols—it was what they always did on Christmas Eve, what they were supposed to do, even if no one felt like it this year. Her mother poured them each a cup of her traditional spiced tea. "Nice service."

Paige's father nodded. "Sure was."

"Beautiful." Paige tried to work some enthusiasm into her voice, but didn't really think it came through.

The room fell into silence as they sipped their warm drinks and stared at the tree. Paige couldn't help but wonder if they were all having the same thought. The same nagging, ugly question. Would this be their last Christmas together?

Paige stood and walked over to the tree. She put her hand on an ornament made out of plastic beads and pipe cleaner. "I can't believe you've still got this ugly thing."

"That is not ugly. It's beautiful. You made that for me when you were in kindergarten."

"Oh yes. Miss Charlton's class. Best teacher I ever had. She must be getting pretty old, I wonder how she's doing these days."

"The question is, how are you doing these days?"

Paige turned to look at her mother. "I'm doing just fine."

"We all know that's not true. It's time you told us what's going on."

Paige shrugged. "It hardly matters compared to your news."

"It matters plenty to me. To both of us."

Paige looked at her father, noticed the grim set of his jaw. He was prepared to meet this new crisis and do everything in his power to fix it, just like always. Only this time he couldn't fix it. None of them could.

"I've been fired."

His head snapped back. "Do what? I thought you were up for that promotion."

"Yeah, well, so did I."

"What happened?"

Paige had practiced all the ways that she would explain the whole process to her parents. Break it in a gentle way, explain the story slowly and logically, without any emotion. Somehow, sitting before the twinkling tree on Christmas Eve next to her mother, whose body had once again betrayed her, she forgot every word.

She looked at her father, unable to bear the shock in her mother's eyes. "They fired me because I killed a man."

chapter **one**

Ten Weeks Later

Paige Woodward contemplated the reinforced back door of Nashville's Free Clinic and the patchwork of blue covering the exterior. Each shade of navy, indigo, or azure covered another level of graffiti. The defacing spray paint wasn't gone, simply hidden beneath a layer of color that didn't quite match the original. Patch jobs. They didn't change the truth; they only covered it up.

She shook off the thought and put her key in the door. The musty odor never seemed to fade here, in spite of the janitorial crew's best efforts. This dingy lobby would soon be packed to capacity with illness, hunger, and hopeless faces looking to Paige for help—but she could only do so much. Some pain went beyond the bounds of medicine. She had been living that truth for the last few months.

Rufus Toskins emerged from a back hallway, wearing his usual overburdened expression, baggy suit, and bow tie. Paige stopped and waited for him. Today, at least, would bring good news, and now would be a perfect time for him to walk over and deliver it.

Rufus did not acknowledge her presence. In fact, he jerked his head around and blitzed through a door to the opposite hall—like a medical resident rushing toward a code blue.

Strange. Her stomach tightened, just a little. *You're imagining things. Get busy.*

The usual array of workers from the Richardson Construction Company passed through the lobby as they went from one wing to the other. One of the men—older than the rest, perhaps late sixties—walked over to her. "I need to take some measurements in the pharmacy. Okay if I come back there with you?" He wore a faded flannel shirt, scuffed boots, and a friendly smile.

Paige unlocked the glass door and held it open for him. "Have at it."

He nodded, then walked to the back wall of the dispensing area, measuring tape in hand.

Why was Rufus acting so funny? The thought would not leave her mind. She removed the stack of yesterday's prescriptions from their tray, put them in numerical order, then filed them in manila folders. She picked up the phone and retrieved voice messages, wiped down the faded surface of the chipped countertop, and washed her hands. Still, the door to the back hallway remained closed, with Rufus somewhere on the other side. *It's just not like him to turn away like that.*

A mistake? Just the thought of the word caused this morning's bagel to sink in Paige's stomach.

It couldn't be. She checked everything so carefully now. Please no. She jerked open the file of yesterday's prescriptions and flipped through it, one white rectangle of paper at a time. The doctors' black scribble varied in legibility, form, and neatness, but her own blue-inked initials beside the date and the drug manufacturer remained constant. She checked and rechecked what she'd written, looking for any hint of a slip. There was nothing. Of course there wasn't.

She allowed no room for error in her work. None. Never again.

At nine o'clock, Rufus emerged from the back hallway, unlocked the front door, and edged toward the pharmacy. He began to twirl a ring of keys in his hands, the keys jingling through repeated somersaults. Why wouldn't he look at her? "Paige, there's something I need to tell you."

"Something to tell me?" She adjusted the lapel of her lab coat. "Something like I'm off probation, I hope."

He put the keys in his pocket and looked up, but not quite at Paige. "Oh, well, yes, of course you are. But there's more to my news, unfortunately. Bad news."

Paige didn't want to hear any more. All that mattered to her was that she had completed her probationary period. She'd get a pay increase and full benefits. More important, she'd be returned to the ranks of the worthy for the first time since Atlanta.

Rufus tugged at his tie and shifted from side to side. Whatever it was, he obviously didn't want to say it any more than she wanted to hear it.

"Out of my way. This is an emergency. I'm dying." A shriveled woman in a filthy denim dress shoved Rufus aside and plopped her elbows on the counter. She pounded against her chest, coughed once, and pointed a bony finger at Paige. "I need you to give me one of these right now. I know all about the procedures, but give me a pill now, or I'll be dead and all that paper work won't matter." She wheezed again, as if to illustrate the point.

Paige took the prescription from the woman's hand. When she looked at the words scrawled in black ink, she took care to keep her face solemn. "Of course, Mrs. Stonehenge."

She hurried to the metal shelves, found the right bottle of pills on the lowest shelf, and tapped out a single capsule, blue on one side, clear on the other to reveal the dozens of blue and white beads inside. She put the capsule into a paper cup and rushed back to the woman. "There's some water just around the corner."

"Humph, if I live that long." Mrs. Stonehenge grabbed the cup from Paige's hand and bulldozed a path toward the water fountain.

Paige avoided eye contact with Rufus and began hammering out the label on their ancient typewriter. The behind-the-counter door squeaked and Rufus came to stand beside her.

"One of the funding sources for the foundation just dried up. So . . . no raises this year. That means you'll stay on probationary pay, even though you're off probation. In fact, after next month's budgetary meetings, everyone will likely take a pay cut."

The homeless clinic offered a small enough salary as it was, and probationary pay was ten percent less. *Don't they understand that my mother has cancer and my parents can't keep up with the bills? Don't they understand that I'm just now digging out of debt from being unemployed?* "They can't do that."

"This clinic is run by a private charitable foundation. They can do whatever they wish—including withdrawing all funding if it suits them. Given some of the rumors floating around here, I'd say we need to be grateful they're still paying us at all."

"Grateful? I have responsibilities. I need that money."

"That's the way life works. May as well accept that while you're young, because it'll only get worse by the time you're my age." He let himself out of the pharmacy without another word.

Mrs. Stonehenge returned, still thumping against

her chest, but no longer wheezing. "Good thing that stuff works so quick. I thought I was a goner there for a minute."

Paige forced herself to smile, although she felt her irritation rising. "I'm glad you're feeling better."

"Oh, child, just pray you never get as sick as I am."

The woman walked away, carrying her bottle of placebos that she believed to be a miraculous heart remedy. Sometimes just a little positive thinking worked better than medicine. *A good thing to keep in mind.*

"I've been watching you work the last few weeks. You're good with people."

Paige startled, having forgotten all about the man with the measuring tape in the back of the pharmacy. She wondered how much of the conversation with Rufus he'd overheard. "It's just part of the job."

"Maybe so, but some people have a gift for it, and some people don't. Name's Lee, by the way."

"I'm Paige."

"Well, Paige, my granddaughter's a pharmacist in Shoal Creek—she's brilliant when it comes to all the medical stuff, but dealing with the public is not exactly what you'd call her strong suit. You should go to work for her, so she could learn by example."

"What, and miss all this?"

He smiled as he pushed open the glass door that led to the lobby, then stopped at the customer counter. "You think about it over the weekend. I'll be back sometime next week, we'll talk more about it."

Paige laughed to herself. She'd think about it, all right. How could she help but be charmed by the man who thought he could hire help for his grand-daughter? She must be a very lucky girl to come from such a supportive family.

chapter **two**

Clarissa Richardson pulled into her father's driveway. Even in the late winter, the lawn looked manicured and inviting, the French country exterior warm and welcoming. The warmth and welcome ended right about there. Her fingers itched to turn the car around. But she couldn't.

She needed to get this done now. Most likely, her father and newest stepmother were either hosting a Friday night gathering or preparing to go to one. She should be able to make a quick getaway.

Alejandra, dressed in the usual black skirt and white apron, met her at the door. "They're on the sun porch, miss."

"Thank you." Clarissa walked toward the glassed-in room at the rear of the house, where she found her father and Becky sipping cocktails.

"Care to join us, sh-weetheart?" he slurred, eyes already starting to glaze.

Few things were more unbearable than Clarissa's snockered father, and since Becky was one of those things, the invitation held absolutely no temptation. "No, thanks. I just stopped by to pick up that set of china from the attic. I'm trying to get my condo all set up so I can get in touch with my domestic side."

"Good for you, sh-weetie."

Becky, wearing a skin-tight black skirt and a low-cut silk blouse, walked across the room and poured a healthy serving from the pitcher. "I had Alejandra empty all the stuff out of the attic last week so we could sift out the junk. Most of the boxes are still stacked in the garage. You may have to look around."

"Okay."

The doorbell chimed. Which group of social climbing, backstabbing acquaintances was coming over tonight?

Clarissa's uncle walked into the room, debonair as always, his boyish charm creating a welcome contrast to the overstuffed atmosphere. He looked at her and shoved his bangs away from his eyes. "Sweet Pea, no one told me you were going to be here. I'd have come a little earlier if I'd known."

"Tony!" She threw her arms around him.

"You look beautiful. The pharmacy business must be agreeing with you."

"Well, you need a haircut, so the construction

business must not be agreeing with you." She laughed, then drew back from the hug. "What are you doing here?" *Surely you're not spending a Friday night with these two.*

"Just talking a little business with your dad." He sat in an upholstered rattan chair and patted the one beside it. "Sit down. Tell me how things are going down south."

"What kind of business?" Clarissa knew her family too well to believe that this gathering was some nonimportant issue. More than just age separated Tony and her father. They never saw each other socially. Something was up.

"Weren't you heading toward the garage?" Becky looked at her pointedly.

"As a matter of fact I—"

"I'll walk with you, Sweet Pea." Tony, ever the peacemaker, started for the hallway, pulling Clarissa along before she said something she'd perhaps regret not regretting.

They found the garage and both began looking through boxes.

Tony said, "Our little meeting should be done in an hour or so. You want to come over and hang out? Pizza and a movie?"

"I'm meeting some friends downtown. Join us. You need to get out more." It was true. Besides, he was dressed for it. Nice jeans. Simple polo. Great shoes. He was more of a handsome older brother than an uncle.

"I'm too far past my prime for carousing. Your old uncle can't keep up like he used to."

You kept up just fine before the divorce. "Don't use that 'old uncle' stuff on me. You may be my uncle, but you're not that much older than I am."

"There's a lot of difference between thirty and twenty-two. Trust me."

"I'm twenty-five, and no there's not." She got to the final pile of boxes and looked through them all again. "I don't see it anywhere. Guess I'll have to go ask the step-monster."

He followed her back down the hallway. "So . . . you never answered my question."

"What question?"

"How are things going with the pharmacy?"

She shrugged. "About like you'd expect, I suppose."

"You know, Dad only wants the best for you."

"I know, but I wish he'd told me what he thought was 'best' before I declined that residency at Johns Hopkins. I stayed because I wanted to open a *Parrish Apothecary* franchise, in *Nashville*, in the *exact building* where Grandma used to work. I know that probably sounds ungrateful, but don't you think he could have let me know his plans sometime before graduation day?"

When they neared the sun porch, Becky's nasal voice echoed down the hallway. "I'm telling you, he's giving it all away. There won't be anything left of an inheritance if he doesn't stop it. Maybe we should look into his mental state. Has he been seeing a shrink? A doctor? Anything?"

"Good idea. We should look into that."

A low growling noise came from Tony's throat as they turned the corner. "Dad's as sane as anyone and you know it. He earned his money, he has the right to do with it as he sees fit."

Clarissa understood the meeting now. It was all about trying to keep Granddad's money in the family and out of the ledgers of charities nation-wide. Since Grandma's death three years ago, his way of dealing with the pain had been through phi-lanthropy—something that caused her father increasing alarm. Something that had also sen-tenced Clarissa to a pharmacy in a podunk town, with parole only possible after a year of good behavior. Or more correctly, after a year of meeting nearly unattainable goals.

As much as she felt bad about abandoning Tony to face all this alone, she knew better than to stay. She needed to get her stuff and get out. "Becky, I didn't find the box in the garage. Is there some-where else it would be?"

Becky gasped. "I hope you didn't mean that old set of Wedgwood that was in the back corner."

"Of course that's what I meant."

Becky contorted her face into the fakest look of shock Clarissa had ever seen. "I got rid of it."

"You what?"

"I sold it to that used china shop several weeks

ago. I'm sure those place settings are scattered all across Tennessee by now. I never realized you wanted it."

"It said 'Save for Clarissa' all over the box in big red letters."

"Did it? You know how it is, after a few hours all those boxes start looking alike. I must have missed it somehow."

"That china belonged to my grandmother. She gave it to me. It was *mine*."

"Then maybe you should have stored it yourself, rather than leaving it to clutter things around here." Becky took a long swallow of the drink in her hand and looked evenly at Clarissa. She'd taken Grandma's china, just to prove she could. "I really am sorry. Just an honest mistake."

There was no *honest* or *mistake* about it. Clarissa looked at Becky's throat and pictured her hands wrapped around it, squeezing with every ounce of her strength.

"You know what, Sweet Pea, downtown sounds like a good idea, after all. Come on, I'll walk you out to the car, and we'll figure out where to meet up." Tony took her arm and gently pulled her away from the room.

He waited until she climbed into her car to say anything more. "I'll call you on my cell when we're done here. Believe me, it won't be long. I can't deal with this, even if he is my brother."

"Tell me about it." She turned the key in the ignition. "Okay, I'll be waiting for your call. No backing out this time, promise?"

"Promise."

As she pulled from the driveway, she could still see him in her rearview mirror, standing on the porch of her father's home. It suddenly occurred to her that of all the people she'd ever loved or who had ever loved her, her uncle Tony was all she had left.

chapter **three**

Paige made the hour commute from the Nashville Clinic to her parents' home every few weeks, yet it didn't surprise her a bit that the first thing she noticed when she pulled into the driveway was the white paper banner taped to her parents' white garage door. WELCOME HOME PAIGE.

Ever since her mother had taken an adult ed computer class, she looked for excuses to demonstrate her prowess at the printer. This particular banner consisted of four sheets of paper taped together, with hot pink letters making up the words and a picture of a banana split printed faintly in the background. A masterpiece of clip art if ever her mother had created one.

In the front bay window she saw her old lab, Dusty, push himself up on his three good legs to bark. Her father came to peek, disappeared, then flung open the front door. "There's my girl." He came down the porch steps as fast as his arthritis would let him. "I am so glad to see you." He put his arms around her and didn't let go. There was a hint of desperation in that hug.

"Dad, are you all right?"

"It's going to be okay, Paige, it's going to be okay. We're gonna get through this just fine."

Get through this? When her mother's cancer relapsed three months ago, it had been hard on all of them. But something else was going on here, something fresher. Something worse. "What are we going to get through?" She pulled back so that she could look at her father's face.

He squinted his eyes against the March sun. "Your mother . . . she did call you, right?" He rubbed the back of his neck and looked everywhere but at Paige. "I was sure she called you."

"What was she supposed to call me about?" Fingers of dread began to wrap around Paige's heart. When she looked into her father's eyes and saw the absolute despair in them, the fingers began to squeeze. Hard. This could only mean one thing.

"The treatment's not working this time. Doctor says we're almost out of options, but he's looking into some clinical trials. He said he'd call us on Monday and let us know if he could find anything."

She wanted so much just to collapse against her car. Anything that could support her. But she knew what that'd do to her father. "Well, all right then.

That's what we're aiming for." She squared her shoulders. "Where is she?"

"Out back, sitting on her bench."

Paige nodded. "I'll go talk to her." She reached down to pet Dusty. "Come on, boy."

He hobbled alongside her around the back of the house and across the weathered patio. The surface was faded and worn from years of family picnics, roller skating, and late evening gab sessions. How could the same woman whose joy of life could wear out concrete be losing the fight to keep that life?

Her mother was seated on the bench at the corner of the property, in the dull shade of her favorite oaks. Her eyes were closed, her hands clasped in her lap. Was she resting or praying? Dusty went to lie at her feet, while Paige sat beside her. "Hi, Mom."

Her mother's eyes flew open. "Oh, sweetie, you're home." She threw her arms around Paige and squeezed tight. The cherry-almond scent of her Jergens lotion brought back a wave of happy memories so strong that Paige had to swallow back the tears.

"I wasn't expecting you this early."

"Really?"

"Let me guess, your father called you with the news and you got all upset and left work early. That's why I wasn't planning to tell you until later." She cut a hard look at her husband, who was leaning against the nearest oak.

He folded his arms across his chest. "I did no such thing. I said I wouldn't, and I didn't. I thought you were—"

"Mom, he didn't call. It's seven o'clock, I've been off work for almost two hours."

"Oh dear, the time must have gotten away from me."

A cold wind blew, causing the tree limbs above them to bend with the force. The sound of a crow's *caw* came from nearby as it searched for something to eat in the bleak landscape of late winter.

Paige reached over and held her mother's hand. "I'm just glad I'm here now."

Her mother looked into the tree above them. "Do you remember when we used to have a swing on that limb?"

"Yes, Daddy spent hours getting it set up just right."

"You and I would spend hours out here. I can still see your hair flying behind you—no wonder it was always so stringy when you were a kid. You would sing that song about the daring young man on the flying trapeze at the top of your lungs, swinging so high you'd sometimes get caught up in the branches. I'd sit right here on this bench, and knit, and read, and sing right along with you."

The limb above had two smooth places, its bark stripped away by the ropes once tied there. If friction and pressure could wear down a giant tree, what chance did Paige and her family stand? "That was a long time ago."

"Yes, it was. But it doesn't seem like it's been any time at all, it just moves too fast." Her mother ran her hand down the length of Paige's hair. "Who would have thought that stringy-haired kid would grow into such a beautiful young woman?" She covered Paige's hand with her own and squeezed. "Oh, honey . . . we all knew this would happen."

"Did we?" Paige whispered.

"Of course we did." Her mother's tone sounded as crisp and clear as if she were announcing a planned trip to the market. "That's part of the fun of being 'treatable not curable.' "

"I fully expect your doctor to call first thing Monday morning, having found the perfect clinical trial that will put you in remission and keep you in remission."

Her mother looked at her father. "I bet you didn't tell her that other part, right?"

"What other part?" Paige looked at her father.

He shrugged in response. "Doesn't matter."

"What other part, Mom?"

"A lot of clinical trials aren't covered by insurance, since they are considered experimental. Your father and I don't have extra money to be throwing around, looking for some miracle cure that doesn't even exist."

"I can help."

Her father shook his head. Her mother wouldn't hear of it. But Paige insisted and insisted that she'd do anything for them, and by the time dinner was ready they'd both agreed.

Now she'd just have to figure out a way to find the money they needed.

chapter **four**

Clarissa stood behind the counter of the pharmacy in this place that she hated and wondered how she got into this. She knew the answer full well, and it all began on what should have been one of the happiest days of her life. Graduation day.

She still remembered walking across the platform, shaking the dean's hand. It's funny, she could still see the sheen of sweat on the former senator's bald head as he droned on and on with all the usual "go forth and conquer" rah-rah. She could still smell the tang of whiskey on her father's breath as he announced his engagement to Becky.

Granddad's voice was the only sound she still heard clearly. "Well done. Mighty proud of you, young lady." This was as high as the praise came from Granddad; Clarissa accepted it for the gift it was. He shook her hand and smiled. "I've got some good news."

"Really? What?" She had known—or at least thought she knew—what was coming here. She knew her grandfather had been spending lots of time with Milton Parrish, and if anyone could talk someone into selling a franchise, it was her grandfather.

"We're going to put a pharmacy in the theater we bought in Shoal Creek."

"A theater? Shoal Creek?" Several heads turned in their direction, and Clarissa knew her voice had risen above the crowd.

"It's a small town about an hour south of Nashville. Milton Parrish and I have been talking. We agree that Shoal Creek will be a great place for you to get started, you know, get your feet wet in a small stream before you try surfing the ocean. The theater has such beautiful architecture; I know you'll love the building."

"A Parrish Apothecary franchise, in Shoal Creek? What about the Lancaster Building?"

"Not a Parrish Apothecary, exactly. We're going to name it Richardson Apothecary, I'll own seventy-five percent, Milton is buying twenty-five percent interest. You'll have the same buying contract with the drug companies that his apothecaries do, this one just won't be so high-end—it will cater more to the small-town everyman. It's something he'd been wanting to try anyway, this presented the perfect opportunity. If it succeeds, he plans to launch several more stores under the Richardson Apothecary name, all falling under the umbrella of his franchise."

"But I just bought a condo in Nashville. I was planning to open a *Parrish Apothecary* in the

Lancaster Building as soon as I've worked off my intern hours."

"Don't worry, I still own the Lancaster Building, it's not going anywhere. I've extended the current tenant's lease by eighteen months. In the meantime, you'll work off your six months of intern hours in Nashville as planned, then you'll commute an hour to your new store in Shoal Creek. Lots of people drive longer than that each day. And you *will* open a Parrish Apothecary—if you work hard and prove yourself. Milton says if you can make the Shoal Creek location a success within a year, he'll sell you exclusive franchise rights for Nashville, maybe even all of Tennessee. I think that's a fair deal. Don't you?"

"I . . . guess so." Clarissa hugged her grandfather, trying to be truly grateful. He was building her a pharmacy, she knew that it was more than most of her classmates would receive. But . . . it wasn't what she wanted. "Thank you so much." She could only picture what the city of Shoal Creek would be like. Away from her friends, no support of any kind. Yet she would do what she always did, work hard and hope to earn her family's approval.

And that's just what she'd spent these last months trying to do. Now as she watched her grandfather walk down the aisle of the pharmacy, she found herself hoping once again. Hoping maybe this would be the day.

He walked back into the dispensing area. "How's your day been?"

"Fine. Good. We're getting a little busier every day."

"That's what I like to hear. We want to do everything in our power to make this place a success, don't we?"

Make it a success at least long enough to get me out of this place. "Yes, we do."

"Do you have the reports ready for me?"

"Back there on the desk."

He went to the desk along the back wall and began to pore over the financial reports from her first three months of business. His mouth tightened at every line. "I can't believe you're still losing money at this rate, I thought you'd have a much better customer base by now."

"People stick with what they're used to. I told you up front it would be nearly impossible to do anything better than break even by the end of the year. Do you believe me now?"

Her grandfather shook his head. "You have to do what it takes to bring people here to shop. Make them see that it is worth the drive to the town square because they'll get much better service here. Milton's apothecary chain is so famous for its customer-oriented service that people don't care that they are paying more for their medicine."

"Parrish Apothecary has locations in Beverly Hills, Los Gatos, and Manhattan. The people there don't care if they're paying more, because twenty extra dollars doesn't mean a thing to them. This is Shoal Creek, Tennessee. The people here work in factories, they farm, they make their own clothes. Customer service hoopla doesn't mean anything here, a low price is the only thing that matters."

"Customer service matters to everyone. I think you should hire some more help. It would make things less pressured, more friendly."

"I've got a technician for back here and a clerk out front. That's more than I can afford."

"How many hours you working a week?"

"Sixty, seventy sometimes. But that's why I'm telling you, Granddad, I'm doing everything humanly possible in here. It's not working yet, but we do move closer every month."

He looked at the numbers again. "I'd really like to see you make some great efforts in projecting a more friendly, small-town image. That's what'll bring the people in."

How dare he tell her how to run a pharmacy. He'd hardly stepped foot in one. Even when Grandma was sick, he always sent Clarissa to pick up her meds.

Funny, she could still see Felicia's knowing expression when she handed her the prescription blank, the way she walked with complete confidence, the way she spoke as if she had all the answers. Clarissa had known then that she wanted to be a pharmacist, to be someone as smart and assured as that. And here she was. But something wasn't working the way it was supposed to.

"I'm telling you, it's going to take more time."

"Well, we don't have it, as you know. Milton Parrish has given us until the end of this year to make this place work. As if that's not enough, now I've got your father pestering me because that new wife of his wants to put a yoga studio in the Lancaster Building."

"A what?"

"Yoga studio. He says that since that part of town is considered chic right now, it would be a surefire hit."

"What did you tell him?"

"I told him you were working hard down here and I would wait until the end of the year to decide. When the current tenant's lease is up, I'll give the new lease to the person most deserving."

Clarissa looked at her grandfather and wondered what exactly she had to do to be deserving in his eyes. Whatever it was, she didn't think she'd found it yet.

chapter **five**

Monday afternoon, Paige sat at the kitchen table listening to her parents' end of the phone conversation. How she wished they had a third extension. She wanted to take the phone from her father's hands—after all, she was the trained medical professional here. She should be the one talking to the doctor. But she knew that was not the way her parents wanted it. They wanted to run their own lives.

Finally, they hung up. "Well?"

"There is a clinical trial he thinks she would be a good candidate for. It's happening in Houston, at M. D. Anderson Cancer Center. It involves a stem cell transplant, some radiation, I don't know. So far, there have been eight other patients with your mother's kind of lymphoma to go through it. Five of them have done real well, the other three, well . . . I guess they were sort of like us, they didn't have much to lose."

"So, what's the next step, looking for a donor match?"

"Your aunt Opal's already won the donor lottery. They tested her a while back, thinking we might need a transplant at some point. For some reason siblings are better than husbands or daughters. That woman is so competitive, she even wins blood-typing contests."

"Well, I won't begrudge her this victory if she can help Mom. When do we get started?"

"We don't," her mother said. "We can't afford it, so there's no use thinking about it."

"How do we know?"

"There's already been some conversation between the hospital and the insurance company. They've apparently convinced them to cover a portion of it, but it'll still be about twenty thousand dollars out of pocket. They want her to fly in next Monday for some preliminary tests. I, for one, think she should go."

Twenty thousand dollars.

Paige thought about the raise that she didn't get. She thought about the small nest egg she'd put away for a house someday. Still, she would do without food and shelter if that's what it took to get her mother treatment.

"They said we'd be in Houston for almost four months. We can't leave the house alone that long, not to mention poor Dusty." Her mother reached down to scratch Dusty's waiting chin.

"What if I moved in here? I could take care of the house and Dusty, and I'd still be in commuting distance to work." *Okay, it would be a really long commute, but doable.* "It will be good for me to be living here with the two of you, for when you need . . ." Paige stopped the sentence, but it was too late to stop the thought. She affected a bright voice and tried to undo some of the damage. "My lease is up in a month anyway. I was going to renew, but now I can just pay you guys rent instead."

"Rent?" Her father looked positively scandalized.

"Daddy, I'd rather pay for a whole house than half of a tiny apartment somewhere."

"Most people pay someone to house-sit for them, they don't have the house sitter pay them rent. Especially not their own daughter."

The doorbell rang. Paige jumped to her feet, more because she needed to move than she cared who was at the door.

The man standing on the front porch had a couple of days' growth on his face and wore frayed jeans and a T-shirt that said *Jackson Plumbing*. He smiled and said, "Evening, beautiful."

She tightened her grip on the door handle in case she needed to slam it shut in a hurry. "Can I help you?"

"I talked to Norman this morning, told him I'd be by for a look-see."

"A look-see?"

"Well, you know, don't want to buy anything sight unseen." He winked at her and snorted what she supposed was meant as a laugh.

"What, exactly, are you planning to buy?"

"Truck, tools—the usual. I'm Sam Jackson. He didn't tell you I was coming?"

Paige looked him straight in the eyes. He appeared perfectly sane, no shifty glances like he was lying. Still, he had to be. "Just one minute, please."

She closed the door in Sam Jackson's face, taking care to lock it behind her. She walked into the living room and looked at her father. "Daddy, there's a man named Sam Jackson here. What are you selling to him?"

"Paige, you can't do everything for us. I've got to make sacrifices, too. Anything to make certain your mother gets the help she needs."

When they opened the door, Sam Jackson was already circling her father's truck. They walked out to the driveway to join him. "You got some real nice stuff here." He opened a tool box and removed a set of prized wrenches. "Really nice stuff."

Paige stood with her father for the next half hour, watching Sam Jackson look through every compartment, touch every tool. "I'll be in touch."

"You have my cell number, right?" her father asked.

"Yep, got it right here." The man patted a piece of paper in his T-shirt pocket and climbed into his filthy white truck.

"How can you consider selling to him, Dad? Look at his truck."

Her father's truck was always pristine as a matter of pride. Just the thought of it belonging to this man, whose own truck was covered in dirt, windshield dotted with grime, caused her stomach to ache.

"Honey, I'm sixty-seven. Most men my age are already retired. Besides, I'm not really planning to sell right away, I'm just covering my bases. If things get worse than we expect, I want to know exactly what I have and what I don't have to work with. Knowing what my stuff'll bring gives me an idea exactly how much of a fallback I have."

"Promise you won't sell."

"I promise I won't if I don't have to."

She stared into the sky. *God, help us get through this. Help me get a raise, so my father doesn't have to sell his things.*

chapter **six**

Paige came into work the next day a woman determined. She would go over Rufus's head straight to the charity board of directors if that's what it took, but she was going to get that raise. It had been part of the deal when they hired her. She'd kept up her end of the bargain; it was time for them to live up to theirs.

Without even putting her things away, she headed straight for the administrator's office. The hall was coated with fine sawdust from the construction, and she left footprints in her wake. Rufus's door was open when she reached it, and inside he was shaking hands with a beautiful woman in an expensive red pantsuit. She wore three-inch heels, and her blond hair was perfectly shaped to reveal the diamond earrings that sparkled at her ears.

"Oh, sorry, didn't realize you had company."

Rufus's face was as grim as Paige had ever seen it. The woman barely looked at Paige. Just said her farewells and clicked her way down the hall through the mess.

"The good news just keeps on coming," Rufus said when the woman was out of sight.

"What now?" They began making their way back through the dusty halls to the pharmacy.

"They found mold in a back wall yesterday. We're open the rest of the week, then they're shutting us down for two weeks to deal with it." The monotone in Rufus's voice reminded Paige of a robot reciting words whose meaning it couldn't understand or begin to feel.

"Shutting us down?"

"Without pay."

"Rufus, I need my raise and I need the money for those two weeks. As much as I hate to go over your head, I have to. I'm going to call the Weber Foundation and take this to the board of directors."

"Call all you'd like. That was Susan Weber who just left. She came to deliver the news personally."

Paige unlocked the pharmacy door and sank into the chair behind the desk. "Why would they do that?"

"Because they choose to." Rufus looked around as if to confirm that no one else was watching. "Word is, they want to sell this building and use the money to fund one of their new pet projects that the country music stars are all excited about. If I were you, I'd get my résumé together."

"That doesn't make any sense. Why would they go to the expense to renovate it, then?"

"The answer is obvious. A higher asking price." Rufus reached inside his coat pocket and pulled out a folded section of newspaper. "I've already ripped out the part that applies to me, I thought I'd leave the rest with you."

Paige flipped open the fold to see *Want Ads* at the top. The same numbness that she'd heard in Rufus's voice seeped into her limbs. "Thanks, Rufus."

"You're welcome." He walked away, his shoulders even more stooped than usual.

Paige started her usual morning tasks, amazed that her body could still function when her mind could not. Closed for two weeks. Without pay. How was she supposed to help with her parents' twenty-thousand-dollar debt without a paycheck coming in at all?

As for the résumé, she knew exactly what would happen in a job hunt. She'd experienced it through dozens of job interviews before coming to the clinic. As soon as potential employers punched her name into Google, any chance of a job disintegrated. The story never vanished. There was no easy alternative for her.

"Can I come back there? I need to do some work up in the ceiling." Lee, the old contractor she'd met last week, stood smiling at the counter.

Paige opened the door for him. "You're starting to make a habit of this."

"Yeah. This is the nicest place to be in the whole building, far as I'm concerned."

Customers streamed through the newly opened doors, and the first three came straight to the pharmacy. Paige started to work at the typewriter, grateful to be too busy to think.

"Hello there. You haven't changed your mind about marrying me, have you?" Joe dropped his container on the counter and waited. No last name, no nothing. Just Joe. Every few weeks he came in to get his asthma inhaler, and to propose to Paige. In truth, he was the closest thing to a friend she had in Nashville.

She smiled at him but kept typing. "Not this time, Joe, but you're looking mighty dapper today. Is that a new shirt?"

He rubbed his wrinkled hand across the blue plaid flannel and grinned. "Yep. Got it last week, but didn't put it on until today. Wanted it to look good for you."

"That's a nice color on you." She finished typing and put the label on a bottle.

"That's what the lady at the mission said. Said it makes my gray hair look brighter."

"It sure does." She walked over and picked up his container. "Why don't you have a seat? It'll be a little bit."

Joe winked and walked toward the waiting area.

Paige turned her attention to the seat beside him. "Mr. Tims, yours is ready."

Paige opened the drawer and looked at the stack of plastic cards. She reached for the one on the top, but drew back her hand. She needed every penny she earned right now; she couldn't afford to be helping people who had made bad life choices. Still, as she watched the skeletal man in threadbare pants and dirty coat push from his chair and pad toward her, she picked up the card and dropped it into his bag.

Probably no more than fifty, a life hard-lived left him looking old and defeated. "'Bout time." He stretched out his hands, gnarled from arthritis and years on the street.

"Be sure to take that with some food or milk, okay?"

"Not much of that on the streets these days." He turned and shuffled across the lobby.

Paige got busy working on the next order in line.

"Thanks! Thanks a lot!" Everyone in the lobby turned toward the sound. Mr. Tims stood at the front entrance, waving the card in the air.

Paige smiled and waved. She could feel every eye in the place locked on her. So much for being discreet.

Lee took a step down the wooden ladder and nodded toward the door. "What was that all about, if you don't mind my asking?"

"I put a Kroger gift card in his bag. Not much, but enough to get him something to eat."

"Really?" He took another step down. "You do that for all your patients?"

"Can't afford to." In fact, she couldn't afford the one she'd just given out.

"So, how do you choose then?"

41

"I don't know. Sometimes it just feels—right. In this particular case, his medication works better if it's taken with food. And, you can tell by looking at him he hasn't had much to eat lately."

"Like I said, you're good with patients. You think any more about my offer?"

"What offer was that?"

"Working with my granddaughter, of course."

"I'm sure I'd love to work with your grand-daughter, but don't you think she'd prefer to hire her own help?"

"Maybe so, but I own the place. I can hire who-ever I like." Lee smiled smugly, climbed back up the ladder, and stuck his head above the acoustic tiles.

Paige knew that Lee was just talking; she knew better than to hope, but it was the only particle of anything remotely resembling hope that she'd seen in several days now. She pressed a label onto the container in front of her. "Joe, got you ready."

Joe shuffled to the counter. "Thank you, pretty lady." He leaned forward and whispered. "Got Mr. Richardson himself working back there with you, huh? You must feel pretty important."

"No. His name is Lee. He just works for Richardson."

"Name's Lee, all right. Mr. Lee Richardson. That's the big man himself."

Joe couldn't possibly know what Lee Richardson looked like, and Lee Richardson couldn't possibly be some guy in flannel and boots. Richardson Construction trucks were all around the city. The man who owned the company undoubtedly spent his days in designer suits in a big corner office. Not climbing ladders. "And how would you know that?"

"Worked for him, once. Long time ago." The crinkles around his eyes turned down. "Nice man. Fair." His head nodded slowly as if lost in memory. "Well, I'll see you soon." He winked and disappeared out the door.

"Okay, all done." Lee folded the ladder and tucked his arm between two rungs. He walked over to Paige. He picked up the newspaper, folded on the counter with a big red circle around the ad for a pharmacist at Centennial Hospital.

"I didn't think you wanted another job."

"We're about to shut down for two weeks without pay, and finances are beyond tight for me right now. Centennial has a full-time position with a rather generous signing bonus. I could use that money."

"How much did you spend on that homeless man's gift card?"

Paige shrugged. "More than I probably should have, but he's desperate, too. Maybe that's why I wanted to help him."

"What if I offer a twenty-percent pay raise over what you're making now and a signing bonus. What was the hospital offering?"

"Three thousand dollars. Half on hiring, the other half after three months."

"Okay, I'll offer five. Same deal. Half on hiring, half after three months."

This was a dream job, with better pay, at a critical time. It all seemed too good to be true. What was the catch? Paige knew the answer.

Lee Richardson did not have all the facts.

Paige knew she could open her mouth right now, and in less than a moment's time, the job offer would be withdrawn. "Has your granddaughter been looking for someone else to hire?"

"No, she's working a lot of long hours, trying to do it all herself." He smiled then, a smile of true pride. "Comes about that trait honest enough. And she's doing well. I just think she needs a little more of what you're so good at. Someone that takes the time to see her patients as real people, not just someone to help keep the bills paid. Know what I mean?"

"Maybe she won't agree."

"Maybe not at first, but it won't take her long to come around. I started my own company over forty years ago, and gut instinct has never proved me wrong. Bringing you into that store is just what it needs. How soon can you start?"

If Lee Richardson's gut didn't tell him to ask some more questions, there was no reason Paige should volunteer anything, especially given the unfairness of the situation. She didn't want to leave the clinic, but if the ship was sinking she needed off. And Shoal Creek would be only minutes from her parents' house. The signing bonus alone would make up a big chunk of what her mom needed, and her mom came first right now. After all, hadn't she just been praying for an opportunity like this? "How's Monday?"

"Great. Here's the address. I'll meet you out front and take you in and introduce you to Clarissa." He handed her a piece of paper with the address written on it. "I'll see you Monday morning."

Paige could barely wait for him to walk out of the pharmacy before picking up the phone. "Dad, don't you dare sell your things. You're not going to believe what's just happened."

chapter **seven**

Paige sat with her mother on their garden bench for one last time before they said good-bye.

Her mother leaned her head over onto Paige's shoulder. "What's the pharmacy like? In Shoal Creek, I mean?"

"I haven't seen it yet, but I gather it's a little independent set right on the square inside the renovated old movie theater."

"Oh, I've heard about that. Some construction company from Nashville bought up most of the square—restoring it into something beautiful, I hear."

"That's right. You know, it's pretty close to my

dream come true. A quaint pharmacy in a small town, where I know my customers by name."

"'Delight yourself in the Lord and he will give you the desires of your heart.' That's from Psalms—somewhere. I wish I could remember references better. Anyway, point is, we trusted God through all this and He has provided."

"I wish I had your faith, Mom. And your memory for Bible verses." Paige smiled, realizing how true it was. God had provided yet another job just when she needed it. She could count on Him to make everything else work out, too. Right?

Her father called from the back door. "Okay, Doris, we're ready to go."

Paige helped her mother to her feet, and the two of them made their way toward the car. "Make sure to walk Dusty twice a day. He'll pretend he's too old and crippled to go, but once you let him know you're not falling for it, he'll go a pretty good distance. Let him roam around the backyard, too."

"Don't worry, I've got it covered. And yes, I'll keep an eye on the roses if they need watering. Now, get in that car and go to Houston. I don't want to see you around here again until you are all better. Understand me?"

Her mother sank into the passenger seat, too weak to continue the pretense of resistance anymore. "I'll do my best."

Paige gave her father an extra-long hug. "Take good care of her."

"Course I will." He kissed Paige on the top of her head. "See you in July."

July. How could four months sound like such a long time?

Her mother rolled down her window. "Keep praying."

"I will." Paige wondered how her mother never seemed to lose faith. She hoped she would possess that kind of strength someday. In fact, she hoped for some of it before she started her new job. She had no idea what she would be facing when she got there.

She watched her parents pull out of the driveway and suddenly felt very alone.

chapter **eight**

Paige spent the rest of the weekend packing up her closet for her move. She'd still have the apartment for a month, so the rest could wait, but she needed her wardrobe. She talked with her parents daily as they drove across the country, and then before she knew it Monday arrived. Driving into Shoal Creek that first morning, Paige couldn't help but remember all the times she'd driven the same road as a teenager. High school friends crammed in a car, singing some terrible pop song at the top of their lungs. Those days didn't seem that long ago, but times had changed so much.

Arriving at the pharmacy, she sat in her car for an extra few moments, praying for the courage to open the door. A new job, a new location, a chance for a fresh start. She couldn't afford to blow this. "God, help me make a good impression."

What time I am afraid, I will trust in thee. The verse popped into Paige's mind. She laughed aloud. "Mom, I know what you mean. I assume it's from Psalms somewhere, but I can't remember the reference, either." Somehow, between the verse and the connection with her mother, she felt bolder, stronger.

She took a deep breath and climbed out into the morning and a new life. "I will make a good impression. I will get back into life. I will make new friends." She found herself almost afraid to hope that this time would be different.

At the square, the former grand movie theater dwarfed the surrounding buildings. The weathered brown brick stretched skyward, the sign above the glass doors looked like the original movie marquee. *Theater Center Shops*, it said. The sounds of hammering and electric saws came from the tiny windows upstairs.

Lee Richardson stood waiting at the front of the store, the same smile creasing his face, the same jeans and flannel shirt. As before, his shoulders were back, his head held high—more like a brave general than the retirement-age contractor that he was. "Hello there, young lady. Glad you're here."

"I'm glad, too." And terrified. And thrilled. And nauseous.

"Clarissa will learn a lot from working with you."

"I'm sure I'll learn even more from her." Time to stop this line of conversation before it went any further. "What made you think of turning a theater into a pharmacy?"

He opened the set of double glass doors, which led into what still looked like the lobby of a movie theater. "For the last couple of years, my company has really been working to give back to communities. Refurbishing the Nashville Clinic was one way, revitalizing the downtowns of more rural areas is another."

A small coffee counter stood against the wall where the snack bar had obviously once been. Cozy tables and chairs filled most of the area, and the air was thick with the smell of roasted coffee beans. Across the lobby there were two sets of double doors, which Paige supposed had once led down the two main aisles of the theater.

She could almost feel the presence of moviegoers of years past. What dreams had walked through these same doors? How many hearts had broken inside these very walls? How many lives changed by something they saw on the screen? She shook off the thought, but the faintest aroma of buttered popcorn salted the air and prolonged the nostalgia.

Lee pulled open one of the doors to the far left. A blue sign above them announced *Richardson Apothecary* in scripted white letters.

Once inside, she was amazed at the beauty of it all. They had managed to incorporate the giant round wall lights into the back of the pharmacy, so it looked almost like an old cathedral. The woodwork gleamed; the craftsmanship was amazing. A small shop of over-the-counter items and medical supplies stood neat and tidy before the dispensing area.

"This is lovely."

"Thought you'd like it." He ran a wrinkled hand across the doorframe, and then nodded toward the back. "Here comes Clarissa now."

A young woman floated down from behind the pharmacy counter. Her exotic beauty could easily have graced the screen that once stood in this building. The glossiness of her black hair would surely have sent Elizabeth Taylor screeching for the hairdresser, and the flawlessness of her complexion would have compelled even Ava Gardner to race for the makeup chair. Paige couldn't help comparing her own thin blond hair and freckled face. Perfection versus plain. Glamour versus ordinary.

When Clarissa shook her grandfather's hand, her whole face seemed to glow with happiness. "Granddad. Good morning." She nodded toward Paige, still smiling. "Who's your friend?"

Who's your friend? Paige took an involuntary step backward. Surely Clarissa knew . . . surely Lee would have told her.

Clarissa had hummed all morning as she moved about the pharmacy. Obviously, her grandfather had finally come to his senses and realized what a good job she was doing. A great job, even. She knew him well enough to know that he would never apologize for doubting her, but today was the equivalent.

She could still hear the excitement in his voice when he called yesterday. "I'll be there in the morning. I've got a surprise for you. Just you wait, it's exactly what you need."

Of course, she didn't know exactly what he was bringing, but she knew what it had to do with. He would be bringing something that declared he was about to begin work on the Lancaster Building for her. Would it be a blueprint of the building so that she could have design input like she did for this place? Or maybe even a set of keys to the building? Or a contract from Parrish Apothecary?

She allowed herself to savor one of her most vivid memories from childhood. It was after her mother had already left to find herself, her father had started drinking heavily to lose himself, and Clarissa spent most of her time by herself. Until she'd gone to live with her grandparents.

Her grandma made every day an adventure. The

51

very best adventure of all was the day they climbed into Grandma's car, drove into the city of Nashville, and parked on a street in front of a tired-looking brown-brick building. Trash gathered in the gutters and a couple of rather scary-looking adults loitered against a far building. And Grandma had led her inside to what was a small ice cream shop.

"Darling, this used to be a pharmacy. Not just any pharmacy mind you, it was Regency Pharmacy. All the fashionable people from Nashville used to come in here, they'd get an ice cream at the soda fountain, just where you see the ice cream shop today."

"Ice cream in a pharmacy?" To a five-year-old, it sounded like heaven.

"Oh, things were different in those days in a lot of ways. Mr. Bannister hired me to work here, and lots of people thought he was crazy for doing it."

"Why would they think that?"

"Because in those days, women didn't become pharmacists so much. I guess no one thought we were smart enough. Anyway, it was quite the big news when I started here."

"I bet Grandpa was proud of you."

"That was before I knew your grandfather, when I first started anyway. He came in not long after I started work and asked me where the aspirin were. Before he left the store, he had a bottle of Bayer and we had a date for dinner." She smiled in a dreamy way and nodded toward the back wall. "That was all open then. What was the pharmacy counter is now just a storage room, I suppose. Oh, I'd give anything if you could see this place the way it once was."

And starting today, Clarissa would begin making that dream come true. She could almost feel her grandmother smiling at her.

Oh, and just the thought of Becky's face after the announcement was enough to cause the sun to shine today. According to rumor, Becky was so sure that she would be setting up her yoga studio in the Lancaster Building that she was already privately interviewing instructors. Personally, Clarissa would burn the place to the ground before she saw that bimbo owning anything near there. After today, she wouldn't have to worry about it anymore.

That's when she saw her grandfather coming through the door, wearing the broadest smile she could ever remember. The time had finally come. Everyone's dreams were about to come true. She stepped out of the dispensing area and walked with the slow rhythm she'd learned for graduation: *one, and, two, and, three*. It was the only way she could keep herself from running.

Only when she met him halfway down the aisle did she notice he wasn't alone. Accompanying him was a young woman who looked to be about Clarissa's age. She had stick-straight blond hair—

the kind of pale blond that could only be natural. Her nose was covered with a smattering of freckles, her blue eyes were huge and looked a bit frightened.

Clarissa forced herself to smile like this person was the greatest thing to enter her pharmacy. After all, she apparently somehow played a role in the delivery of this morning's good news. "Granddad. Good morning." She shook his hand as always, then nodded toward the girl. "Who's your friend?"

"Clarissa, I'd like you to meet Paige Woodward. Paige, my granddaughter, Clarissa Richardson." He turned to Clarissa. "I've hired Paige to help you get this place really up and running."

Clarissa coughed. "Excuse me?"

Paige fought the urge to turn and flee. He hadn't told her?! Anything?! And now Paige stood beside her about-to-be boss, who had no idea she was even coming.

Lee put his arm around Clarissa's shoulders. "I know it's been hard on you, trying to do all this alone. We've talked about the difficulties in projecting great customer service. Well, I've been watching Paige at work at the Nashville Free Clinic, and she's fabulous at customer service— and everything else, as far as that goes. She'll be a huge asset for this place."

The happy twinkle that had been present in Clarissa's eyes only seconds ago disappeared behind the blazing fury of what could only be rage. She looked from her grandfather to Paige, then back again. She opened her mouth to say something to him, then stopped, exhaled slowly, and turned to Paige. "Well, welcome." She mumbled something under her breath, which might have been "I guess," but Paige couldn't say for sure.

"I'm glad to be here." Paige tried to keep her tone perky, but somehow she knew she failed.

"What I want to know is, how'd Granddad persuade someone so 'fabulous' to come to Shoal Creek? I'd give anything to be back in Nashville. Even working at a homeless clinic there has to be better than being in the middle of nowhere."

So much for making a good first impression. Paige looked toward Lee and remained silent.

The corner of his mouth twitched as if he was amused. "Paige grew up not too far from here. In fact, her family still lives in Sledge. Right, Paige?"

"Yes, they sure do." She forced her mouth into what had to be the fakest smile ever, but what else could she do? A customer rustled down a distant aisle, a baby cried in the background, and the trio stood looking at each other.

Clarissa flinched. "Maybe Shoal Creek feels like the big city to you then, huh?" She rubbed the fingernails on her left hand with her right thumb, then held the hand up to the light as if to check the polish. "Personally, I don't think I'll ever get used to it. But Granddad said I needed to get my start

55

away from my friends and have absolutely no fun. You know, you've got to be miserable if you want to succeed in business, that kind of stuff."

"I said no such thing."

"What did you say then?" She folded her arms and skewered him with a look.

"I said, if I was going to invest the money it took to get you started, I wouldn't do it somewhere that you could spend all your time running around with your friends and not focused on your work. You need to start small, prove you can do it, then work into something bigger."

"Which is basically what I just said you said, isn't it?" She flipped her hair over her shoulder and smiled in victory.

Lee laughed. He turned to Paige. "I'll leave my granddaughter to show you around. I'm going to inspect the renovations upstairs. I'll stop back in to check on you ladies later."

"Well, come on back." Clarissa walked away without turning to see if Paige followed. She pushed through the door to the dispensing area and let it swing shut behind her.

Paige watched the barrier close between them. It felt more than a little symbolic, and she suddenly longed for the smell of sweat and liquor, the poor lighting, and the dingy work space of the clinic. Things made more sense there—or at least followed a predictable pattern. She squared her shoulders and pushed through the door.

Clarissa stood at the counter, staring at Paige. She opened her mouth as if to say something, shook her head, and then shut it. She continued to shake her head slowly, as if having a silent argument with an unseen opponent. Finally, she took a step forward. "Wait here just a second." She pushed through the door, ran down the aisle, and disappeared out the front. Even from the back of the pharmacy, Paige could hear Clarissa call, "Granddad, hold on a minute."

chapter **nine**

Clarissa hurried out of the store, her adrenaline pumping so fast she was surprised she didn't levitate above the floor. Did her grandfather really think so little of her that he would do this?

She caught him at the bottom of the stairs. "Granddad, can I talk to you for just a minute?"

He smiled and turned. "Sure. Really surprised you good, didn't I?"

"You can say that again." She looked toward the door of the pharmacy. "I'm working as hard as I can here."

"I know you are, that's why I brought in some help. It'll give you the time to do some of the things you need to get done to get the business going. You can learn from her, she can learn from you. It'll be a win-win situation."

"Who's paying her salary?"

He looked surprised by the question. "Well, the store of course."

"I can't afford another salary right now."

"You can't afford to *not* have another salary right now. Sometimes in business you have to invest a little extra up front for the big payoffs in the long run."

"But how am I supposed to make this place profitable if you keep adding unexpected expenses?"

He smiled. "I told you all along, customer service has to be king. This will pay off big in the long run."

But time was something Clarissa didn't have much of. She wasn't worried about dividends over time. She was worried about here and now. And here and now she didn't have the money for this new girl.

"So, it doesn't matter whether or not I think we can afford her?"

"I was running my own business long before your father was even born, much less you. These kinds of things you'll just have to trust my judgment on. You'll see. It won't be long until you're thanking me for hiring her."

"Somehow, I doubt that very much."

"You can handle this, you can handle this." Paige whispered the words over and over, yet each time she said them she became more and more convinced they weren't true.

A frazzled-looking young mother entered the store, holding a toddler by one hand, a crying baby on the opposite hip. With every step the woman took, Paige fought the increasing urge to duck behind the shelves. What was she supposed to do? Clarissa had been gone almost ten minutes now, and Paige had no idea about the setup of this pharmacy, and not even a clue how to work the computer system.

She forced herself to make the walk to the patient counter. "May I help you?"

The mother put the baby up on her shoulder. "There, there, stop your crying now. Andrew, hand the nice lady the piece of paper, okay sweetie?"

The little boy reached into the pocket of his jeans and pulled out a crumpled prescription. He handed it to Paige with a serious expression on his face. "My brother needs some medicine."

"Your brother?" Paige looked at the baby on the mother's shoulder, wearing pink and ruffles.

The mother nodded toward the door. "His older brother. He's waiting out in the car, so if you don't mind hurrying, I'd appreciate it."

"I . . . well, I'll get this as fast as I can." Paige walked back up to the dispensing area and looked at the crumpled prescription blank. Amoxicillin 250 mg capsules shouldn't be hard to find. She walked down the first aisle and began to read labels. Everything appeared to be in alphabetical order by generic name; of course she could do this. When she saw the white plastic bottle with the words *amoxicillin 250* on the label, she almost cried with relief. She could count these out, put them in a vial, and hope that Clarissa showed up in time to work the computer.

She poured the capsules on the tray and started counting. Five, ten, fifteen . . .

The pharmacy door squeaked open. A rumpled girl walked behind the counter, red hair frizzed and untamed, pale face splattered with freckles. Someone looking for drugs?

Paige summoned up her most authoritative voice. "I'm sorry, no one is allowed up here. You need to wait below." She looked toward the front door, willing Clarissa to appear. The door remained shut tight.

"Last time I checked, I worked here. Unless you know something I don't?"

"Work here?" This waif in the low-cut jeans and wrinkled shirt couldn't be more than twenty.

"I'm the tech."

Paige suddenly felt foolish. "Oh, sorry, I'm Paige. I'm the new pharmacist. I just started today." Paige extended a hand, which the girl eyed suspiciously.

"Yeah, I just saw Clarissa out front. She told me all about it." She reached out and gave Paige's hand a brief shake. "Name's Dawn."

Did Paige imagine the undertone of hostility in

Dawn's voice? The same undertone she'd imagined from Clarissa? *Stop being paranoid.*

Dawn dropped her oversized purse into a bottom drawer. "I'll go check the refill line." Had the room just grown colder?

"Uh, wait. Do you know how to work the computer? There's this new prescription here, the kid is waiting in the car, and I don't know how to do it."

Dawn went to the terminal without another word. In no time, the label printed. Paige put it on the vial she'd already filled with the medicine and hand-initialed the label. Dawn rang up the purchase at the back register. "Okay, now I'm going to listen to the refill line." She walked to the back counter and didn't say another word.

Just then, Clarissa came stalking down the aisle, looking even less happy than she had when she'd followed her grandfather out. "So, did Dawn show you the setup?"

"Uh . . . no. She went to listen to refills."

"Right. Okay, so come on, I'll show you around."

The tour was impressive. Behind the counter were the fast movers, while the rest of the shelves were arranged alphabetically by generic name. Liquids lined the back wall, and to the right the shelves held inhalers, ophthalmics, and everything else. Somebody knew what they were doing when they laid this space out.

"This place is really streamlined," Paige said

when they'd finished. "It's got to be the most efficient pharmacy design I've ever seen."

"I did the layout myself." Clarissa almost smiled, but not quite.

"You're kidding. Wow, you've got a gift."

Clarissa looked at her, studied her face as if expecting something to suddenly appear. "Can I ask you a question?"

"Sure."

"What would possess you to take a job in a place that you've never seen, with people that you've never even met?"

"Well I . . ." Paige pushed against the corners of her lips with all the strength she possessed, but she knew that nothing even resembling a smile was there. "The clinic was going to be closed for a while due to renovations. I needed the money. Your grandfather was very nice and offered this job. It's closer to my parents' than Nashville."

"You intentionally moved closer to your parents?" Her sarcasm left no room for misinterpretation.

"I . . . yeah." There was no reason to go into the rest of the story.

"Well, okay then. I guess that says a lot."

Dawn came walking from the back counter while several labels spit from the printer. She pulled them off without saying a word.

Clarissa nodded at her. "How are the refills?"

"Thrilling as usual." Dawn looked at Paige then

back at Clarissa. "So . . . I'm just going to start filling these."

Paige reached out her hand. "I'll be happy to take some of those. It'll be a good way for me to get my feet wet."

"Sure." Dawn tore off a couple of labels. "Knock yourself out."

A moment later, Paige was walking down the third aisle, looking for metoprolol, when she heard the unmistakable sound of whispering coming from the next aisle over. A higher-pitched voice, obviously questioning, then the lower-pitched answer—Clarissa's voice and full of anger. "Can't believe he'd do something like this," followed by other words she couldn't make out, then, "What kind of person takes a job in a place she's never even seen? Not someone I want to work with."

chapter **ten**

Her second day on the job, Paige returned from lunch determined to keep up the pretense of being perfectly happy in this unwelcoming place. Surely her co-workers would come to accept her presence here eventually.

Clarissa was standing at the counter, talking to a woman who had just approached with a prescription in her hand. "Mrs. Magnusen, this prescription is not from your regular doctor, is it?"

"Nah, I just went to the walk-in clinic so I could be seen right away. Why, something wrong?"

"Did you tell the doctor you saw today anything about your past medical history?"

"No. The nurse gave me that fill-in sheet with all those check-a-box questions."

"Did you mark 'yes' beside kidney disease?"

"Um, well, now that you mention, I think I got so busy going down the list and marking no, I might have forgotten."

"Let me call them for you. I think they'll probably want to decrease the dose. Have a seat."

Clarissa walked around behind the counter, dialed some numbers, and waited. "Yes, this is Clarissa at Richardson Apothecary. I've got Susie Magnusen here right now and she's got a prescription for Cipro 750 every twelve hours. I wonder if Dr. Stone is aware that Mrs. Magnusen has kidney disease?" Clarissa rolled her eyes as she waited in silence. Paige guessed the nurse was trying to track down the doctor.

"Hello, Dr. Stone. Yes, according to her primary care physician Susie Magnusen's creatinine clearance is down around twenty. Do you want to change her Cipro strength to 250? Yes. Yes. Thank you." Clarissa marked out the 750 mg and changed it to 250 mg, then began counting out the pills.

Mrs. Magnusen came to the counter. "Everything okay?"

"Yes. Make sure you always mention your

kidney issues to a doctor you're seeing—especially when it's outside your usual clinic. The good news is, he cut your dose, which will cost you less. So, how about that?" She rang up the purchase and handed Mrs. Magnusen her prescription.

"Thank you so much, young lady." Mrs. Magnusen walked out beaming.

Paige looked at Clarissa, amazed at what she'd just seen. "How did you know about the renal disease?"

"Last month her physician called about renal dosing of some of her other meds. I noted it in the computer."

"Yeah, but you hadn't even been back to the computer yet when I walked in, you were still at the counter."

Clarissa shrugged. "I just remembered, that's all."

The same way that she'd remembered that Cipro's dosage needed to be adjusted without the computer warning her. Paige realized that whatever else she might be, Clarissa was one smart pharmacist. Once they got past the bumpy start, she'd be a great person to learn from.

Paige said, "Well, now that you've gotten that all taken care of, why don't you take a lunch? With Dawn here, I can handle it." Even though Paige still felt very awkward in this new place, Dawn was a proficient tech in every aspect of the word. Maybe this gesture would help bridge the gulf.

Clarissa looked toward Dawn, then back at Paige. "I'll do a quick sandwich out front." She looked at Dawn. "I've got my cell. You know the drill."

Paige watched Clarissa walk out and tried to make small talk with Dawn. "So, did you grow up around here?"

"Yeah."

"Your family still here?"

"Yeah."

Paige couldn't force the girl to talk no matter how awkward it was, so thankfully there were several refills to keep her occupied. Paige kept telling herself it would just take a little time, that's all. This time next week, they would all laugh that there had ever been a problem.

An older woman in a gardening hat and faded jeans entered the store, carrying a prescription bag. Paige walked down to meet her at the counter. "May I help you?"

The woman removed the plastic vial from the bag. "Hope so. I picked up the refill of my blood thinner a while ago, and the pills aren't the same color they usually are."

The strangest sense of detachment came over Paige. She saw herself lean forward, heard herself speak. "Really? Let me see."

The woman handed her the bottle. This other Paige, the one who moved like a robot, performed tasks but felt nothing, looked at the label.

Clarissa's initials were printed in the corner. Inside the bottle rested pills that were supposed to be warfarin 2.5 mg but weren't. Paige felt herself lift her head to look at the customer.

"See, they're purple. Mine are usually green."

Thankfully, this new Paige kept her composure, smiled calmly, spoke in a soothing voice. "Just one minute, Mrs. Harris, let me see what I can find out. Have you taken one of these?"

"No, I always take 'em at bedtime. Don't know why I even looked at 'em, but I did."

Paige could not look at Dawn when she came behind the counter, went to the shelves, and got the warfarin 2.5 mg bottle. She poured the green tablets onto the tray and counted a double portion for good measure. She put them in the bottle and fastened the safety lid in place. There, now everything was fixed as good as new.

She went back to the counter, a cheerful smile on her face. "Here you go, Mrs. Harris. I have your green pills ready for you. I gave you an extra month's supply for free to make up for the inconvenience of having to come back in."

"What happened? Did I get the wrong stuff?"

Paige put the bottle into the bag in the woman's hand. "Nothing like that. Sometimes the manufacturers try a new color. In this case, they did, and found out all their patients were upset, so they switched it back. It should always be green from now on, but don't ever hesitate to come back with questions like that." This new Paige, the detached one, felt no remorse at all for the lie. It was simply something that had to be done—for everyone's sake.

Mrs. Harris smiled. "Thank you, young lady. And thanks for the free month's supply. Every little bit helps when you're living off your retirement." She walked out of the store, seemingly unfazed.

Dawn stared at her, mouth open. "Why did you tell her that? About the color change?"

Only now did any hint of the old Paige return. It started with the smallest twinge, nothing really. But as each second ticked past, it grew into an ache, then an all-out stabbing pain inside her.

"I . . . it . . . I'll be right back." Paige ran into the bathroom and locked the door behind her. She stared at the girl in the mirror, wondering who she was. Where had this person come from? This person who so coolly told lies, who hid truths from the people she worked with. Actually, it was obvious where this person had come from. She had been created. Created by the very system that had ruined her life, the system that she now felt no remorse about working outside of. She took a few deep breaths and walked back into the pharmacy, head held high.

Clarissa stood waiting at the counter, watching her. "Dawn told me what you did—that you covered up for me."

Paige shrugged. "I knew she'd be all upset if she knew she'd gotten the wrong thing. Fact was, no harm was done. It was Coumadin 2.0 in the bottle." *And what was half a milligram of difference? The increased chances of stroke or heart attack would have been slight. . . . Okay, even if the decreased dosage did pose a significant risk, fact was, the lady hadn't taken any. End of story.* "I figured a little fib wouldn't hurt."

Clarissa nodded. "Thank you. I . . . was distracted when Dawn filled that a little while ago, I didn't check it as carefully as I should have. I've never had a mistake come back before." She toyed with a piece of paper on the counter, then looked up at Paige again. "Really, I know I haven't exactly been overflowing with warmth toward you since you've been here—and it's nothing personal. It's just that, well . . ."

"I understand."

"Why would you have done that? For me?"

Paige looked out through the store. "You're a good pharmacist. I've seen that already. I knew a pharmacist once—a good one. A single mistake combined with a greedy lawyer cost her everything. I don't want to see that happen to someone else." Paige stared at the computer screen, and the world around her faded away into the world in which she lived not so very long ago. Still in Atlanta, still working at Sharitz HMO, still without a blemish on her record. The scene became so clear she could hear the voices as if they were still speaking.

"Paige, will you check these for me? Joanna's caught up with a patient at the counseling window."

"Sure." Paige had nodded at Lacy, the pharmacy technician, and walked to Joanna's computer station. A half-dozen prescriptions lined the counter, a stock bottle beside the handwritten order, and a pharmacy vial with label attached beside that. Paige picked up the first and compared the stock bottle to the label, the label to the written prescription, and then opened the vial to make certain the correct tablets were inside. "Perfect." She put the vial in the bag and put it on the outgoing shelf.

"Phone call for a pharmacist."

Paige picked up the phone, tucked it between her ear and shoulder, and checked the next prescription in line. "This is Paige Woodward, may I help you?"

"This is Dr. Webb's office. A couple of prescriptions to call in."

"Just one second." Paige dropped the next vial in the bag and slid an empty prescription blank across the counter. "Okay, ready."

"The first one is for Mark Schalesky, for medrol—"

"How do you spell that last name?" She scrib-

bled the information as quickly as she could while the technicians and other pharmacists bustled around her.

"Need a pharmacist consult at the window," one tech called from the front. Another tech called from the back, "I need a pharmacist back here to check these refills."

It was a mad rush and when she made it back to her computer monitor, Paige found a row of refills waiting to be checked and a folded piece of paper on her keyboard. She opened the paper to find:

EMERGENCY MEETING TONIGHT,
IMMEDIATELY AFTER SHIFT CHANGE.
FIRST FLOOR CONFERENCE ROOM.
ALL PHARMACISTS MUST ATTEND.

She looked at a colleague who was working at her counter. "What's this all about?"

The woman shrugged. "Got me. One of the administrative assistants came in with a whole stack of these—gave me one, left that one for you, put one in Carl's mailbox."

"I wonder what's so important that it won't hold until the monthly wrap-up next week."

"Whatever it is, I hope they make it quick. The last thing I want to do after work is spend more time here, locked in some boring meeting."

Paige agreed. She had a dinner date with Brian in an hour, and she didn't want to rush to get ready.

Somehow, though, given the suddenness of the meeting, she doubted tonight's subject would be boring.

"Paige, you still with us?" Clarissa laughed as she waved her hand before Paige's face.

"Yeah, sorry. Spaced out there for a minute."

"No problem. I was just about to show you how to run the end-of-day reports."

"Let's get to it." Paige glanced again at the bottle of Coumadin 2.0 mg on the counter. She looked at the bins of refills awaiting pickup, and every nerve in her body twitched with the need to double check the whole lot.

Relax. She said it was her first mistake. It was the wrong strength of the right drug, for crying out loud. None was taken, no blood clots formed. Stop worrying about what could have been.

There was worry enough in what had already been.

chapter **eleven**

Paige glanced at her watch. Again. Eight fifty-eight. Where was Clarissa? Dawn, of course, would not arrive for another twenty minutes, but Clarissa had never been late. At least not for the few days Paige had been at the pharmacy.

Thankfully, Mrs. Trout arrived with the keys to the front end of the store. Otherwise, they would have been stuck standing outside the door, waiting beside the two customers whose silhouettes now cast shadows through the glass.

Hurry up, Clarissa.

Hopefully when they opened the doors in a couple of minutes, neither customer would need a prescription filled. Late starts and annoyed customers were a bad combination for the start of a new day.

The shadows at the door shifted, keys clanked in the lock, and suddenly Clarissa let herself and the customers in. Her voice projected through the store. "Sorry, all. Traffic was terrible. Thought I was going to be late there for a minute."

"You *are* late." An elderly man in a rumpled suit made no effort to keep his voice low as he headed toward the antacids. The other customer, a woman with a red nose, went straight to the cough and cold section.

Clarissa made a face behind the man's back, then smiled at Paige. "I was thinking you should be ready to start opening by yourself. If nothing else, maybe this little arrangement will get me out of Nashville's rush hour. If you open, I'll wait an hour, and save a ton of stuck-in-traffic time. You're up for it, right? Dawn'll be here, and I'll come in by eleven to give you a lunch break. Then maybe Saturday, I'll leave after noon and let you get your feet wet with closing shop. Saturdays are always slow back here, anyway."

Paige exhaled slowly. "I . . . guess so." She didn't have a full grasp of the computer yet. Dawn did, but she was consistently late for work. Quite late, usually. Still, Paige could at least open on time. "I don't have keys."

"That's *right*. I keep meaning to get the extra set from Mrs. Trout and give it to you."

"Mrs. Trout?"

"Mrs. Trout. The front-end clerk. Let you in here today." Clarissa looked at Paige as if she were an idiot.

"I know who she is. What I meant was, 'Why does Mrs. Trout have all the keys?'"

"Because she sometimes gets here before I do, like today. And she sometimes comes in on Sundays and does a little merchandising work up front."

"But she has the key to the dispensing area, too?"

"Well, yeah. They were on the same ring and I didn't want to separate them. I was afraid I'd lose one if I did. It's not like she's up here selling narcotics. I mean, look at her. She's hardly the criminal type."

"I didn't say she was. Still, it's *against the law.* What would happen if a state board inspector just happened to be around that day?"

"Like board inspectors are going to spend their Sunday afternoons in this town, looking for Mrs. Trout and her kind to be wandering free in a pharmacy."

It did sound foolish. Why should Paige make waves? She could still feel the joy from mailing her signing bonus just in time for her mother's first payment. Just being employed was a blessing. But disaster sometimes came unexpectedly. "You never know."

"I do. Look, I've been doing the work of three people here. If Mrs. Trout is willing to come in on her day off and help me, I'm not going to get all ballistic on her. I'm going to appreciate the gift for what it is and get on with my life—which has enough issues without inventing more to worry about."

Paige looked at her young boss, hoping the bravado proved true. The worse-case scenario had already played out in her own life. She vowed never to go through that hell again, no matter what she had to do.

Clarissa poured thick red syrup into the bottle. On the floor above them, construction teams rattled and banged. She was on the verge of a headache. How much longer would this day last? She looked toward Paige, and her annoyance grew.

Paige mumbled under her breath as she looked from prescription, to label, to stock bottle, to medicine vial. "Yeah, looks good. One more quick check."

Aaagh! She was so meticulous it was maddening. It took her forever to do anything. Did the girl ever laugh? The only word that came to mind was *dull*. The more she thought about it, the more it really burned her that her grandfather had hired this—what did he call her? A hard worker? Slow worker was a more accurate description. It didn't take much to look busy if it took you an hour to do anything.

Her grandfather had been deceived by slowness and freckles—that little smatter of freckles across Paige's button nose. Yep, combined with her wide-eyed innocence, it took the girl-next-door look to a whole new level. Cuteness. It fooled old people every time.

Clarissa sighed, put the label on her bottle, and took it to the counter. "Alana, your prescription is ready." She knew if she didn't get away now, she was going to say something she'd regret. Who knew if Paige was reporting back to her grandfather; she needed to at least be civil and hope for the best. But that wasn't going to happen if she stayed beside Paige for another second. She was going to blow. Where could she go that wouldn't be overly conspicuous? From upstairs came some more clanging and she had her answer.

Cory.

He was the one distraction in Shoal Creek that made it almost bearable. And he hadn't called in over a week now. It was time to heat things back up.

"Hey, Paige, I'm going to check on the work

upstairs—find out when they're going to stop making all that noise. It's driving me crazy."

Paige looked up from the computer screen. She glanced pointedly at the line of prescriptions waiting on the counter, then back at Clarissa. "Do you think now is the best time for that?"

"I'll be right back." Honestly, it was only three prescriptions. Maybe Paige would move a little faster if she didn't always have someone there to carry the load for her.

Besides, the noise *was* annoying, and it served her patients' best interest to check on progress. Of course, the fact that the supervising carpenter was such a premium specimen of manhood would make the fact-finding mission less painful.

She went up the steps to what had been the theater balcony. It was now the staging area for all the work going on in the building—the travel agency next door was almost complete, then they were putting in a boutique up here.

When she reached the top of the stairs, she could see the men busy at work. Unfortunately, Cory was not among them.

An electrician leered down from his ladder. "Can I help you, or'd you come up here to see me?"

Disgusting.

"Just checking progress." She wasn't about to ask for Cory.

She walked back down the stairs, resigned to her fate of boredom. But when she opened the door to the pharmacy, she saw him. At the counter. Stuck talking to the Dull One. Better mobilize a rescue.

She smoothed her hair with her fingers and walked up beside him. "Hello, Cory. What brings you here?" She smiled at him, tilting her head just enough so that she knew her upturned eyes produced maximum effect.

"I heard a rumor there was another beautiful girl working down here, and thought maybe this was changing from a pharmacy to a modeling agency. Decided I better get down here and see what all the fuss was about." He spoke loud enough for Paige to hear, and he grinned back and forth between Clarissa and Paige, his dimples working their effect. "Of course, Ken always exaggerates about these things, but this particular time, I'd say he got it right."

Paige's cheeks turned pink, but she never looked up from the computer when she said, "Cory, will you cut it out and let us get back to work? You do want your mom's medicine today, right?"

Cory looked at Clarissa, cleared his throat, and sobered just a little. "Turns out, my mom needs a refill. Paige said she can call the pharmacy in Sledge and get it transferred over here."

"I told you I could do that three months ago."

"Did you? Must have slipped my mind. Of course, no surprise there. Lots of things slip my mind when there's something more interesting to think about."

Clarissa did not like the way Cory grinned at Paige. Obviously he was trying not to be rude, but still, if he didn't watch out, he would give Paige the impression he liked her or something. *That's all we need, to have the Dull One mooning over Cory. It would make her even slower than she already is.*

"Well, I'll leave you ladies to your work." He tapped once on the counter. "Thanks, Paige." He winked at Clarissa as he walked past, but somehow it felt dismissive. Condescending even. The way a jock in high school would wink at the homely-but-smart girl who had just done his homework for him.

Clarissa watched him walk away, wishing she could think of an excuse to follow. When he reached the door, he stopped and turned. Of course, it had all been an act. A macho act. He'd give her a knowing smile now, to let her know they'd hook up later.

Instead, he waved toward Paige and disappeared out the door. Was that a blush on his cheeks as he turned away?

Clarissa licked her lips and walked up beside Paige. "So, you've met Cory now."

Paige continued to count pills with her spatula and didn't answer until she was done. "Actually, I met him about twenty years ago. He was a couple of years behind me in school, but I've known him all my life."

"Where did you say you're from again?"

"Sledge. It's about fifteen miles south of here. Small town, a lot like Shoal Creek."

Clarissa thought of Becky, probably planning even now the new yoga studio in the Lancaster Building. She thought of her father, drinking his way into another oblivion. She looked at little Miss Apple Pie before her and remembered Cory's obvious attraction to her. What would it take to make something go right?

She knew the answer. It was always the same. Stay focused and work hard. It was the Richardson way.

chapter **twelve**

Dawn groaned at the beeping alarm. She should have left last night's party a little earlier.

The snoring lump beside her remained motionless, his breath thick with stale beer and cigarettes. She poked his shoulder. "Jack, wake up. Time to get ready for work."

"Hit the snooze."

"I promised Paige I'd be on time today."

"Like you care what she thinks."

"Get up."

He rolled toward her, his eyes still closed. "Call my boss and tell him I'm sick."

"You promised you'd stop that. Come on."

"Shut up and let me sleep."

She shoved him so hard he nearly fell off the

bed. "Nothing doing. I'm not working to pay your child support while you stay home in bed."

He pulled the pillow over his head. "You are today."

"You are such a loser."

He flung the pillow at her, hitting her square in the face. "You should be more grateful. I'm the only one who would take you in after your parents kicked you out."

She looked at the unshaven face and bloodshot eyes that had once seemed so charming. "Grateful? *You're* the reason they kicked me out."

He grabbed the pillow from her side of the bed and rolled away from her. "Hey, if you hate it here so bad, feel free to move on. I'm sure you'd be real comfortable living in your car. Now shut your mouth and let me sleep."

"I hate you." She meant every word. Mostly because he was right. She had nowhere else to go.

With no time for a shower, she stumbled forward and opened the closet door. It loomed before her like a cave: dark, eerie—and empty. Dirty clothes lay in small heaps across the dirty carpet. She bent to pick up a white shirt. A smear of ketchup marred the front, so she tossed it back to the ground. The second attempt, a green striped button-up, smelled of sweat and cigarettes. Finally, she picked up a short-sleeved blue pullover that didn't look half bad—if you didn't count wrinkles. It would have to do. Like everything else in her life.

● ● ●

Paige arrived on her fourth day ready to settle into her routine. She'd brought a coffee maker, and now that she had her keys, she wouldn't have to wait at the door until someone else showed up. No, from here on out she could arrive a little after eight, brew a fresh pot, and spend some time getting ready for the day ahead. She set down the box at the pharmacy door, flipped through her keys, and unlocked the door.

As she bent down, she looked at the index card she'd set on top of the box. Maybe she had trouble memorizing Bible verses, but she kept hearing about the power of praying Scripture. Her mother needed the strongest kind of prayers right now, and Paige planned to do her part. She glanced at the card again. *Acts 3:16—By faith in the name of Jesus, this man whom you see and know was made strong. It is Jesus' name and the faith that comes through him that has given this complete healing to him, as you can all see.* It was verses like this that she planned to pray and claim, over and over again, until she got God's attention.

She swung open the door and punched the code in the alarm keypad. The empty darkness inside the store felt all too familiar. *God, please help Mom. We do have faith, please make her well. We need her so much. And if You're still listening, please send me a friend.*

82

Someone.

Anyone.

"You open?"

Paige turned and found herself looking up into the bespeckled eyes of an elderly woman. In spite of her age, she stood erect, wearing a wool skirt and boots with heels.

"No, not until nine. I'm just getting things set up. You need something?"

The woman sighed. "Honey, I need lots of things. But mostly, I was hoping for a refill of my angina medicine."

It would at least provide some company for a few minutes, and the woman seemed nice enough. "Where did you get it filled last?"

"Right here."

"Come on in. It's silly for you to have to come back in an hour."

The woman gave a brisk nod. "That's what I like. Someone with a little common sense. Wasn't sure there was any of that left in your generation."

Paige saw the woman to the sitting area, then proceeded behind the counter. "I have to get the computer fired up. It'll take just a few minutes."

"You planning on making some coffee?"

"Yes, but don't worry, I'll get your medicine for you first."

"Nonsense. I don't want any half-awake pharmacist filling my prescription. You make that coffee *first.* You can pour me a cup while you're at it.

Personally, I'd die before I'd drink that frothy stuff out front. Plain old coffee's good enough for me."

Paige nodded. "Well, okay then. You got it." She turned on the computer, then carried the coffee maker to the back shelf, measured out the first pot, and set it to brew. Once she pressed the *on* button, she walked down to her customer. "Do you know your prescription number?"

The woman reached into her oversized quilted purse. "Got my bottle right here." She fished through the cavernous space for a moment, then produced the green plastic vial.

Paige looked at the name on the top of the label. Ora Vaerge. "How do you pronounce your last name?"

"Like the noun. You know, I'm on the *verge* of something great."

Paige laughed. "I like it. It's pretty."

As Paige navigated the computer to find her record, the woman strained to look over the counter. "How's that coffee coming?"

Paige set the bottle beside the terminal and walked to the back counter. "Nearly ready. Do you want cream or sugar?"

"Nope. Black's good. No need for anything else."

Paige carried a steaming mug for the woman. "I'll get to work on your prescription now."

"What's that paper you were carrying around?"

"The what?"

"Paper. You know, the index card. You were reading it when I first walked up."

"Oh, it's a Bible verse. I'm praying about something very specific in my life. I'm writing out verses that help me."

"I've never been able to quote verses. I remember references like you wouldn't believe but can't quote a word. I have to go look them up."

Paige laughed outright. "My mom's just the opposite. She can remember all sorts of verses but can't tell you where any of them are found. I don't know that I've ever heard of anyone besides you with the opposite problem."

"Not a problem at all. A reference comes to mind, it's easy as can be to go look it up. Don't have to carry a bunch of cards around with me, neither."

"I guess you're right." Paige finished with the refill. "Here you go, Mrs. Vaerge. Your prescription's ready."

The woman swung her arm in a dismissive manner. "Ora. Call me Ora. I'm too young to be Mrs. Vaerge." She winked a left eye that had easily seen eighty years pass. "So, what are you praying about? If I have a reference for it, I'll give it to you."

"My mom has cancer. I'm praying through verses on faith and healing."

"Let's see, let me think a minute." She rubbed her chin, then gave a brisk nod. "Got just the thing.

Second Timothy, chapter four, verse twenty. Can't remember what it says, but I remember it's about faith and healing."

As much as Paige was ready to get on with her day, this was just too intriguing to ignore. "How about I look it up?" She walked to the back computer and typed in the web address for an online Bible. "Let's see, 2 Timothy 4:20, got it right here, it says 'Erastus stayed in Corinth, and I left Trophimus sick in Miletus.'" Paige looked at the woman and resisted the urge to giggle. "Uh, I guess your memory for references didn't quite work this time."

"Course it did. It says, 'I left Trophimus sick,' doesn't it?"

"Yeah."

"It was Paul doing the talking, right?"

"Yeah, I guess so."

"Course it was. It was from Paul's letter to Timothy. Now, back to my point, lots of sick people were made well when Paul touched them and prayed for them, right?"

"Yeah."

"Well, there you have it, clear as Vicks VapoRub." She put her prescription bag in her purse, then looked up at Paige as if she were an idiot. "Sometimes healing doesn't happen, even when the faith is there. Sometimes The Big Man just has other plans, and those plans don't involve the person in question getting better. See?"

Was that supposed to be encouraging? Time to get this lady out of here. "Well, thanks, Ora. I'll walk you out so I can lock up behind you."

Ora set her empty mug on the counter. "Next time, use cold water."

"Excuse me?"

"In your coffee maker. If you start with cold water, the coffee tastes better. Yours isn't very good."

Paige bit her bottom lip. "Umm, thanks for the tip."

"No problem. You opening tomorrow morning?"

"Yeah."

"Good, I'll come by then. You can try again." The woman turned and disappeared out the door.

Paige looked at the ceiling. "God, what is going on? I'm claiming Your Word, I'm doing all I can, and You seem to be answering every request with the complete opposite. I asked for a friend, and You've sent me a crotchety old lady who criticizes my coffee and gives me bizarre Bible references that have nothing to do with anything. Do you even hear me anymore?"

chapter **thirteen**

Monday morning marked Paige's first full week at work. Things felt almost normal, though it still hurt to head home every night to her parents' empty house. She was washing out her coffee pot when Clarissa arrived and began to scrub everything that didn't move. As she wiped at the counter for at least the tenth time, Paige walked over and put her hand on Clarissa's arm. "Is everything okay?"

Clarissa continued to rub at an imaginary spot. "You ever heard of Parrish Apothecary?"

"Yeah. Isn't that a boutique pharmacy? Great service but higher prices, and doesn't take insurance?"

"Milton Parrish is coming in today. *The* Milton Parrish. He's part owner of this store along with my grandfather, but he's never actually been here before. He's also sole owner of the Parrish Apothecary chain. He's decided to sell franchise rights to a select few people, and I want to be one of them."

Paige nodded. "Got it. Something special you want me to do?"

Clarissa straightened the Zithromax Z-Paks on the shelf. "Tidy up anything that needs it. When he's here, provide your best service and try to look happy."

Paige saluted. "I'll give it my best."

Clarissa did not acknowledge the attempt at humor. Instead, she looked toward the door and began to drum her fingers on the counter. "I hope Dawn shows up wearing something halfway nice today. I told her to dress her best, but looking back, I think I should have been more specific."

"Maybe she'll surprise you." In truth, Paige had never seen Dawn in anything besides faded jeans and wrinkled shirts, but now was not the time to say as much.

When Dawn arrived at ten after nine, quite early by her standards, she was wearing a long khaki skirt and a black turtleneck sweater. "If either one of you says a word about these clothes, you're dead. Let's just understand that up front."

Clarissa snickered. "Can I ask just one question?"

"Ask at your own risk."

"Did that actually come from your closet, or did you borrow it from someone?"

"My closet, unfortunately. My mother gave it to me for high school graduation, she just knew it was the perfect ensemble to wear to job inter- views." Dawn looked down and grabbed a fistful of skirt at the side seam. "Personally, I wouldn't want to work for anyone who would hire a person wearing something this boring, but you did say the most conservative thing in my closet, and this is it. Now, I'm going to listen to the refills so I can hide in the back. I'd die if any of my friends came into the store today and saw me in this."

By the time noon arrived, everything in the pharmacy had been rearranged at least twice. Clarissa had grown increasingly agitated and short-tempered, obsessively staring at the door. Paige tried offering a word of comfort here and there but nothing seemed to get through. Finally,

Lee Richardson walked in, followed by a distinguished-looking man in a gray suit.

"Here he is now," Clarissa hissed. She looked from Paige to Dawn, took a deep breath, and smoothed her hair. "Best foot forward, everyone."

The two men walked through the front end of the store aisle by aisle, talking the whole time, pointing at things, gesturing. Every now and then, snatches of phrases like "profit margin," "lower overhead," and "liability" could be heard, with an occasional bit of laughter.

A steady flow of customers kept Paige too occupied to worry much about what they were doing. When they finally stepped up into the dispensing area, they ignored Paige and Clarissa altogether and continued their tour as if no one else was even there.

"This is a terrific layout." Milton Parrish's voice came from the back of the pharmacy.

"Clarissa is the one who designed it all. She told me what she wanted done, I just followed orders." There was a moment of quiet before he continued, "Tell you what, Milton, the girl's got a keen eye for efficiency. We could use her in the construction business if she ever gets tired of pharmacy." There was no mistaking the pride in Lee Richardson's voice.

Paige looked at Clarissa, who was typing at the computer. Her face remained serious, but her eyes began to sparkle.

Paige concealed a thumbs-up from the men's view, and Clarissa actually smiled at her.

"This place is well done, no doubt about it," Milton Parrish said. "Let's just pull up a couple of chairs, sit back, and watch awhile. I always seem to learn the most that way."

"Sounds good to me."

Clarissa turned toward Paige and opened her eyes wide. Panic time.

Paige picked up a pen and wrote, *It's going to be fine,* slid it across for Clarissa to see, then tossed it in the trash before working on the next prescription in line. And then the next. And the next.

After what seemed like hours, the men finally stood up and walked into the back room.

Paige grasped Clarissa's wrist and squeezed. "The pharmacy's been busy all day, the patients have all been happy, Mr. Parrish is impressed with your layout. Sounds like things are looking good for you."

Clarissa looked at her. "I . . . hope so."

The store's front door opened. An obese young woman in too-small clothes entered the store, a sticky-faced baby on her hip. The woman never lifted her eyes above the bottom row of shelves.

"Oh, no. Look what's coming. This is just what we need right now." Clarissa looked at the door to the back room. "Get her out of here as fast as you can."

Paige met the woman at the counter. She looked at the prescription and cooed at the baby. "You must be Jonas. Don't worry, we'll have you feeling better in no time. And it'll taste good, too." She nodded to the mother. "It'll be just a few minutes. Please, take a seat."

"Be right back." Clarissa disappeared into the bathroom with a hairbrush in her hand.

Paige measured distilled water and poured it into the bottle of powder. When she shook it, a thick pink liquid took form. She attached the label and the *refrigerate and shake well* sticker and dropped it into a bag. She walked to the counter. "Okay, Jonas's prescription is ready."

Lee Richardson and Milton Parrish came back into the pharmacy. They took a seat at the back desk, looking over some sort of sketches.

The mother wearily approached the counter.

"Here's a dropper. Fill it to this line." Paige showed the woman the half-teaspoon mark. Keep it in the refrigerator, and be sure to give it a good shake before each dose. Okay?"

The woman nodded. "Thanks."

Paige reached out to touch the baby's soft cheek. "Good-bye, Jonas. I hope you feel better soon."

The mother walked away, her steps heavy and slow. Still, she turned to give Paige a little wave before she walked out the door.

Clarissa came out of the bathroom relieved to see the woman and her baby leaving before her grandfather and Milton Parrish came from the back room. She walked up beside Paige and nodded toward the door, thankful to be able to let out a little steam. "People like that drive me crazy."

"People like what?"

"You know. Charity cases. All the extra paper work makes our lives miserable, and for what? I'm at work, why isn't she?"

"Maybe she does work. My grandmother was a sharecropper and she worked harder than most anyone. She was on welfare because she didn't make enough to keep food on the table and her medical bills paid, but she was a great lady. The greatest I've ever known." Paige looked again toward the door and blinked hard.

"Well said." Milton Parrish's voice came from directly behind them. "Every customer deserves respect, no matter their financial situation."

Clarissa cringed. When had they come out of the back room? "Of course. I simply meant . . ." She looked toward her grandfather, her eyes wide.

"We've always valued hard work in our family. Haven't we, Clarissa?" He smiled at her then turned toward Milton. "Sometimes that translates a little harshly when spoken aloud."

"Yes, it does." Milton Parrish turned and smiled at Paige. "You did a fine job. You're the kind of pharmacist that makes me proud to be in the profession."

"I told you she was good, didn't I?" Clarissa's grandfather smiled proudly at Paige.

What? Clarissa looked at her grandfather and pasted on the biggest smile he'd likely ever seen. "Granddad, you are so right. I just think she's the greatest."

"See, I told you it wouldn't take long until you agreed with me." He nodded toward Milton Parrish. "Shall we go get some dinner?"

"Sounds good." He shook Paige's hand. "A real pleasure to meet you, young lady. I can see that you measure up to the great things I've been hearing." Then he turned to Clarissa and shook her hand. "You've put in a lot of hard work here, just make certain you don't lose sight of the customers behind it all."

"Thanks for the reminder." Clarissa smiled and shook his hand, pretending as she never had before.

Somewhere behind her, Paige wasn't having to fake her smile. Well, she'd better enjoy it now, because never again would she be shown to be anything but inferior. Clarissa would make certain of that.

chapter **fourteen**

Ora was waiting by the door when Paige arrived on Wednesday morning. Paige looked at her watch, then back at the older woman. "Am I late or are you early?"

"Neither." Ora stood perfectly still, neither smiling nor frowning, just . . . watching.

Okay, then. "Is that a new dress?"

The blank stare disappeared behind the glow of a satisfied smile. Ora looked down and rubbed the green cotton fabric between her thumb and fingers. "Yep. Got it yesterday. They brought in a new bale up at Jackson's."

"A new bale?" Paige unlocked the door and tried to think of a reply to that. She punched in the alarm code, let Ora in, then locked the door behind them.

"You know, at the dig store. They get in a new bale of clothes once a week or so. You can usually buy by the pound. Don't cost too much."

"Wow, I'd say you got a good deal on that dress then. It looks brand-new."

"Once, I got a pair of pants, just casual mind you, to wear around the house. Got home and found twenty dollars in the pocket. Didn't pay but two dollars for the things."

"Wow. *That* was a good deal." Paige started the coffee and the computer, and went about her morning routine. Several minutes later, she poured them each a cup of coffee and walked down to the waiting area, wondering if today's brew would finally meet with Ora's approval—something that had yet to occur. "Here you go."

Ora eyed the cup suspiciously before taking a sip. She scrunched her lips together. "Blah." More coffee-making tips were obviously on the way.

Paige took a sip from her own cup to see if she could guess what might be the subject of today's critique. Nice and hot. Strong enough but not too strong. Tasted good to her—but then it always did. She looked at Ora and waited.

"What's the story with that red-headed girl?"

The abrupt departure from the usual subject matter sent Paige's thoughts scrambling. *Red-headed girl?* "You mean Dawn?"

"Don't know of any other redheads around here."

"Well, she's a hard worker, quick and efficient with most anything, and she's usually late for work. That's about all I know for sure. Why do you ask?"

"She a real pharmacist, like you?"

Paige shook her head. "No. She's a technician. She just helps with data entry, counting, and pouring. We check everything she does."

"You reckon everyone sees it that way?"

"Of course they do." The acid of the coffee suddenly began to burn Paige's stomach. "Why would you ask that?"

"I realized yesterday afternoon I needed a refill of my blood pressure medicine. Came in, gave my bottle to the redhead. She filled it, gave it back."

"I'm sure Clarissa looked it over first. You just didn't notice."

"Think so?" Ora took a long sip of her coffee and contorted her face. "Ick. This is even worse than usual." She took another short sip as if to confirm, then looked toward Paige. "I'd say it's kind of hard to look something over, when that *something* is in the pharmacy, and you're sitting outside at the coffee shop talking on a cell phone, now wouldn't you?"

Paige set her cup aside. "Clarissa was out in the coffee shop while Dawn was in here working?" How many pharmacy laws would that break? Two that Paige could think of, maybe a few more. "Not for long, surely. Just a quick trip."

"Can't say. I was here maybe ten minutes, and she was out there at a table when I went in and out there at a table when I came out."

Paige fought to think through all the implications. An untrained twenty-year-old handing out prescriptions without a pharmacist's double check? The store could lose its license. Clarissa could lose her license. And that wasn't even considering the danger it put the patients in. When she asked the next question, she wasn't certain that she wanted an answer. "Were there any other customers in the pharmacy?"

"Didn't pay that much attention. There might have been one or two others."

The coffee burned all the way up Paige's esophagus now. Ora had to be wrong. Clarissa was smart to the point of brilliance; she would never do anything this idiotic. It was all a big misunderstanding, that's all. It had to be.

A memory flashed through her mind of her first week at work. What was it Clarissa had said to

Dawn before she left for lunch? Something to the effect of, "I've got my cell. You know the drill."

If Dawn already "knew the drill," that meant there had to be a precedent. Didn't it? No, it couldn't be. Maybe Ora just misunderstood.

Or maybe she didn't.

Paige spent the morning watching the door. She stopped what she was doing the very second Clarissa, wearing a pale pink skirt and a whimsical ponytail, walked in. Dawn was in the back room unloading supplies, so there would be no one to overhear anything that was said. Now was the perfect time to talk. She waited only until Clarissa took her first step into the dispensing area. "I need to ask you about something."

Clarissa put her purse in a drawer. "Yeah, like what?"

There was no way to phrase this question without it sounding like an accusation. Might as well be done with it. "You would never leave Dawn alone in the pharmacy, would you?"

"What would make you ask that?"

Paige did not want to go into all the details of the truth. No need to get Ora on Clarissa's bad side. "I heard a rumor that maybe you do."

"Yeah, well don't listen to idle talk. I was probably in the bathroom or something."

Paige nodded. "That's what I figured. I knew you would understand how reckless it would be to leave her here without you—like while you went to the coffee shop or something." She looked Clarissa directly in the eye, wanting her to understand that she did know the truth.

Clarissa took a step closer, putting her face only inches from Paige's. "Listen, before you got here, I was the only pharmacist here. A nine- to twelve-hour day without a break is a bit much to expect of anyone, wouldn't you say? Maybe I go out to the coffee shop sometimes, but what of it? Dawn calls my cell if something comes in she doesn't understand. Otherwise—you've seen her work. She's good."

In spite of the fact that Clarissa loomed uncomfortably close, Paige suppressed the urge to take a step backward. She needed to stand her ground. "Clarissa, you can *not* leave her alone like that. You're risking everything you have—your store, your license, other people's lives—just to get a latté. Especially now that I'm here, there is absolutely no excuse for it. If you want something from the coffee shop, send Dawn after it."

"I think you are forgetting who is the boss here and who is not."

"Clarissa, I'm not trying to be your boss. I'm trying to keep you out of trouble."

Clarissa folded her arms across herself and looked the other direction. Surely, she knew that Paige was right. This was not a gray area—it was deepest ebony. "I don't have time for this. I've got work to do." Clarissa went to the desk at the back of the pharmacy and began slinging papers from one pile to the other. "Get busy on the refills, that's what you're getting paid for."

Paige went to the stack of labels that waited on the counter. Other than the occasional drawer slam, the only other sound for the next half hour was the faint rustle of the labels, the thunk of capsules in the counting tray, and the soft footfalls of customers in the front part of the store.

Dawn finally emerged from the back room. "I didn't think I'd ever get that OTC order sorted out. What a pain." Dawn looked from Paige to Clarissa. "Everybody okay up here?"

Paige poured tablets into a pharmacy vial, almost afraid to break the silence. She looked at Dawn and shrugged.

"Dawn, check the refill line," Clarissa called from the back desk.

"I just listened an hour ago."

"So listen again."

Dawn rolled her eyes and walked toward the back, mumbling something under her breath.

A few hours and several cold stares later, Paige grew desperate to break through some of the hostility. She walked over to stand behind Clarissa, determined to make some small talk. "Have you heard anything from Milton Parrish?"

Clarissa turned to look over her shoulder. "Why? What are you hoping I've heard?"

"About the franchise. I was hoping you've heard that it's starting to come together."

Clarissa pivoted in her seat to face Paige more completely. "Is that what you wanted to know, or are you really asking if he's said more about what a great person you would be to run a pharmacy?"

Paige took a step back, shaking her head. "No. No, that's not at all—"

Clarissa wheeled around and grabbed her purse from beneath the counter. "I'm going to take a lunch break now. I am still allowed to do that, right?" She stormed from the pharmacy without a backward glance.

chapter **fifteen**

That night, Paige sat in the silent living room and stared at the same pale blue phone that had sat on the same oak table for the last twenty years. All she had to do was reach over and pick it up, punch the buttons, and work up the enthusiasm to convince her parents all was well. It shouldn't be that hard. Why was it that her hand would not reach for the receiver?

The old grandfather clock clanged out the quarter hour. Then the half hour. Paige thought back to Atlanta, to the emergency meeting and the long conference table where her best friend, Rachelle, had come to sit beside her.

"We were swamped upstairs. I swear, every kid in Atlanta has an ear infection this week."

"We were busy, too. So, any idea what the big meeting's about?"

"None. But Helga has been especially uptight every time I've seen her today. And given how uptight she usually is, that's saying a lot."

Just then, Helga Parker walked into the room, her plump face even more serious than usual. Rachelle was right about that. "Okay, people. I know you all have things you'd rather be doing right now, so I'll get directly to the point. Because of Glenda Prescott, we are announcing a complete and immediate change in policy."

Groans sounded all around. Busy as this HMO was, there were some patients that everyone knew, because those patients were such chronic complainers. Glenda Prescott was such a patient.

"She has been on Vasoretic for a few months now. When she came in two weeks ago to get a refill, she was given Vasotec instead. Apparently, she took it for a couple of weeks, then noticed some swelling in her ankles."

"Come on, Helga, tell 'em the whole story. It's worth repeating." Josh Hart, the assistant pharmacy director, was as laid-back and jovial as Helga was uptight and stern. "She came walking into administration yesterday, screaming about how we were trying to kill people. I asked her

what was wrong, and she . . ." He started laughing and took a moment to compose himself. "She pulled up her pant leg and said, 'THIS is wrong.'"

He snickered again. "Tell you the truth, I guess her ankles were a little edematous, but not enough that I had a clue what she was talking about."

Helga grimaced. "A patient receiving the wrong medication is a serious matter, regardless of whether or not it was a life-threatening event. The fact is, if her ankles had not swelled, alerting her to the fact that she was getting only the beta-blocker without the benefit of the added diuretic, her blood pressure could have gone significantly higher. We all know that."

"Did her blood pressure go higher?" Rachelle asked.

"About five points systolic." Helga drummed her fingers across the thick chart that sat on the table in front of her.

Helga rapped her knuckles on the table for attention. "And she's started talking to one of those fast-talking TV lawyers. Likely there's going to be a lawsuit. Of course, our in-house legal team wanted a copy of anything pertinent, just in case. I pulled up her file, and saw PIA in the pharmacy comments of her profile. Anyone want to tell me what that means?"

Dead silence. Furtive glances cast at each other, but no one dared to look at Helga.

"Rachelle, how about you? What do you think it means?"

"It means pain in the . . . uh . . . backside."

Several sniggers sounded from around the table.

Helga glared at the assembled group. "Since you were good enough to tell me what it means, Rachelle, maybe you can be so kind as to explain to me why you think this might have happened."

Rachelle shrugged. "Just so everyone knows what they're dealing with when she comes to the window. You know to expect complaints and problems, so no one gets caught unawares in dealing with her."

"This . . . PIA. Is it in other profiles, too?"

Rachelle looked around the table at her silent co-workers. "Probably. Maybe a couple dozen or so?"

"A couple dozen?" Helga's whole face quivered with the force of the words. "A couple dozen of our patients have something derogatory like this in their profile?"

"Not to be disrespectful, but we fill a thousand prescriptions a day in this clinic. If only two dozen people are singled out as being hard to deal with, then I think that says more about those people than it does about us."

Helga looked hard at her for a minute, as if she wanted to say more but couldn't think of a valid argument. She finally changed subjects. "Anyway, back to the problem at hand. One thing we've real-

ized is that we have no idea who made this mistake. Paige's initials were printed on Mrs. Prescott's bottle, but we all know that any pharmacist in here could have been the one who actually did the final check. So, we're implementing some new policies—actually, we're enforcing the existing policy that we've been much too lax on. Effective immediately, every single label must be hand-initialed by the pharmacist who does the final check. Understood?"

Everyone around the room nodded.

"Great. This new policy will be enforced, effective immediately. I'll be coming around doing spot checks for the next few weeks, just to make sure we're on track.

"Any questions?"

Silence.

"That's all for now, then. See you all tomorrow." Helga walked from the room, taking her thick file with her.*

The grandfather clock chimed the hour, and still Paige had not touched the phone. Maybe she just needed a little practice. She finally picked up the phone and punched some familiar numbers.

Rachelle answered on the fourth ring. "Can my caller ID be correct?"

"Oh come on, Shell, you know it's me."

"She lives!" Rachelle sang out the words as if she were announcing the resurrection of Lazarus to an entire village. "I haven't heard from you in so long, I'd started scanning the Tennessee obituaries."

The familiar lilt of her old roommate's voice hit Paige like an unexpected kick to the gut. Whether from joy or pain she didn't know, but the force of the reaction doubled her over. *Put on a brave face. Sound happy. You've got to do this now, or you'll never make it work on your parents.* She drew herself upright and spoke in a bright tone. "Yeah, well, it took you so long to answer, I thought you must be out for the night."

"Going out is highly overrated."

"Since when?" When Rachelle walked into a room, heads turned. In spite of her commitment phobia, she never lacked for a date, even on a Wednesday night.

"Oh, just thought I'd stay at home, recharge my batteries. Maybe watch a little TV—ESPN or something."

"Aha! That's it. It's that Braves center fielder—what's his name—Steve Jensen. And you're sitting home to watch him play? Wow, this must be serious!"

"I don't do serious." She paused a split second too long to give her words credibility. "So, what's up with you? How's the new job?"

Time to get down to the practice session. "It's going great. It's a beautiful pharmacy in a quaint location, and I work with some great people. Couldn't be better."

"Translation—doing hard time. Beautiful place but minimum bonding with fellow pharmacy personnel."

"How do you do that?"

"You're easy."

"That's what I'm afraid of. I'm about to call Mom, and I don't want her to worry."

"She'll worry anyway, that's what mothers do. One small tip—leave off that 'couldn't be better' part. It's a dead giveaway."

"Thanks."

"And tell her I'm praying for her, okay?"

"I will." Hopefully Rachelle's prayers would get a few more results than Paige's had lately.

The two friends exchanged another minute of small talk, then Paige was left alone with the phone again. She looked at the number written on yellow sticky paper stuck to the receiver—the line for the temporary apartment where her parents now lived. She picked up the receiver and punched the keys before she could think to change her mind.

Her mother answered on the first ring. "How's my girl?" Shuffling noises came from the other end of the line, then her mother's low whisper, "Norman, it's Paige. Go get on the extension." Her voice returned then, with full strength. "You didn't answer my question. How are you?"

Keep it upbeat. Light. Happy. "I'm just fine. How are you?"

"Right as rain. I'm glad to get this thing started."

From the tone of her voice, Doris Woodward gave no indication that what she had started would almost kill her. Could kill her, in fact.

What had the doctor said? "The reason I have such a good success rate is that I will take you as close to death as I possibly can before I turn it around." Paige thought of the massive chemo her mother was about to undergo before Aunt Opal's healthy stem cells would be infused into her veins. The sickness. The pain. The hope.

"Paige!" Her father's voice came from the extension. "How's that job coming along?"

Paige would pull this off—she had to. "Still great. After the first week, I know it's going to be even more than I had hoped. You got the money I sent from the signing bonus, right?"

"Sure did. Carried it over to Patient Accounts myself—three days before it was due, I might add. Maybe I had to ask 'em for a little financial help up front, but never let it be said that Norman Woodward doesn't pay his bills on time. I'm going to do that every single month—pay early, I mean."

Her mother said, "I can't wait until I can come see that pharmacy myself. I bet it's beautiful."

Some things you just don't tell your mother while she is in the fight of her life—things like an undercurrent of anger that you can't understand, cold stares, and your fellow employees whispering behind shelves. "How about your place? What's it like?"

"You should see this little apartment. It's so cute. Reminds me of the place your father and I lived when we first got married."

"Only thing it's missing is the leaky roof," her father said from the extension.

Paige laughed. "Well, that's something we can be thankful for. How's Aunt Opal?"

"Good," her mother answered. "They drew her stem cells today and everything went well. They said she produced even more than they needed."

"Didn't surprise me none. She's always done everything over the top—from Christmas decorations on down. Anyone who goes so far as to iron her skivvies is gonna produce extra stem cells, it just makes sense."

"Oh, Daddy." Paige laughed and then found her voice catch a little. "I wish I could be there with you."

"You rest easy. Your mother's in the best of hands here. I'm practically an expert in all of this now. You couldn't ask for any better. Tomorrow they're going to remove her old port and put in a . . . let me see . . . a central venous catheter. They'll use it for chemo, blood draws, the works. And I guess I'm supposed to go to some sort of class about how to help take care of it."

"Oh, Dad, it's just so wrong that you're mixed up in all this."

"Nonsense. She's *my* wife, isn't she? Besides, this is more or less what I've done for the last forty years, unclogging drains and such. Only difference I see is the size of the pipes."

Paige couldn't bring herself to laugh, but she did smile. "Poor Mom."

"Poor Mom, nothing. Downright lucky if you ask me."

But they both knew better. There was nothing lucky about what Paige's mother was about to go through.

chapter **sixteen**

Clarissa sat in the coffee shop, thumbing through a magazine, pretending her lunchtime wasn't long over. So what? Let Perky Paige handle the crowd for a while. After yesterday's condescending tirade, she deserved it.

The magazine jerked from her hand. "Hello there." Tony waved it in the air. "What are you reading?" He flipped through a couple of pages of *Vogue* before tossing it back on the table. "Very highbrow."

"Tony! What are you doing here?" She jumped to her feet and threw her arms around him.

"I used the excuse that I needed to check the progress upstairs, but the truth is, I came to see my favorite niece."

She swatted his arm. "I'm your only niece."

"Even if there were a dozen, you'd still be my favorite."

"Good answer. A lie, but still a good answer."

"I'll buy you lunch, what do you say?"

She pointed to the mostly untouched salad on the table. "Just ate. How about dinner?" At least something good would come from this day.

He rubbed his chin. "I'll buy dinner if we can order pizza."

"You eat entirely too much junk food. There's a decent steak house just outside the city limits. It's actually a pretty nice place, considering it's in this dump of a town."

"You've soaked me for one too many expensive dinners lately. I say pizza."

She laughed and stood. "Well, come on, I have to get to work. We can argue about it while I show you the latest upgrades in the pharmacy."

When they walked in, the place was empty of customers, and no one seemed to be in the dispensing area, either. "Come on back." Clarissa opened the door, wondering if Paige had tired of waiting for her and left for lunch. No, she would have seen her go by, and besides, Paige was too perfect to do anything like that. "Anybody home?"

"Dawn's still at lunch. I'm back here." Paige's voice came from the back.

"What are you doing back there?" This was one of those times that Clarissa was glad for the Richardson gift of being able to carry on a perfectly normal sounding conversation in a perfectly normal tone, even when there was enough tension in the air to suffocate the average mortal. She'd talked to Tony on the phone about the situation but never let on how fully she was beginning to dislike Paige. Hopefully he'd see how unfair everything was on his own.

"Wiping down the shelves." Paige, too, seemed to possess the gift for falsely light conversational tone. She emerged from behind the shelves, carrying a wad of paper towels in her hand. "Oh, sorry. Didn't know we had company."

"Paige, this is my uncle. Tony, this is Paige."

Tony went perfectly still and simply stared at Paige. Finally, he took a step forward and offered his hand. "Uh . . . hello."

Tony at a loss for words? Clarissa had never seen it before—and she didn't like it now. She looked at Paige to see her reaction.

"Uh . . . just a second." Her cheeks flared pink as she dropped the towels in the trash and went to the sink to wash her hands. She came back, smiled at Tony, and shook his hand. "Sorry about that." Her cheeks were still pink.

Tony looked from Paige to Clarissa and something sparked in his eyes. "I was just telling Clarissa I'm planning to stay for the rest of the day, thought I might grab some dinner before I leave. You want to join us? I hear there's a nice steak place on the edge of town."

Clarissa almost snorted. "Steak house, really? I wish I'd thought of that."

He had the most charming smile when he chose to use it, as he did now. "How often do I get the chance to take my favorite niece and her co-worker out for a special dinner?"

Clarissa was going to kill him. What did he think he was doing?

Paige toyed with a bottle on the counter and didn't look up. "I don't want to take you away from your time together. Thanks for the offer, though."

Tony walked right up beside her and nudged her with his shoulder. "Oh, come now. You two should spend time together outside of work, and besides, it's a free meal. It's hard to argue with that." He looked back toward Clarissa. "Clarissa sure never does. Do you, Sweet Pea?"

"Even if you do have to put up with the likes of Tony to get it." Her fingernails dug into her palms.

"It's all settled then. I'll meet you ladies here at closing time."

"But I—" Paige's expression looked so genuine as she started another fake protest.

"No more arguments, my decision is final. I'll be back at closing." He flashed that charming smile once again and Paige dropped her eyes. But she couldn't hide a grin.

"Come on, Tony, I'll walk with you to the door." Clarissa grabbed him by the arm and pulled him away from the blushing Paige.

"What, you afraid I'll get mugged on the way?"

He grinned back over his shoulder. "What's this world coming to?"

Paige's answering giggle seemed to follow them down the aisle of the store. Clarissa waited until they were at the front door before whispering through clenched teeth, "So, what made you invite her to dinner, the blond hair or the blue eyes?"

He waved and smiled toward Paige in the back, then pushed through the door into the lobby. When the door swung closed behind them, he put his hands on Clarissa's shoulders. "Neither, actually. It was the repeated phone calls from my favorite niece, who thinks her co-worker is out to get her, that she's gunning for brownie points with my father, and possibly even out to conquer the free world with her evil schemes. I came down to check it out, and the best way to check it out is to spend some time actually talking to this person."

She studied his face, from the firm set of his jaw to the earnest slant of his eyes. "Really?"

"Of course. Why do you think I'm here today? I'm not really involved at all in running this job. I told Dad I wanted to come see it, made up some vague excuse, and came down here to see what's going on."

"So, this whole 'I'll take you both to dinner,' it's . . ."

"Just my way of checking things out—incognito like, you know what I'm saying?" He wiggled his eyebrows up and down for maximum effect.

Clarissa giggled and hugged him. "You're the best."

"Of course I am." He nodded toward the pharmacy door. "I have to say, she looks harmless enough to me."

"Yeah, well, that's the kind you've got to watch out for." Clarissa went back into the pharmacy determined that Tony would see the real Paige tonight. The only way to do that was to make certain that Paige relaxed and let her guard down, which probably meant eating some crow about the argument yesterday.

Paige thought through the list of excuses she could give for backing out of dinner tonight. There were plenty of choices; all she had to do was pick one. Given the way Clarissa had charged down the aisle after her uncle, she had no doubt given him an earful of how wrong the invitation had been in the first place. They would be relieved with whatever reason she chose.

She was typing a prescription into the computer when the squeak of the door told her Clarissa had returned. She didn't even look up. "You know, I really should go home after work. I need to walk the dog, all that. You two go on without me."

"Oh, please come with us."

This made Paige stop what she was doing and look up.

Clarissa walked up beside her and stared out

across the pharmacy, the fingers of her right hand tapping against the fingers of her left. "You know, you were right about what you said yesterday. I shouldn't leave Dawn here alone, I know that I shouldn't." She dropped her hands to the counter and leaned. "I'm sorry I got so defensive about it."

"Uh . . . no problem."

"Good." Clarissa's expression immediately brightened. "Since that's settled, of course you're coming to dinner. Like Tony said, we need to spend some time together outside of work. I mean, after all, we hardly know each other."

This amazing transformation in Clarissa's attitude was more than a little unsettling, but Paige couldn't afford to ignore the gift that it was. Whether or not she wanted to go, she needed to make this effort.

Clarissa hummed all afternoon long, happier than Paige ever remembered seeing her. Could it be this easy? Maybe this dinner out was just the thing they had needed all along. A tiny shaft of hope seemed to light somewhere inside her.

The rest of the afternoon passed almost pleasantly, and when they locked the door for the evening, Clarissa took off her lab coat and hung it on the hook. "So, you're not seeing anyone, right?" Her voice sounded so casual—a little too casual.

Paige finished wiping down the counter. "No, I'm not. Why do you ask?"

"What do you think of my uncle Tony?"

"Seems nice enough."

"Nice enough? Is that all?"

"Since he's married, I'd say nice enough is plenty." Paige threw the paper towel in the trash. Subject closed.

"Is not."

Paige looked at her. "Then what's the gold ring on his left hand?"

"Oh, that." Clarissa waved her hand dismissively. "Ancient history. He's been divorced a while now. His ex left him for some fat old partner in her law firm. What an idiot."

Paige wondered at the woman who would leave those broad shoulders and that stubbled face with the boyish smile for anyone, much less a fat old law partner. Of course, what did she know about it?

The thought of tonight's dinner began to grow increasingly uncomfortable. Tony was handsome, magnetic in his charm, and most of all he was Clarissa's uncle. What was on that list of excuses again? Time to pull one out and get out of here. Lean Cuisine at home sounded just right, and a whole lot less complicated than the alternative.

"I'll go out front and wait for Tony." Clarissa disappeared out the door before Paige had a chance to spout out a reason why she suddenly couldn't go. Well, she'd just have to say it to both of them now.

When she walked out the door, she saw Clarissa and Tony across the lobby—her dark elegance next to his roguish charm, her willowy frame next to his athletic build. They were too busy talking to see Paige come out the door, but their voices carried across the room.

"Oh, she's just finishing up a few things. She'll be right out."

"Ever heard of a place nearby called Frederick's? Some of the guys upstairs were telling me about it."

"Oh yeah, it's supposed to be really nice. Romantic, you know?"

That's it. Time to get out of this one and head for home.

"Hi, Paige."

Paige jumped at the sound of Cory's voice so close behind her. She turned to see him leaning against the wall beside the pharmacy door. "You scared me to death."

"Sorry." He pushed off the wall. "Hey, I was about to go get some dinner. You want to come?"

Paige knew she couldn't very well make an excuse to Clarissa and then go to dinner with Cory. "Oh, thanks. I can't tonight. . . ." Her excuses died without voice. She locked the pharmacy door, then pulled on it once to double check.

"Paige, there you are. Will you hurry up? Tony's about to starve." Clarissa's voice came through even louder this time.

Cory sized up Tony and then glanced back at Paige. "You've got plans, huh?"

"Cory, I—"

"Forget it." He stalked off, walking right past Clarissa and Tony without acknowledging that he'd seen them.

Clarissa glanced over her shoulder toward Cory. She turned back so quickly Paige thought maybe she'd imagined it.

She walked over to join them. "Sorry it took me so long."

Tony smiled at her. "So, I was just telling Sweet Pea that I heard about this place, Frederick's. What do you think?"

This was the chance she'd been waiting for. "You two go ahead. Frederick's is a little out of my price range."

"Nonsense. I would never invite a lady to dinner and then allow her to pay. Dinner's on me."

Paige shook her head. "I wouldn't feel right. You've come to visit your niece, and somehow ended up with me in the bargain. That's not fair to you."

Tony offered her his free arm. "Unfair in a totally fabulous way, I assure you. You are simply the icing on the cake."

Paige took a step back. "I don't think . . ."

Clarissa let go of her uncle and grabbed Paige by the arm. "Stop thinking and let's get moving. Come on, we're wasting time and I'm hungry."

"Well said." Tony took Paige's other arm, and the duo made a show of pulling her through the lobby.

"Okay, okay, I give." It might be fun. Maybe tonight would be just what she needed to finally break through with Clarissa. *Thanks, God, sorry I doubted You.* She looked at Clarissa and smiled. "Sweet Pea?"

"What can I say? Tony is one of the few people who appreciate my finer qualities."

Tony jingled the keys in his hand. "I'll bring the horse from the barn. You ladies stay right here."

Less than a minute later, a midnight blue Porsche pulled up to the curb. Tony hopped out of the still-running car, walked around to the passenger side, and opened the door. "Allow me, ladies."

Paige climbed into the back. Clarissa sat in the passenger seat and turned. "Sorry about that. Tony's car is built for two people—and their really short friends."

Paige smiled. "I'm good."

Tony drove through the square, and soon they were following the ribbon of Highway 43 into northern Alabama. "So Paige, tell me about yourself." He glanced at her in the rearview mirror, his amber eyes almost glowing with intensity.

She shivered and looked out the window. "I grew up just down the road from Shoal Creek in a little town called Sledge. That's where I live now, in fact."

"Okay, born and raised in a small town. Got it. Where'd you go to pharmacy school?"

"Samford."

"Ah yes, Birmingham, we're moving on to the bigger cities now. Got that. Where'd you work after that? Before here, I mean."

"Maybe you should have told me there was an application process for this dinner." Paige hoped that her tone sounded light, but in truth, she wanted to stop the questions before they dug any deeper. She looked in the mirror and found him staring at her, surprise playing out across his face.

He threw his head back and laughed. "All right, Clarissa. This is the kind of woman you need to be working with. Someone that won't take all the usual Richardson guff." He laughed again. "Sorry about that, being overly inquisitive and overly direct tends to be a family trait, I'm afraid."

Paige said, "Then tell me about Tony Richardson."

Clarissa groaned and slouched down in her seat. "Oh no. You've done it now. Neither one of us will get in another word for the rest of the evening."

Tony nudged Clarissa with his elbow. "That's likely true. But she asked for it. And I am fascinating."

"Fascinating? Since when?" Clarissa leaned her chin on her elbow and grinned at him.

"Since now. I make a decree that from this

121

moment on, I shall be nothing less than fascinating, captivating, and charming."

Paige didn't doubt for a moment that he could pull off all three.

chapter **seventeen**

Paige hummed as she walked through the lobby. The sun seemed a little brighter today, the air sweet with the promise of spring. It was the nicest morning she remembered in a while. When she reached the door of the apothecary, she stopped and stared.

There, in a Mason jar, was a bouquet of wildflowers. She looked around the room. No one seemed to be watching her—or even aware of her existence. She picked up the jar and looked for some sort of note.

Nothing.

"Looks like you got yourself a secret admirer."

The glass slipped through Paige's fingers. She managed to regain her grip just in time. "Ora, you scared me to death, sneaking up like that." She took a deep breath, then smiled at the unpredictable woman. "Did you bring these?"

"Wouldn't have used the word *admirer* if I brought 'em, now would I? I'm an old woman, not an admirer. Wouldn't be *secret* either." She reached out a wrinkled hand and touched a purple blossom. "They're right pretty. Hard to find this time of year. Who's your young man?"

Paige turned the key in the lock. "Got me. Probably someone left them for Clarissa."

Ora followed her inside the pharmacy and took a seat in her usual spot. "Not likely. That girl's too uppity for something this special."

Paige started the coffee. "I'm not so sure. From what her uncle said last night, the guys are practically fighting over her."

"Didn't say they weren't. But her kind of admirer would most likely send a dozen roses, not go out and handpick wildflowers. He'd be too afraid of getting his nice shoes dirty."

Paige set the flowers on the counter and went about the business of getting ready for the day ahead. When the coffee finished, she poured cups for both of them and did her best not to give the flowers another thought. Still she couldn't help but look at the colorful spray every few minutes. The beauty of the arrangement, the effort it must have taken—of course, those flowers could have been meant for anyone and for any number of reasons.

The morning progressed, through Ora's coffee-making tips, three customers, and very few phone calls. The slow pace gave Paige time to think. And wonder some more.

When Clarissa arrived, she walked into the dispensing area, a smile on her face. "What did you think of my uncle Tony?"

Paige tried to keep her voice noncommittal. "He's nice."

Clarissa quirked her eyebrow. "Nice? Admit it. You like him."

"Of course I like him. Why wouldn't I?"

"Um-hmm."

Paige felt the heat in her cheeks. "What?"

"Where'd these come from?" Clarissa pointed at the flowers.

"Don't know. Someone left them at our door this morning."

Clarissa looked toward the door, then back at the flowers. Her eyes narrowed for a split second, a spark of what looked like anger flamed then disappeared. "Really?" She put her hand over her mouth. "I hope it's not some weirdo stalker or something. I say we throw the whole thing away."

Paige laughed outright. "Get a grip. I am not throwing them away—they're beautiful. Someone went to a lot of trouble for these."

"If it will make you feel better, I'll take them home with me tonight so you won't have to worry about the 'stalker' coming in and seeing them."

The pharmacy door opened just as she said it, but the man entering didn't look like a stalker. He carried a huge bouquet with several colors of roses and other flowers Paige couldn't name. It was gigantic.

Clarissa went to the counter, already reaching, a smile on her face. "And who might these be for?"

The man looked at his clipboard. "Paige and Clarissa—pharmacists at Richardson Apothecary."

Clarissa jerked the card from the bouquet without acknowledging the clipboard awaiting her signature.

Paige signed the form. She fumbled in her pocket for a tip and handed it to the man with a smile. "Thank you so much."

He nodded. "Enjoy 'em."

Clarissa turned and leaned against the counter, card still in hand. "They're from Tony. It says, 'I enjoyed our time together last night. Let's do it again soon.' "

She held the card up to Paige's face. "Notice how the names are listed? *Paige* and Clarissa, not *Clarissa* and Paige. See it? Your name's first. You know what that means."

"That the person in the flower shop took it down wrong?" Paige took in the colors of the bouquet, then looked at the little Mason jar. "Maybe he brought the wildflowers, too."

"Not a chance."

Paige looked at her, wondering where the sharp tone had suddenly come from. She sniffed the bouquet. "This is nice. My uncles never send me flowers after they buy me dinner. Come to think of it, my uncles never buy me dinner."

"Yeah, I'm just lucky I guess."

Clarissa walked to the back of the pharmacy. There was no mistaking the way Tony had flirted last night. Maybe he was here to check out Paige, but he had crossed the line into *checking her out*. The order of their names on the card gave all the proof she needed. She was going to lose him, too.

The scraggly bunch of weeds called wildflowers stared at her from the pathetic excuse for a vase. She knew they were from Cory, she'd seen the way he'd been watching Paige. Last night he had obviously been waiting for her at the door, and then he left in a huff when he realized the three of them were going to dinner. Yeah, this was a jealous-about-Tony kind of gift. Why couldn't they have been for her?

She could still remember those weeks before the pharmacy opened. The smell of fresh paint and sawdust lingering in the air, gleaming cabinetry, spotless carpets. While she stocked the shelves and generally set things up, Cory supervised the finish construction work. He would sometimes stop what he was doing and spend an hour helping her unpack office supplies or arrange displays, or just talking. The lingering looks and flirting had eventually led to phone calls, dinners, and staying out late enough to watch the sun rise on a new day.

Then Paige showed up. The cute new girl in town. Suddenly, the old one didn't measure up.

When she walked to the front, a middle-aged woman smiled as Paige was explaining her medicine. The woman had probably waited half an hour for Paige's ridiculous amount of rechecking, but she smiled and laughed. Why did everyone love Paige?

The transaction complete, Paige walked up beside her. "Hey, Clarissa, you all right? You seem like you're not feeling so well."

Clarissa shook her head. "Just tired."

"It looks like it's going to be a slow day. Why don't you go home and get some rest. Take Tony's flowers with you. That will cheer you up."

"Oh, you know, I think it will do me good to stay the whole time. Sometimes nothing works better than staying busy, you know what I mean?"

Paige nodded. "I feel that way a lot."

Yeah, I'll just bet you do, Miss Perfect Life.

chapter **eighteen**

At noon on Monday, hunger forced Paige to stand in line at the coffee shop. She could not afford this, had no business spending six dollars on lunch, but she hadn't made it to the grocery store over the weekend. She went up to the counter and ordered a sandwich and a bottled water, vowing to skip a meal to make up for the expense.

"My treat." Before Paige could get her wallet out of her purse, Lee Richardson was handing the girl at the counter a twenty-dollar bill.

"You don't have to do that."

"Of course I don't have to. I want to. You're doing me a great service by working here with my granddaughter."

Paige smiled at him. "You keep saying that, but

you did the service for me by getting me this job. This place is beautiful." She looked at him. "I didn't realize you were here today."

"Just got here. About to go check in upstairs. Mind if I come down and talk to you for a few minutes while you're eating?"

"Not at all. There's a bench out front that's in a nice sunny spot. I was planning to sit out there."

"Good, I'll come find you."

As he walked away, Paige noticed an extra heaviness in his gait today. Something else felt different too, but she couldn't pinpoint exactly what. His eyes maybe. Yeah, that was it, they looked so dull.

When he came outside a few minutes later, she decided to come right out with the question. "Lee, are you all right?"

"All right?"

"I don't know, you just seem sad. The sparkle's missing from your eyes today."

He looked at her for a minute then shrugged. "It's a long story."

"I'm sorry. I wasn't trying to pry."

"No, you weren't prying. You see—" he took a sip of water "—today is my fiftieth wedding anniversary."

Paige put a gentle hand on his shoulder and squeezed. "I'm sorry. You must really miss your wife today."

"Yeah. I had promised to take her on a cruise through the Greek Islands for our fiftieth. She loved archaeology, traveling, sightseeing. I hated all of those things and did as much as I could to put off doing them. I kept promising her that for our fiftieth anniversary, I would go wherever she wanted, she could call all the shots. She had brochures for Greek cruises in our house for the last five years, had figured out every last detail, down to which cabin she wanted on which ship."

"When did she pass away?"

"Three years ago. It's been the hardest three years of my life."

Before Paige could offer her regrets, a shadow fell across their table.

"Hey, boss. Hope I'm not interrupting anything." Cory walked up to Lee. "You did invite me to join you, right?"

Lee looked at Paige. "Hope you don't mind. Thought I'd catch up on the news at both places at once."

"Not at all." She scooted over. "Have a seat, Cory."

Cory sat beside Paige, a little too close. She inched further down the bench. "Did your mother get her medicine okay?"

"Yep. She said you did a superior job of refilling and to tell you thanks."

Lee smiled, but when Paige looked directly at him he coughed—as if he could cover it up that easily. He held up his empty water bottle. "I'm going to throw this away, be right back." He walked toward the trash can so slowly, it was obvious he'd left the two of them alone on purpose.

Cory shifted so that his arm rested against hers. "Nice day, hmm?" He grinned and took a bite of his sandwich.

Paige knew that her discomfort would only encourage Cory to be more bold. Time to put him off balance with a new topic of discussion, one that Cory couldn't manipulate into something that it wasn't. "What happened to Lee's wife?"

"She died a few years back."

"I know that. I mean, how did she die?"

He stretched his arms up, then locked his hands behind his head. "Malpractice." The word sounded so matter-of-fact. So . . . clinical. "I'm surprised you didn't know that. Once he gets started talking about the carelessness in the medical profession these days, he can go on for hours. The man's intense, but you've probably already noticed that."

Paige tried to swallow a gulp of her water, but it could not get past the lump in her throat. She began to cough.

Cory reached over to thump her on the back. "You okay?"

Lee returned just then, his chuckle even louder than Paige's gasps for air. "What do you think, Cory, do you need to try the Heimlich?"

Paige looked up at him and tried to breathe. "No. I'm okay."

Nothing could have been further from the truth.

• • •

Clarissa looked toward the door for the tenth time. "I'm starving. Where is Paige?"

Dawn shrugged. "She should be back in about five minutes. You want to go ahead and get a head start?"

"Yeah, maybe I'll just do that. Leave everything out for her to check when she comes in, okay?" So what if it bothered Paige. It was time she learned the realities of small retail.

Clarissa was picking up her purse when her cell phone vibrated in her lab coat pocket. "Hello."

"Have you heard about Kelsey?" Alexa's shrill voice came through the phone. It only added to the annoyance of the whole situation.

Clarissa sighed. "Yes, I've heard. What's she thinking? She hardly knows the guy."

"Oh, I think it's romantic. A love that would not suffer separation." She said the last part in her best movie announcer voice, then she sighed. "Yep, it's the kind of thing they write about in novels, my friend. Aren't you excited for her?"

Clarissa turned her back on the store and leaned against the counter. "Yeah, right."

Dawn poked a bottle and prescription under Clarissa's nose for checking. Clarissa nodded and waved her away.

"She's running off to marry some guy she hardly knows. I don't know that *excited* is the right word."

"But she's happier than I've ever seen her."

Dawn was back, this time holding a rectangle of paper in front of Clarissa's face. The words were written in blue ink. "Look over your shoulder. The man in the suit is acting kind of weird."

Annoyed, Clarissa turned around and immediately saw the man in question. His brown hair was arranged in a bad comb-over, his suit looked rumpled and cheap. He snapped his gaze away and started browsing through the cough and cold section.

"Hey, Alexa, I've got to go. I'll talk to you later." Clarissa hung up and whispered to Dawn. "What's he doing?"

"He's been in here for a while now. Every time I look over at him, he's watching the pharmacy. As soon as he sees me looking, he starts acting like he's browsing through the aisles, but I'm telling you, he's watching us."

Clarissa thought about the narcotics locked in a safe just a few feet away. Small pharmacies made prime targets for addicts, and there was nothing more dangerous than a druggie with a weapon. She looked around the store. There were three customers in various places. Was he waiting until the store was empty? She turned to Dawn. "I'm going out to talk to him. Keep your hand on the phone. Dial 9-1-1 if he so much as twitches a finger."

Dawn put her hand on the phone. "Got it."

Clarissa drew up her shoulders in an effort to

appear taller than her five feet five inches. She walked directly up to the man, who was pretending he didn't see her coming. "Hello there. I've noticed you've been looking for a while. Something I can help you find?"

"As a matter of fact, yes." His words were not slurred as she'd expected, and when he looked up, his eyes seemed clear. No hint of desperation in his voice.

Whew. Her shoulders relaxed a bit, easing the straining muscles in her back.

He reached into his back pocket and drew out a fake lizard-skin wallet. He flipped it open and pulled out a business card. "My name is Gary Powell. State board inspector."

Clarissa felt the smile droop off her face. A board inspector?

Although she'd heard stories of how they sometimes stood out front like just another customer and observed store operations anonymously, she'd never expected it to happen in this little place. She quickly offered the most sincere smile she could muster and took care to use her sweetest southern accent. "Oh my, an inspection. To what do I owe this great honor?"

Gary Powell didn't smile. "Routine."

When she thought of how close she'd come to leaving Dawn alone while he was watching, she almost cried. Wouldn't Paige have a fit if she knew.

She took a quick mental inventory of everything that had transpired in the last half hour. She'd been on the phone a good bit of the time, but there was no law against that. Dawn had brought everything over to check, even while Clarissa had her back turned. He would have seen that. Okay, so far, so good.

"I'm Clarissa Richardson." Her hand shook as she extended it to him.

Gary Powell offered a courteous shake. "Nice place you've got here. I was just admiring the workmanship."

Clarissa tried to relax. "Thanks. My grandfather's company did it. Richardson Construction."

He nodded, first at her and then at the dispensing area. "Mind if I see your files?"

Like she could refuse. "Oh, please, come on back."

As she led the way, she could see Dawn watching her, on the alert. Clarissa opened her eyes as wide as possible, trying to communicate an all-out alarm. Hopefully, she'd get the message. When she reached the counter, she beckoned with a smile. "Dawn, please come meet Inspector Powell. He's with the state board, he's going to look over our files."

Dawn walked over and shook his hand. "Nice to meet you."

He nodded. "You too, young lady." He looked at Clarissa. "Where can I sit so I won't be in your way?"

Clarissa led him to the desk along the back wall. "Right here. Make yourself comfortable. Anything in particular you want to see?"

He paused for a second and scratched his chin. "Why don't I start with what you've done today."

"Sure." She lifted the stack of papers from the black plastic tray. "Here are today's offerings. We've not been terribly busy, as I'm sure you saw, but there's enough here to give you a good idea of how we do things."

He started flipping through the prescriptions. "Thanks."

Clarissa nodded toward the front. "I'm going to work on some refills. Call me if you need anything." She walked up to the counter beside Dawn and motioned her behind a shelf. She leaned over to whisper, "Listen, you've *never* been left to work alone, got it?"

"Duh. I'm not stupid."

At that moment, Paige rushed into the store, pulling on her lab coat and finger brushing her hair at the same time. "Sorry I'm late. I lost track of time."

Clarissa froze, wishing she could send Paige away again right now. "Paige. Glad you're here. I want to introduce you to somebody."

Paige looked puzzled and then caught a glimpse of the man sifting through their records. Clarissa thought she saw almost a hint of panic in Paige's eyes for a second.

"This is Gary Powell. He is a state board inspector, here just on a routine visit." Clarissa strolled toward the back desk, in no hurry at all to reach the destination.

He looked up from the stack of paper, saw them approaching, and stood to introduce himself.

Paige shook his hand, and this time the color truly drained from her face. "Nice to meet you."

"You as well. So, have you worked here from the beginning?"

"No. I just started a few weeks ago."

"Where did you work before?"

"In Nashville. At the Nashville Free Clinic."

"I was sorry to hear they shut that place down. It did some good work." His whole face relaxed into an expression of downright affection. He had met Paige barely a minute ago, and she'd already won him over. How did she do it?

"I was sorry about it, too. But then again"—she gestured around the pharmacy—"it brought me here."

"Clarissa, Dr. Janke's office on the phone for you," said Dawn from the counter.

"Take a message."

Gary Powell smiled affably. "No, please. Take it. I don't want my presence here to interrupt your work."

Clarissa walked to the counter, her ears trained toward anything that might be said behind her. Just before she picked up the receiver, she heard Gary Powell ask, "So, Paige, how do you like it here?"

Paige looked toward the counter and waited until she was certain that Clarissa had answered the phone. "I like it just fine."

He shifted in his seat and spoke in a lower tone. "The problem we have in a lot of these small-town pharmacies is that they tend to bend the rules a little. I guess the theory is that it won't matter much, because no one will notice. Is there anything here that you've seen that the board should know about?" He looked directly at her—not a threatening look, but an expression that wanted answers.

"I . . . uh . . ." Paige wondered if he knew something or if he was just throwing out questions, hoping to snag something he might have missed. The bitter taste from the unfairness in Atlanta might have faded, but it was far from gone. She didn't want to ever get another dose. So, she took a deep breath and tried her best to smile. "No, I think Clarissa is very conscious of doing things the right way."

He nodded and jotted something in the notebook on the desk. "That's what I like to hear."

Paige exhaled slowly and returned to the dispensing counter. Clarissa emerged from the back shelves, and Paige realized at once that she had been eavesdropping on the whole conversation.

She mouthed the words *good job*, then went back

to the work at the counter as if nothing significant had happened at all.

Not ten minutes later, Gary Powell returned the stack of prescriptions to the front counter. "Everything looks to be in order. Nice job, young ladies."

Clarissa smiled up at him, and Paige had the distinct impression she was considering batting her eyes. "That wasn't painful at all. Honestly, inspectors get a bad rap."

They watched him walk out the front door, then Clarissa went to the stool and collapsed. "Whew. That was more stress than I needed for one day. I'm glad that's over."

"So am I." But the turmoil that had kicked up in Paige's mind was far from over. She had just lied. To a board inspector.

"I think I'll take my lunch now." Clarissa needed to get out of the pharmacy for a few minutes and de-stress. She stepped out into the bright sunshine and felt the unseasonable warmth of an early spring day. What a nice day, a good day for a walk around the square. She started to hum, until she turned the first corner and saw her grandfather's truck parked along the side street.

How long had he been in Shoal Creek? And why hadn't he come to see her yet?

She went back into the building and started up the stairs, almost running headlong into Cory, who was on his way down. "Is my grandfather upstairs?"

"Yep."

"Did he just arrive? I missed him somehow."

"He ate lunch with me and Paige. Far as I know, he'd just gotten here then."

"Ate lunch? With Paige?"

"Yeah, and me. The two of them sure do seem to get along well."

"You have no idea." She ran the rest of the way up the stairs, still not believing what was happening. How could Paige possibly have wormed her way into the respect she seemed to get from Granddad? And Tony for that matter. When she reached the top of the stairs, she saw her grandfather in the middle of the room, a set of plans rolled out on a small table before him.

She walked over to him. "Granddad, you didn't tell me you were coming today."

He looked up and smiled. "Didn't want to spoil the surprise."

"Well, you surprised me all right." *More than you know.* "I'm on lunch break, you want to come grab a bite with me?" She kept her eyes locked on his face, waiting for the tiniest of reactions. Would she see a twitch of guilt in his cheek? A flicker of regret in his eyes?

She saw nothing.

"No thanks, I've already eaten. I'll be down to check on progress in a couple of hours, okay?"

There was no escaping the fact that she'd been dismissed. She squared her shoulders and smiled brightly. "Well, all right. I guess I'll talk to you later."

When her grandfather came in that evening, he went straight to the weekly reports. "Hmm, looks like last week was your best yet." His eyes gleamed as he looked up. "See, I told you having Paige here would help, but even I didn't expect it to work this quickly."

"Granddad, last week was a good week because half of Shoal Creek got flattened by the flu. It had nothing to do with Paige." Even though she was whispering, Clarissa turned to confirm that Paige was not nearby. Satisfied that they were not being overheard, she continued, "In fact, I find her work, if you call it work, is both slow and even a little careless. She's going to hold me back from getting that franchise next spring, and I really need to get it before the lease is up on the Lancaster Building."

He looked at her, anger in his eyes. "You're taking a lot for granted. I haven't promised you that spot in the Lancaster Building."

"Tell me you're not going to give it to Becky."

"I'll give it to the person who is most deserving. The other yoga studio that Becky opened has been very profitable. She's shown she can do it." He nodded toward Paige, who was down at the counter talking to a patient. "Look at her. She makes sure no one leaves feeling like they haven't had complete service. That's what I like to see."

What was it going to take to prove to everyone that Paige was all an illusion? Did no one see the truth for what it was? Clarissa was the hard-working brains behind the operation, but Paige somehow managed to stumble into the right place to be caught in a good light. Time to make certain that everyone got a good look at the dark side.

chapter **nineteen**

Paige was driving down a busy four-lane road, horns blaring from somewhere behind her. Faster cars *whooshed* past, leaving a blast of cold air in their wake. She knew she needed to accelerate to keep up with the flow of traffic, but her foot didn't seem to cooperate with her decision. "Come on, we've got to move a little faster." She tried again, and this time the car jerked forward.

But now her hands felt shaky. They trembled despite themselves. She looked at the steering wheel and did not recognize the hands that were grasping it. Papery, translucent skin hung in veined wrinkles all over the back of her hands, and the shaking had crept through her body, her arms and legs quivering in rapid jerks.

A car horn blared directly behind her, and she knew she was about to crash. She swerved to the side of the road but turned too hard. She saw a tree trunk directly before her and whipped the wheel back around, and directly toward a green SUV. She saw the huge blue eyes of the toddler in the back seat before she heard the crunch of metal. Suddenly her whole body catapulted toward the broken windshield, and it was the last thing she saw before the world went black.

Paige splashed cold water on her face. "Get a grip, Paige, it was just a dream." The same dream she had lived through dozens of times. Still, the wrenching of the seizure seemed so real, the smell of hot metal so pungent, how could she just forget it?

She walked back into the living room and sank onto the sofa. The same reality show that she'd been watching before she fell asleep played on the television. Just more women and men scheming against one another. Paige pushed the power button and dropped the remote onto the side table.

A quick glance at the bronze hands of the grandfather clock told her it was only eight p.m. It was time to change the focus back to the here and now, the only thing that really mattered. Her mother. She picked up the phone.

Her father answered on the second ring. "Hello."

"How are things going?"

He paused a moment before answering. "Best I can tell, things are going according to plan. Your mother's sicker than all get-out, but I guess that's what's supposed to happen, hmm? They pumped her full of some sort of chemo today, and she got her first radiation treatment yesterday." A mumbling sound came from the background. "Your mother would like to speak to you."

"Don't listen to your father's exaggerations. I'm not too sick." She paused a minute and Paige could hear her take a shaky breath. Across the miles, Paige could feel her frailty. Her eyes teared without warning. It was so hard being apart. "You should see me, though. They've got me all marked up for my radiation treatments. . . . There are dots and lines all over the place. . . . Looks like a two-year-old got hold of me with a set of markers and tried to play connect the dots."

Paige choked out a laugh. "Now there's an idea. Dot to dot on your mother. I never thought of that."

"It's about the only thing you didn't think of when you were a kid." The pauses were agonizing, but Paige knew her mother wanted to talk. She waited. "I never did get the marker stain out of my best tablecloth."

"Maybe not, but wasn't I a cute little thing?"

Her mother started a laugh, but it turned into a cough. "Sorry about that." She coughed again. "I can't seem to shake this annoying little cough."

Paige's fingers tightened around the phone. There was no such thing as an annoying little cough to someone undergoing the kind of treatment her mother was undergoing. Any bacteria, the tiniest of viruses, had the potential to wreak tremendous havoc on a body whose defenses were being decimated by chemo. "Mom, I'm going to let you go rest. Is Dad staying with you at the hospital tonight, or is he going back to the apartment?"

"I think he's planning to stay here, but I keep telling him to go get a good night's sleep. Nobody listens to me anymore."

Paige's father came on the line. "I told her, for the first time in our lives, you and I have a choice in the matter. Personally, I plan to take the chance while I've got it. Soon as she feels better, she'll be bossing us all around again."

Paige could hear her mother saying something in the background. She was glad to know that cancer had not taken the good-natured teasing from her parents.

Not yet at least.

"Morning, young 'un. How are ya?"

Paige smiled at Ora as they walked into the lobby together. "Fine." She fumbled through her purse for the keys and thought of the upbeat tone in her mother's voice the night before. She was determined to let that memory overtake the return of the recurrent nightmare. "Quite good, actually."

"That sounds promising." Ora's boots clacked against the floor as they walked. "And *that* looks promising. Hello there, young man. You look like you've got something on your mind."

Paige looked up to see Cory standing at the pharmacy door, looking from Paige to Ora then back again. "I . . . uh . . ." He shifted on his feet but didn't continue.

"Does your mom need a refill?"

"Not exactly."

Ora pulled gently on his arm. "You need to scoot, she can't open the door while you're standing there."

"Oh yeah. Sorry." He moved two steps to the right.

Although Cory was not particularly a quiet person, in Ora's presence, he seemed downright tongue-tied.

Paige opened the door, killed the alarm, then wondered what she should do. He obviously needed something.

Ora glanced toward him. "Well, young man, you coming in or not? Paige needs to lock the door behind us. Too early for customers, you know."

Cory followed obediently, looking suspiciously at Ora. "Aren't you a customer?"

She plopped into her seat in the waiting area. "Of course not. The pharmacy doesn't open for another hour. How rude do you think I am?"

Paige would have given money to read Cory's thoughts at that question. His face had gone bright red. "Well, I . . . I . . . probably need to get going."

Ora crossed her arms, her lips set firm. "Nonsense. You came here for some reason, right? Get on with it. Don't mind me. I'm just waiting for my coffee."

"Your coffee?"

"Yep. Name's Ora Vaerge, by the way." She extended a hand.

Cory shook it. "Uh, pleased to meet you. Cory Griffin's mine."

"You like coffee, Cory? Paige always makes a pot." She looked over his shoulder toward Paige. "Go ahead and get it started. I'll keep young Cory company in the meanwhile."

Paige held her giggle until she got to the coffeepot, then allowed her shoulders to shake with the force of it. It took all of her willpower to remain focused on coffee making. She really wanted to watch the exchange that was taking place behind her.

When the Mr. Coffee started sputtering, she walked out to the front in time to hear Ora saying, "I drink a cup with her every morning. She doesn't make very good coffee, but I'm working with her on it."

Paige laughed outright this time. "What can I say? I'm a slow learner." She looked at Cory. "Sorry to keep you waiting. What's up?"

"I . . . uh . . ." He looked toward Ora. She tilted her head ever so slightly toward Paige.

He licked his lips. "There's a new deli on the other side of the square. You want to try it at lunch?"

Ora shifted in her seat. "Kids these days. No idea how to ask a girl for a date."

Paige willed the earth to open up and swallow

her right then. Could this be any more embarrassing? She looked at poor Cory and realized it was even worse for him. "Well . . . sure. I usually take my break about noon."

"I can go anytime. Why don't you just come find me upstairs when you're ready?"

She nodded. "Sure. Thanks."

"Okay, see you then." Cory nodded toward Ora, then walked out of the store.

Ora cackled. "That one's got it bad, I'd say. Anytime they lose their tongue like that, you can count on it."

"You're the one who intimidated him into silence, not me."

"Girl, you need to open your eyes." Ora set down her cup. "I'd say he's a prime candidate for the mystery flower man. Wouldn't you?"

"You gave me the wrong stuff."

Only the fourth customer of the day and disaster loomed. Paige felt her breath go shallow, her blood leave her hands as she looked at the middle-aged woman who stood across the counter. She wished the robot Paige would take over as she had once before. Today . . . the robot did not come to help. It was the flesh and blood Paige, the one who was terrified. Alone. *Put on a professional face, be courteous, get to the truth.* Deep breath. "What seems to be the problem?" Her voice caught twice in the short sentence.

The woman smelled of sweat and fried foods, and she ran her fingers through her short, dirty curls. "I said—" her voice grew louder with each syllable "—you folks gave me the wrong thing. Like to have killed me, is what you did."

Stay calm. Be professional. Turn and run. Paige somehow managed to shut off the last voice and reached out her hand. "May I see that?"

The woman pulled her hand back. "You ain't taking it from me. I might want to show it to my lawyer, and this here is evidence."

"I promise I'll give it back to you, just let me take a look."

The woman finally handed the bottle to Paige.

Take one tablet daily. Zebeta 10 mg.

Paige opened the container and saw the white, heart-shaped tablets with B3 on one side. She looked at the name on the prescription label. "Ms. Feldhouse, this *is* Zebeta 10 mg in your bottle. This is the correct medication."

"No it's NOT! I felt all light-headed this morning."

Warmth seeped back into Paige's fingers. This was not about mistakes. "That can be a side effect with Zebeta—most beta-blockers, in fact."

"I'm sure you're right. And if I needed a . . . whatever block, I'm sure I'd have to deal with that. But I don't need no block."

"Your doctor must think—"

"My doctor does *think*, you're right about that. I

went to see my doctor this morning. He says this stuff you gave me is for blood pressure. My blood pressure's just fine—in fact he says that's the reason I'm dizzy, because it's too low after this stuff you gave me."

"I don't understand."

"I have high cholesterol. You were supposed to give me THIS." She thrust a piece of paper in Paige's face with the words *Zetia 10 mg* written on it.

Paige's stomach knotted. "Ms. Feldhouse, why don't you have a seat. I'll pull out the prescription and call your doctor's office. We'll get this all straightened out."

"Get *your mistake* straightened out. Yeah, why don't you do that." The woman remained at the counter. Paige frantically ran to the filing cabinet, praying that she would find the doctor's handwritten prescription that called for Zebeta. She could show Ms. Feldhouse that the mistake was his, not theirs, call the office, get everything worked out. Soon she'd be going about her day, perhaps even with an apology from Ms. Feldhouse for being so rude.

She fingered through the numbered files until she pulled out the 25200 file. She set it on the counter and looked through until she found 25232. When she saw what was on the paper, she concentrated all her efforts on keeping her knees locked and her self upright.

The order had been called in to the pharmacy two days ago, taken on one of their blank pads. The handwriting was not Paige's, for that she was thankful. But she also knew that it did not belong to Clarissa. That left one alternative.

Clarissa's eyes looked red when she came into work that morning. "I think I'm catching a cold," she sniffled and put her purse away.

Paige didn't care if Clarissa had the pneumonia at this point. But she knew she needed to wait until Dawn wasn't around before she asked Clarissa about the prescription.

"Can I pay for this back here?" A teenager stood at the pharmacy counter, holding up a bottle of vitamins in her hand.

"Sure you can." Dawn bounced down to the cash register and took the bottle from her hands.

Time to act. "Clarissa, I've got to talk to you."

"So talk."

"Ms. Feldhouse came in this morning with a bottle full of Zebeta 10 mg. She'd been taking it a couple of days and felt a little light-headed."

"Yeah, that's a common side effect."

"But *this* side effect was caused because she was taking an anti-hypertensive when she was supposed to be taking Zetia for her lipids."

"What'd the doctor write for?"

"He didn't write for it. He called it in."

"Well, then it's his word against ours. The doctor

can say what he believes he called in, and no one can prove he did or he didn't. That's the unfairness of it all. She's all right, right? Ms. Feldhouse, I mean?"

"Yes, she is all right. But Clarissa . . ."

"What?"

"That prescription was phoned in on Tuesday. The handwriting belongs to Dawn. You promised me you wouldn't leave Dawn alone anymore."

"What, are you a handwriting expert now or something?"

"Come on, it doesn't take a genius to recognize Dawn's loopy cursive, especially since you always print."

Clarissa crossed her arms. "Yeesh. Are we getting a little worked up here?"

"Yes, I'm worked up. It's *illegal,* it's *unethical,* and besides that it's just plain wrong and you know it. There are reasons that only a pharmacist is supposed to take a phoned prescription. Someone could get hurt. Clarissa, if this happens again I'll have no choice but to call Gary Powell and tell him what's going on."

"You can tell him how you lied to him the first time while you're at it." Clarissa's cell phone chirped in her pocket. She pulled it out and looked at the display. "I need to take this." She walked to the back room.

Dawn tried to concentrate on her work, but given Clarissa's current mood it was difficult. Something had happened this morning, and Dawn hadn't quite figured it out yet. Clarissa acted all nicey-nicey when Paige was around, smiling at her, talking to her, teasing her about some apparent dinner with her uncle. But as soon as Paige was out of earshot, Clarissa was nastier than ever. Dawn understood why Clarissa first disliked Paige—Clarissa's grandfather had hired someone without even consulting her, for crying out loud—but she didn't understand why the anger continued, and now seemed to grow worse. Given all the hours Clarissa had been working, you'd think she'd be a little more grateful for the help.

Clarissa sank into a chair. "That's what I hate about retail. One minute you're so busy you can't even breathe. The next, there's nobody here at all." She squeezed her shoulder blades together. "All this standing makes my back hurt."

Dawn stretched and picked up a refill label. "I know what you mean."

"I wonder what's taking Perky Paige so long. I've never seen her take more than fifteen minutes for lunch."

"Oh, I bet she'll take the whole time today. I saw her leaving with that Cory guy from upstairs."

"What?" Clarissa tossed a paper clip across the counter. "I hate this place."

Dawn stared at her, hoping to find some piece of this puzzle that was Clarissa's mood today. She saw nothing. "You okay?"

"Peachy." Clarissa went to the sink and washed her hands.

Paige walked into the pharmacy, carrying a single long-stemmed pink rose. She put the flower in a water bottle and put it on the front counter, humming beneath her breath.

Clarissa walked over and pretended to smell it, but Dawn had the distinct impression she wanted to grind the petals beneath her feet. "My, my. Yet another flower for our darling little Paige? Everyone loves Paige, don't they?"

Paige stepped back and looked at her. "Clarissa, are you all right?"

Clarissa smiled and batted her eyes. "Just peachy. How about you?"

"I've got some not so great news."

Paige rarely answered her cell at work, but when she'd seen her father's name on the caller ID she panicked. His voice, though they'd just talked last night, had lost all its levity. She had noticed the change over the last few days. The strength seemed to be oozing out of him, like a slow bleed that could not be stopped. "What is it?"

"Your mom's blood test came back positive for RSV. Stands for respiratory . . ."

"Respiratory Syncytial Virus." Paige knew what it was. The infection would manifest itself as nothing more than a bad cold in a healthy adult, but in infants or people with compromised

153

immune systems, from chemo, say, it could be deadly. Just the thought of her mother gasping for breath made Paige's own lungs burn. "Is she having trouble breathing?"

"Not yet. Still just that same little cough she's had for a while now. Seems to feel okay other than being sick from the chemo. She's still upbeat as ever."

"What are they doing for her?"

"Well, they're putting her in this tent for a few hours at a time and giving her some sort of medicine through the air in there."

"Can I speak to her?"

"I'm back at the apartment. They don't want me in the room while they're doing the tent treatment, I don't really understand why. Even when they're done I have to wear this big yellow gown and mask. I look like a giant banana when I go into her room. They said I can get—whatever it is she's got—and even though it wouldn't hurt me, I can spread it to other patients around here. They told me I might as well sleep back in the apartment because they're going to come in and kick me out every few hours anyway, so that's what I'm doing. Sitting here and waiting."

"I know how that feels."

"I never realized just how bad it was for you to be back there, just waiting for information, not being able to do anything about anything, until today. I've felt so helpless here all afternoon. I've taken to watching televangelists just to fill the time."

"Oh, Daddy. What are we going to do?"

"Just keep praying. That's all we can do. Doctor says it's a good thing we caught it early—should only need treatment for a few days."

"That's good, at least."

"Yeah. She wanted me to ask you how things are going. She's so worried about you."

"Worried about me? With everything she's got going on?" Paige knew her mother well enough to know it was true. "She never thinks about herself, does she?"

"Honey, as far as she's concerned, you are herself. You're what she's leaving behind when she goes—whether this cancer takes her or old age."

"I vote for old age."

"You and me both."

Clarissa looked around at the pharmacy she'd built. Here, after closing, was when she loved it the most. The peace and quiet after a day hard fought.

She was going to show them all. She was the best person to run any pharmacy, and it was time everyone realized that. But she needed to take steps to protect herself. She couldn't have Paige going to the board because of something as idiotic as a five-minute break.

Time to take the offensive. She pulled out a clean yellow legal pad and rubbed her hand across the smoothness of the top page. "You are my new best friend."

She sat at the desk and tapped the pencil on her chin. *Let's see, what should I write up first?*

chapter **twenty**

"I'm in a hurry." The elderly man pulled on the straps of his overalls and rocked back and forth on his feet. "Could you make it quick?" His forehead creased with agitation, accentuating the lines baked into his skin by a lifetime of hard work in the hot sun.

Paige looked at the paper in her hand. "Mr. Pauling, is this a new medication for you, or have you been on it a while?"

He released one strap in order to slap his hand on the counter. "What's it matter? Quit your blabbing, I ain't got the time for it."

Deep breath. Calm voice. Help him understand. "It matters because the doctor didn't write the strength. If you know what you take, I'll fill it now and confirm with his office later. If you don't, I have to call now."

"I know what I take—the strong one. It's kind of pinkish-orangish."

A tug began to pull in her gut. "Have a seat. I'll get this as soon as I can." She picked up the phone.

He leaned across the counter and drummed his fingers. "What're you doing?"

Dawn came up behind her. "Why are you calling?"

Multiple rings sounded on the other end of the line. Paige pointed at the paper. "He doesn't know what strength he takes."

"He said the pinkish-orangish one. Can't you figure it out from that and get him and his scowling face out of here?"

The phone line finally clicked. "Dr. Janke's office, hold please."

Did no one else understand what was at stake here? Paige shook her head at Dawn. "Ten milligram propranolol tablets are orange, sixty milligram are pink. I think that's too big a difference to guess at, don't you?"

"Thanks for holding, can I help you?"

Paige explained the situation to the receptionist, who sounded bored with the whole thing. "I'll need to transfer you to the nurses' station. One minute please."

Before Paige had a chance to argue, Barry Manilow was singing about a girl named Mandy.

Paige pulled two bottles off the shelf, ten milligrams and sixty. She counted out sixty of each pill so that she would be ready for either answer, and get Mr. Pauling's tapping fingers off her counter that much faster.

The nurse came on the line. Paige repeated the question.

"Let me find the chart. Just a minute."

Mr. Pauling leaned across the counter, his face red. "Are you going to fill my prescription or not?"

"Almost got it." She turned her back toward him. His attitude was too much to handle so early in the morning. Didn't he understand she was going out of her way to make certain he got the right medication? Why should conscientious service make people angry?

Three more minutes ticked past. The music stopped. "Sixty milligrams."

"Thanks." Paige's fingers flew across the keyboard. She rushed to the printer, tore off the label, placed it on the bottle, then opened it to double-check the contents. "Sorry about that, Mr. Pauling. Now that we've got you in our system, we'll know next time."

He pulled out his insurance card. "Forgot to give you this."

She would have to redo everything. Her stomach felt like it was caught between a mortar and a pestle, turning her insides to a powdery dust.

The phone rang. She grabbed it up and put it on hold, frantically typing in the numbers from Mr. Pauling's insurance card. Two more calls came in rapid succession. Five minutes later, she got everything entered and collected his co-pay.

" 'Bout time."

Paige attempted to smile at him, but it felt more like a grimace. "Sorry for the delay."

He stalked down the aisle, almost crashing into a

just-arriving Clarissa and her latté. He stopped, pointed back toward Paige, and spoke loud enough for the entire store to hear. "Slowest service I've ever had. She's just plain incompetent."

Paige barely managed to gulp back the gasp. She busied herself putting away the bottles, but wanted to find a corner and cry.

Clarissa came behind the counter, her lips twitching at the corners. "What was that all about?"

"There wasn't a strength on his written prescription, so I had to call the doctor. He handed me his insurance card after the fact."

"Yeah, I'm sure he's just a grumpy old coot."

Something about the gleam in Clarissa's eye made Paige more than a little uncomfortable.

chapter **twenty-one**

Dawn rolled over to find the bed empty. Not that it surprised her. There was no way Jack could have come in last night without her knowing. Her frustration had grown into fury and kept her from ever falling into a deep sleep. Kept her from sleeping at all for that matter.

Bam! Bam! Bam!

The pounding on the front door shook the windows in her bedroom. Jack had most likely lost his key. Or left it at—wherever it was he'd been all night. Well, Dawn wasn't going to let the two-timing obnoxious jerk in. He could stay outside and rot for all she cared.

Bam! Bam!

The sliding door on the back side of the house rattled. Apparently he wasn't ready to give up just yet. Come to think of it, now might be a good time to have a little face-off. He could see and hear her through the door, but he couldn't get to her.

She bounded down the hallway and leapt into the small living room. "You can stay outside and rot—"

Two sets of eyes stared at her through the glass doors. Rumpled clothes, smudged faces, unbrushed hair. Jack's kids.

Dawn slid the door open, conscious of the shortness of her sleeping shirt. "Nicole, Jeremy. What are you two doing here?"

Jeremy pushed past her and into the living room. "We're staying with Dad this weekend."

Lack of sleep or no, Dawn knew the schedule better than that. "No, it's next weekend. The first weekend of the month. Remember?" She looked out into the backyard. "Where's your mother?"

Jeremy sat on the couch. "She's going to Atlanta to some concert. She and Dad talked about it last week. He said we could stay here."

Dawn ran to the front door and threw it open. She needed to catch Renee before she drove away. Regardless of what Jack might have offered, he wasn't here, and Dawn wasn't baby-sitting.

The driveway was empty, the street quiet. She turned back to Jeremy. "Who brought you here?"

"Mom."

"Where'd she go?"

"She was running late, so she dropped us at the curb."

A pink ballerina backpack rested on the front porch, a Tennessee Titans duffle at the bottom of the steps. Like it or not, this decision was made.

Well, as soon as Jack got home, Dawn was out of here. These kids were not her problem. She would go have some fun for a change.

"Bring in your packs, then go see what's on TV."

She watched the two kids slump past her to the den. How had she gotten stuck with this? Saturday was her day off.

She shook her head. "I'm going to take a shower. You two stay put." She handed the remote to Jeremy.

"I don't want to watch TV. I'm hungry." Nicole's five-year-old face looked up at her, freckles and traces of last night's dessert covering her face. She would look so sweet and innocent if it were not for the defiance shining from her eyes.

"Well, you'll just have to wait. I'm going to get a shower now. Your father ought to be home any minute."

"But I'm hungry NOW."

Dawn turned her back on the whining and started down the hall. "Now sounds like a good time for you to learn some patience." She walked into the bathroom and locked the door behind her.

"I *said,* I'm hungry NOW!" Nicole's voice sniveled directly outside the door.

Dawn turned on the shower full blast. She undressed and put her head beneath the water, drowning most of the sounds of the pounding and demanding at her door. She turned the water up hot, as if the sting against her skin could somehow erase the sting of her conscience for ignoring the hungry child just outside her door.

This was not her problem. These were not her kids. These were not even her step-kids. They simply belonged to the pig she'd been stupid enough to believe when he said he loved her. What a crock of lies he'd fed her. And he'd been so charming and persuasive in the beginning.

She could still remember how furious her father had been when he found out about their relation-ship. The ensuing fight played a vivid reminder across the screen of her memory, anger flashing in his eyes. "That relationship ends now."

"He loves me, and I love him, and you can't tell me what to do." Defiance surged through her like a drug, giving her strength, making her feel alive.

"As long as you live under my roof I can."

"I'm eighteen. I'm an adult."

"All right. If that's the way you want to play it, so be it." Her father turned his back on her and stomped from the kitchen.

She sat at the table, shaking from the exchange, but exhilarated. She had stood up to him. And won. The rush of this newfound strength flowed through her limbs and tingled in her toes. This was the beginning of a new life of independence for her.

Five minutes later, her father came to the kitchen door, his arms filled with her clothes. "We'll call these a going away present, but as an adult, you buy your own from here on out." He walked to the front door, dumped the load in a pile on the front porch, and pointed outside. "Enjoy your life as a grown-up."

Dawn looked at the heap of clothes, then back to her father. "Dad, I . .."

"You've made your choice. Now get out."

She refused to give him the satisfaction of seeing her cry. She walked out, head held high, and had never been back since. How she wished she could return to that moment, do things differently. Her home life had never been great, but it sure beat this. At least then, there had been hope.

Unfortunately, her job at the pharmacy didn't pay enough for her to live on her own. Her friends from high school had mostly moved on—gone on to college or moved to larger cities with more opportunities.

She was broke. And miserable. And alone.

The water began to get cooler, so she turned the spigot toward hot. She scrubbed at some imaginary dirt on her knee. She washed her hair a second time, feeling the bubbles tickle her scalp, smelling the scent of the sour apple shampoo. She took a long, luxurious time to shave her legs, until every last inch of them was completely smooth.

Only now did she realize that sometime during the process, the pounding on the door had stopped, the whining had ceased. Good. She turned off the shower and reached for a towel. Nothing.

Oh, no. She had thrown them in the washer yesterday morning, and that's where they still were.

"I'm hungry." Nicole started banging on the door again.

Well, at least the kid could make herself useful. Dawn walked over to the door and spoke loud enough for Nicole to hear her over her own whimpering. "Nicole, go to the hall closet and get me a towel."

"But I'm *hungry.*"

"Bring me a towel so I can dry off. After I get dressed, I'll see what I can find you to eat, okay?"

"Okay." The girl could turn a single word into a whine, and it grated on Dawn like fingernails across a chalkboard. No wonder this kid's mother needed to go away for the weekend.

Soon Nicole was back, knocking on the door. "Got your towel."

After Dawn was dried and dressed she stared at the door. She wanted to leave it locked and pretend there weren't two little people just outside, depending on her. At least until Jack decided to show up. But, as much as she wanted to, she couldn't.

She finally opened the door to see Nicole sitting in the hallway just outside, her eyes puffy and pink. "Okay, Nic, let's go get you something to eat."

They walked down the hall. Towels were strewn everywhere around the linen closet. "Nicole, why did you make such a mess?"

"I wanted to find you the prettiest towel 'cause you're so pretty."

Dawn looked back at the child and waited for the laughter. Instead, she saw green eyes, still moist with tears. "Well, thanks then. That was a really nice thought." She stacked the towels back into the closet, then walked into the kitchen. "Let's see what we've got." She rummaged through the mostly bare cupboards. "Jeremy, you hungry?"

He didn't answer.

"He's watching TV. Some show with a bunch of girls and boys kissing in a hot tub. It's gross."

Dawn closed the cabinet door and walked around the corner to see Jeremy happily enjoying an R-rated movie.

"Jeremy, turn that off right now."

"Dad lets me."

"When he gets here, you can talk to him about it. For now, he's not here, and I'm in charge."

Jeremy groaned and turned off the television. "I'm hungry."

"Come on in the kitchen with your sister. I'm just about to fix something to eat."

She came up with two cans of chili, a stale pack of crackers, and a box of Cheerios that was easily two months old. "I guess we're going out to get something. Where do you guys want to go?"

"McDonald's!" came the simultaneous reply.

"Mickey D's it is. Everyone load up in the car."

Dawn reached into her purse for the keys, but found something else instead. Her wallet was wide open. And empty.

Jack must have gone through her purse before he went out last night. It wasn't enough that he'd been staying out all night, coming in smelling of perfume. Now he was taking her money, too.

What was she going to do? The kids were whiny and hungry; she was hungry. Jack might not be home for hours yet.

She thought of the pharmacy. Could she bring herself to go begging? Would she be able to show her face on Monday if she did?

Paige was working alone today. Maybe there was some reasonable excuse Dawn could use for needing money. Nothing came to mind, but she'd have the drive over to think one up. Nothing like no choice to make her try.

When she pulled into a parking spot in front of the theater shops, she looked at the kids. "All right. Let's go, but don't touch anything."

She shooed them out of her car and inside the building's main doors. When she walked into the pharmacy she could see Paige at the counter. No customers were in the store. She pushed through the pharmacy door. "Slow day?"

"It's a Saturday, you know how it is." Paige looked around Dawn, then back. "Who's this?"

Nicole and Jeremy had followed Dawn up into the dispensing area. She turned on them. "Get out of here. Go look at something on the counters."

"Candy?" Nicole asked.

"Out! Now!" The kids scurried toward the front of the store. Dawn looked at Paige, knowing what she must be thinking right now. And every bit of it was true. Why hadn't she just fed the kids chili and stale crackers and saved herself this humiliation? Well, she hadn't, and there was nothing left to lose. She might as well just go for it. "I need to ask you a favor."

"Sure. What do you need?"

"Can I borrow a little money? Jack . . . uh . . . had to go in to work early today. His ex dropped off the kids this morning, and I wanted to take them to McDonald's, but I don't have any cash."

That yesterday had been payday pulsed like a neon sign. Paige had to know there was more to this story.

She looked down to where the kids were checking out the candy and smiled. "Sure. How much you need?"

"Ten ought to get us a couple of Happy Meals."

Paige rummaged through her purse. "Here, I've got a twenty. Take it."

"Oh, I don't need . . ."

"You never know, Jack might have to work until late. This will give you enough to make it to the store if he doesn't get home in time."

Dawn stared at the bill. She knew that if she looked up, she'd see Paige watching her with innocent blue eyes. Eyes she couldn't face. She turned and started toward the door. "Thanks. I'll pay you back."

"Don't worry about it." Paige followed her to the counter. "Those kids are lucky to have you in their lives."

Long after Dawn left the store, she remembered Paige's words. "Those kids are lucky to have you in their lives." When she looked at Nicole's huge eyes, sparkling with the thrill of her Happy Meal toy, she walked over and gave her a hug.

Nicole squeezed her tight. "I love you, Dawn."

"I . . ." Dawn's throat closed off further response. It was the first time anyone had said those words to her in more than a year. She kissed the top of Nicole's head. "Want to go get some ice cream?"

chapter twenty-two

Paige looked at the clock, firmly believing it hadn't moved in over an hour. Saturdays were always slow, but today felt especially endless. And with little to occupy her, Paige found she had too much time to think about her mother sitting through the six-hour infusion of rituximab today. She could almost feel the nausea and vomiting that had become such a part of her mother's life, not to mention the too familiar sight of clumps of wavy gray hair on the pillow.

Paige scrubbed the already clean shelves, determined to think of something more cheerful, or at least someone more cheerful. What was Clarissa doing right now?

She pictured Clarissa in Nashville with her friends. They would be gearing up for a big Saturday night on the town by now. Probably primping in some mirror, fussing over each other's cute outfits and new haircuts. She thought about Dawn and wondered if she was watching cartoons with Jack and his kids, maybe eating popcorn on the floor.

Her own plans for the evening consisted of . . . nothing. Another lonely nothing.

"Hello there. Anybody home?" An oddly familiar male voice floated from the area of the counter.

"Coming." Paige stood up, wiped her hands on

a clean paper towel, and looked toward the voice.

Clarissa's uncle stood at the counter, dressed in a sports coat, a smile on his face. He looked around the empty store. "Wow. It's a madhouse in here."

Paige shrugged. "Slow afternoon, what can I tell you?" She walked to the counter and smiled. "What brings you here?"

"Oh, I had some business down this way. Thought I'd stop by and see if Clarissa and you want to do dinner before I go home."

"This is her weekend off, sorry you missed her. I'll tell her you stopped by."

He continued to stand at the counter. His cheeks colored slightly. "Well, I'm here anyway. What do you say? Dinner?" He scrunched his shoulders and held his hands palm up in a most appealing way.

How was a girl supposed to fight that kind of charm? Besides, there was no danger here. Tony was Clarissa's uncle, nothing more.

"Well, I . . ." Paige smiled at the gesture, then froze when she realized there was no gold ring on the extended left hand. He was another problem waiting to happen. A big one.

Still, just the thought of another lonely night won the battle against common sense. "Why don't you follow me over to Sledge? Crockett Twin is having an old movie marathon this weekend. We could grab some pizza and take in *Casablanca*."

A smile seemed to erupt from deep inside him. "You're my kind of woman."

She couldn't think of a single thing to say in response, so she stared at the blue countertop.

"How much longer till you close up this popsicle stand?"

Paige looked at the clock. "Fifteen minutes."

"I'll go wait in the coffee shop." He tapped the counter twice in parting, a grin still on his face.

Paige walked over to the mirror. Her untouched lips had faded into her pale skin, making her look like she didn't have a mouth at all. Obviously Tony was just being polite, because he couldn't be attracted to this mess of a girl. She brushed her hair and put on some lipstick, just because it made her feel better—not because she wanted to look good for him. Right?

When she walked into the coffee shop Tony stood, smiled, and offered his elbow. "I'll follow you to your place, you can park your car, and I'll be the official chauffeur from there."

Not such a great idea, but how to explain without hurting his feelings? "Um, maybe you should leave your car in the driveway, and we'll take mine."

Tony's chin pulled in a half-inch. "What's the problem, my car or my driving?"

"Your driving's fine. The thing is . . . not many people in Sledge drive around in blue Porsches. Bound to get gossip started."

"I get it. Small-town politics."

Paige took his offered elbow. "Thanks for understanding."

A half hour later, they were at her parents' house, Tony's Porsche completely out of place in front of the cozy but simple home. As Tony approached, Paige held up a finger. "I need to take the dog for a quick walk before we head out."

Tony waited for her and she soon reappeared with Dusty. The old dog hobbled in circles around Tony, unsure whether he should be wagging or barking. "What happened to his paw?"

"He got loose one day and went chasing after a delivery truck. It hit him—damaged the nerves in his front leg. He can move it." Paige held out her hand and said, "Shake." Dusty stuck his limp paw in her hand. "He just can't control the bottom joint, or put any weight on it."

Tony bent down and scratched Dusty under the chin. "Aren't you the brave young fellow, fighting through all that adversity. Let's get you out for some fresh air, young man." Dusty lay down, his tail thumping the ground. Tony laughed. "Or we could just lie right here, I guess."

"He can't stand still for long. Between his injury, old age, and arthritis, he's got to be either moving or lying down. Don't worry, though, he'll be game for a little action. Come on, boy." Dusty pushed to his feet and they headed off.

Tony peppered her with questions as they walked. About Sledge. About her parents' home. About Paige herself. Unsure how deep she wanted to let him in, she kept her answers short and tried a few of her own questions on him. But they were back at the house before she'd learned too much. After settling Dusty inside, it was finally time for dinner, and they headed to her car. Tony walked around to the passenger door, but instead of opening it, he leaned on it.

"You know, I wasn't completely honest with you back at the pharmacy. I need to tell you the truth, or I won't be able to enjoy myself tonight."

So much for a nice evening. "Okay."

"I knew." He looked at his feet and didn't say more.

"Knew what?"

"That Clarissa was off work today. I knew it. I didn't have any business down this way either. I drove down 'cause I wanted to take you to dinner. I made up that stuff about looking for Clarissa because I didn't have the nerve to come right out and ask you." He still didn't look at her. Something about him seemed so lost and lonely.

Just like she was.

Although everything inside screamed at her to stop, Paige reached out and touched his arm. "Your lie may have been the nicest thing that's happened to me in a long time."

Tony's smile reappeared and he put his hand over hers. "I was hoping you'd think so." He straightened up and opened his door. "What kind of pizza do you like?"

• • •

Clarissa looked around the crowded room. The sparse furnishings in hues of black, white, and chrome did little to absorb the cacophony of too many people with too little to say. The twitter of put-on laughter came from some idiotic female behind her—most likely hoping to convince the metrosexual sitting across from her that she would be a fascinating person to spend time with, or at least spend some money on.

"I've got to get out of here."

"What? Come on, the fun's just getting started." Kelsey took a sip of her cosmopolitan and leaned a little closer to Reggie, her British transplant about-to-be-husband, whom she'd known all of two months.

"Here, here. Don't be a wet blanket." He leaned over and nuzzled Kelsey's neck, and got a giggle in response.

Definitely time to get out of here. "I promised Tony I'd stop by for a visit. I'll talk to you tomorrow, Kelsey." She adjusted the thin purse strap over her shoulder and walked away, doubting whether Kelsey or Reggie had noticed that she'd gone.

She got into her car and looked at her watch. Ten o'clock. Tony would still be awake and game for a visitor. He always was. Besides, he needed her.

The noise and energy of nightlife faded in her rearview mirror, slowly replaced by the quiet of well-established neighborhoods whose occupants worked too hard and played too little. No thanks. Clarissa's condo with a view was just fine—who needed four thousand square feet to maintain and expansive lawns to tend? It was all so . . . upper-middle-class homey. Boring.

The windows on the front side of Tony's brick house were dark when she pulled into the driveway. Surely he wasn't in bed already. Well, if he was, he'd just have to get up and quit being such a party pooper. It was Saturday night after all. She'd make him get up and watch a midnight movie, just to prove he could. She rang the door-bell and smiled as she began to mentally prepare her lecture about getting old before his time.

Boom-da-boom, boom-da-boom. The deep thump of a really loud bass pulsed behind her. She turned as a small Mitsubishi screeched to a stop in the driveway across the street, a lanky teenage boy emerging a few seconds later, still playing the air drums as he walked into the house.

Clarissa rolled her eyes and turned back to the door. What was taking Tony so long? She rang again. And again. Finally, she walked around and looked through the window into the garage.

The room was dark, but the light from the street-lamp reflected off the silver metal of a wrench hanging on the back wall, and the handlebars of Tony's bicycle, which hung from the rafters. In the middle of the room, no reflection lit the area at all, leaving it shrouded in dark. It took her a moment to realize the reason. Tony's car wasn't there.

Strange. He never went out unless he was with her.

She climbed back into her car and called his cell. No answer.

Well, she wasn't ready to go home yet, so she simply drove around Nashville until she found herself parked across the street from the Lancaster Building. She looked at the façade and tried to picture what the sign would look like out front. Maybe she would hang a shingle, like an old-fashioned doctor's office. Better yet, maybe she could redo it as close as possible to the way it had looked when her grandmother worked there. Maybe she'd even find some old black-and-white photos of Grandma in her pharmacy days and use them to decorate the walls.

Visions began to form in her mind; how beautiful it was all going to be. It would be the talk of the Parrish Apothecary chains, the elegance of the Nashville store. The shining example of a franchise done right.

Franchise.

The thoughts of the store disappeared behind the memory of the latest weekly reports. While the store revenues were still growing steadily, Paige's salary was eating such a chunk out of it that there was no way that she would be able to break even by the end of the year. She looked at the building, thought about the homage she wanted to pay to her grandmother. "I can make it work. I'll just have to work harder, that's all. That's what Richardsons always do, they work harder than anyone else, and it shows in their success."

Clarissa drove back toward home, determined. She could do this. She always pulled through in a crisis. She would sit down tonight, make a plan, and stick it out.

When she walked into her condo, the phone was ringing. "Hey, Sweet Pea. I got your message. Is everything okay?"

"I should ask you the same question. Where are you this late on a Saturday night?"

"Just getting back now. You want to come over?"

"Nah, I think I'll stay put. Where you been, anyway?"

"Oh, you know, I went for a little drive and lost track of time. It's all part of the senility of being thirty, I think."

It was not like Tony to avoid answering a direct question, but just now he had. Twice. There could be little doubt he was being intentional about that. What was he trying to hide?

The phone beeped for call waiting. "Tony, I've got to go. Talk to you later." She pressed the button. "Hello?"

"Miss Richardson, this is Terry, the night watchman. There's a man down here in the lobby telling me he's your uncle and needs to see you right away. I'm saying he don't look like your uncle to me."

Clarissa smiled, picturing Tony somehow caught in the trap of an overzealous watchman. No wonder he didn't want to tell her where he was. "I'll be right down." She ran down the stairs, two at a time, laughing the whole way. She flung open the door and saw the watchman standing beside a man she did not recognize. The man, wearing black sweats and an Oakland A's baseball cap, walked right up to her. "Clarissa Richardson," he said as he held out a manila envelope, "you have been served."

Somehow, her hand reached out and took the envelope, but she couldn't feel the paper in her fingers. They had gone numb.

He nodded at the security guard and said, "Thanks for your help," then walked out the door.

"Get out of here, you filthy liar." The guard's words were plenty loud, but they were much too late. The man had already disappeared.

"Miss Richardson, I am so sorry. I had no idea he was up to something like that. There's no way I would have called you if I'd known. But I didn't recognize the guy, and he kept insisting he was your uncle. I didn't know what else to do but call you."

Clarissa shook her head. "No, it's okay." She pressed the button for the fifth floor, walked zombie-like to her condo, then sat on the couch to open the letter. When she saw the name *Feldhouse* and the words *Zetia* and *Zebeta* situated among the legal jargon, she knew she'd just lost her last hope for the Lancaster Building.

Unless . . .

chapter **twenty-three**

Monday evening after work, Paige sat on the bench in her mother's garden, index cards in hand. *Matthew 17:20—"I tell you the truth, if you have faith as small as a mustard seed, you can say to this mountain, 'Move from here to there' and it will move. Nothing will be impossible for you."*

"Okay God, my faith may only be the size of a mustard seed, but You say that's enough. Please, heal my mother."

What did a mustard seed look like, anyway? She was pretty sure she remembered from past Sunday school lessons that they were quite small. Surely she had more faith than that; a mustard seed didn't sound like much.

But . . . if that's all it took, why weren't more miracles happening today? Surely lots of people had a mustard seed of faith.

She looked at the grass, already turning green because of the unusual summer-like weather they were experiencing here in early April. New growth. New life. Would there be new life for her mother?

She hoped so.

Wait, there was a story somewhere about a man who didn't have enough faith, and he asked Jesus for enough to help him. Right? Where was that?

She went back into the house, fired up the computer, and searched for what she needed. Ah yes! In Mark 9, the father brought his sick son, who had a convulsion right there in front of Jesus. The father asked Jesus if He could do anything to help.

" 'If you can'?" said Jesus. "Everything is possible for him who believes."

Immediately the boy's father exclaimed, "I do believe; help me overcome my unbelief!"

And Jesus healed the boy. Yeah, maybe this little sequence was a good one to write on a card, too. Paige decided to condense it to verse 24: *"I do believe; help me overcome my unbelief!"* She wrote it on her index card and started back outside to continue her dialogue with God.

The phone rang as she slid the door open. She considered letting the machine answer, but what if it was her parents? "Hello."

"Thought I'd drive up there and hang out with you next weekend. What do you say, you up for it?"

"Rachelle?"

"You have to ask?"

"Yes, as a matter of fact." Even for the ever-perky Rachelle, this voice was way too bright. "You can tell me what's wrong right now and save yourself a five-hour drive."

"Nothing's wrong, and I love to drive. You know me—the need for speed, the wind in my face, all that."

"Did I mention that the last two hours are on two-lane highways, frequented by slow-moving tractors? Did I mention we're in the middle of a heat wave, with humidity that feels more like July than April?"

"Ick." The line went quiet for a moment while Rachelle absorbed that little piece of news. "So that's why I haven't come to see you yet." She twittered a laugh. "Well, slow-moving traffic is good, too. And as for the heat wave, it's not like Atlanta's any better, it's supposed to be downright torrid here this week. No, I'm coming. I've been saying I was going to since you moved. It's high time I check the place out, make sure you're main-taining it to your parents' standards, you know."

"Will you please unload? I don't want to spend the rest of the week worrying about what's wrong."

"Relax. There's not a thing wrong with me. Just need a little girl fun, that's all."

Ah. Must be man trouble. This we can handle. "Girl fun it is."

"I'll drive over Saturday morning. How about giving me directions to your pharmacy? I'll come in there, check the place out, and get the keys to your house. I still make the best grilled burgers in the known free world, so I'll have dinner ready when you get home."

"All right, then. But when you come into the pharmacy, there's something you need to keep in mind."

"Such as?"

"Nobody here knows much, uh, about . . . my time in Georgia."

"You're kidding." Her pitch broke sound barriers. She was most definitely uptight about something.

"Well, it's not like I walk around looking for someone to tell about it, and no one's ever asked. So . . . anyway. Just make sure you don't say anything in front of anyone, okay?"

"Not exactly the kind of thing I would bring up in casual conversation. Still, are you telling me your boss doesn't even know about it?"

"You know I really needed this job."

Rachelle made a clicking sound with her tongue, a sure sign there was more to say. "Well, I'll see you in a few days."

"I'm looking forward to it." Paige refused to acknowledge the little pang of guilt that Rachelle's questions had awakened in her. She'd done what she had to do, that's all there was to it.

She hung up the phone and bounced onto the sofa. One of the lingering aftereffects of the whole Atlanta mess was the separation from her friends. The telephone and Internet were not the next best thing to being there, no matter what the commercials said. Whatever the problem that was bringing Rachelle to her, Paige couldn't wait.

• • •

Tuesday morning, Clarissa sat working at the desk, desperately searching for a way out of this legal mess, when the pharmacy phone rang. She got up to go answer it, but Paige had already picked it up.

"Richardson Apothecary." She turned her face toward the wall and spoke in a quiet voice. "Tony, hi."

A blade sliced clear through Clarissa. What did Tony think he was doing? He said he'd come here just to make certain everything was okay for Clarissa, right? He was just checking up, that's all. Besides that, he'd obviously been out Saturday night; he was definitely not calling here because he wanted to talk to Paige.

Cory came strutting through the door but stopped to hold it open for a little lady on her way out. He said something to her that had her twittering like a schoolgirl as she left the store. The boy knew how to charm, that much was sure.

Clarissa sashayed down to meet him, taking care to swing her hips just enough to draw his attention, but not enough to make it obvious what she was doing. She managed to intercept him just before the pharmacy counter. "Cory, what brings you here?"

"Oh, you know," he looked toward Paige then back at Clarissa, "just checking in with you ladies." He shifted on his feet just a little. "I, uh, need to talk to Paige."

No, you really don't. "Really? She's on the phone with my uncle Tony, is there any way I could help you?" She smiled and moved a step closer. "We haven't had a chance to . . . talk in a while. How are things going with you?"

Cory looked over her head toward Paige, who leaned against the counter, her back to them. "Just fine. I've been really busy." Paige's soft laughter filtered through the air at just the right time. Cory's eyes narrowed. Bull's-eye.

Whatever else Tony might be doing, he was at least putting Cory in his place. "Do you want me to give her a message?"

"Um, nah. I guess not. I'll just talk to her later." He turned and walked away without a backward glance.

Clarissa went back up into the dispensing area and smiled at Paige as she hung up the phone. "Was that my uncle Tony calling you?"

A faint blush colored Paige's cheeks. "I think he's just bored." She smiled in spite of her words.

"So, have you two been talking lately?" Nothing good could come of that.

"A little."

"A little?" Clarissa intentionally put a teasing tone into her voice. Better to keep things light.

"He came by Saturday and we went to dinner."

He did what? This was not possible. No way would Tony do that to her. No wonder he'd been so secretive when they talked Saturday night. While she was getting served papers, he'd been out on the town with the person who was ruining her life. "Funny, I don't remember hearing you mention that yesterday."

"I . . . guess I didn't."

I guess not. "You going out again?"

Paige shrugged. "I don't know. He asked about this Saturday, but I've got a friend coming to town."

"That's too bad." She knew the attempt at a light voice was failing.

"Did I just see Cory in here?"

Why don't you rub that in my face now, too? You know he came to see you. "Yeah. He was just checking about some medicine."

Paige looked from Clarissa to the door. "That's odd. I just filled his mom's stuff last week."

"Who knows?"

The morning went on, busy but not overly so. A man arrived wearing a uniform and carrying a couple dozen pink roses. "Delivery for Paige Woodward."

Paige walked over to the counter, feigning surprise. *What a little fake. Tony probably told her he was sending them.*

"Thank you." She walked back, carrying the humongous bouquet in her arms, grinning like a schoolgirl.

Clarissa flipped her hair over her shoulder and tried to look bored. "Tony's going a little overboard. Look at those things, they must have cost a fortune."

Paige pulled out the card, put a hand over her mouth, and pretended to stifle a gasp. "They're not from Tony. They're from Cory. He wants me to go to lunch with him." She shook her head and looked at the flowers. "I wish he hadn't done that."

"What, you don't like him?"

"I like him fine, but these cost a lot of money. All he had to do was ask."

Clarissa watched Paige flounce over to the mirror and check her hair. She always pretended to be so innocent, but she knew exactly what she was doing.

The pharmacy line rang four times before Dawn realized Clarissa must be busy elsewhere and answered. "Richardson Apothecary, may I help you?"

"This is Carla at Dr. Micheel's office. I need to call in a prescription."

"Just one minute, please." Dawn put the phone on hold and called to Clarissa. "It's a doctor's office, new prescription."

Clarissa emerged from the back of the shelves, cell phone in hand. "So, take it. I'm in the middle of something."

Was she joking? Dawn watched, waiting for the punch line. It didn't come. "You told me I couldn't take call-ins anymore, remember?"

"Just for today, I've changed my mind." Clarissa put the cell back to her ear, then pulled it away. "Um, don't take it in cursive, print it, okay? Don't worry, I'll double-check everything."

Dawn picked up the phone. "Go ahead, I'm ready." As she wrote the order for prednisone, ten milligrams, QD, a strange surge of power flowed through her. Clarissa thought enough of her to let her take a phoned prescription. She knew Paige was too uptight to trust her that much. At least Clarissa saw some value in her.

When Clarissa finally got off the phone, she walked over and picked up the prescription that Dawn had just written out. "That's perfect. It's even spelled correctly." Clarissa started working on refills and said no more about it, but she hummed and smiled the whole time.

As soon as Paige returned from lunch, Clarissa reached into the drawer and pulled out her purse. "I'm going to lunch now." She threw the purse over her shoulder, then pushed the prescription Dawn had taken as a call-in across the counter. "Paige, would you mind finishing this one for me? I've been too busy working on refills."

"Sure."

"Thanks," Clarissa said and when she smiled, it was too big, too wide. Dawn didn't know what was happening, but she was just glad not to be Paige right now.

chapter twenty-four

On Friday, Paige could feel the bulge in her lab coat pocket, packed tight with a stack of index cards. She pulled out the pale lavender card at the top. *Jeremiah 32:17—Ah, Sovereign Lord, you have made the heavens and the earth by your great power and outstretched arm. Nothing is too hard for you.* Nothing was too hard for Him, including getting her mother through this day. Today, more than any she could remember, she wanted so badly to be in Houston with her parents. If she walked out the door right now and started driving, she could be there by tomorrow.

"Can someone help me find the right cough medicine for my son?" A tired-looking woman of about thirty stood at the counter in a wrinkled T-shirt and pajama bottoms.

Paige went down to meet her. "Sure, I'll help. Walk with me over to the cough and cold aisle, and tell me about your son."

"We haven't slept for three nights. The kid is hacking until all hours. I can't take another night of this." The woman rubbed her face with both hands. "Give me the strongest thing you've got."

"Does he have a sore throat? A fever? Does his cough sound wheezy or barky?"

"No to all the above, just a constant hacking."

"How old is he?"

"Seven."

"Paige, call for you," Clarissa called from behind the counter.

As Paige picked up a bottle of cough medicine and held it out to the woman, she could feel her fingers starting to sweat. She wanted to run behind the counter and grab the phone right now. Somehow, she forced herself to stay put. "Give him a teaspoonful of this every six hours. Give your doctor's office a call if he doesn't get better soon."

"Thank you."

Paige called, "You're welcome" over her shoulder as she rushed toward the phone.

"At least it's someone besides Tony this time." Clarissa shrugged as Paige stepped back behind the counter to answer. Something in her voice sounded sad, but Paige didn't have time right now.

Paige put the phone to her ear. "This is Paige."

"Well, baby girl, today was a big day—" Her father's voice broke, the squeaky intake of breath the only sign he was crying.

Paige waited quietly for him to gain control. She knew he hated to lose it like this. She counted out capsules for a refill that was waiting, glad to keep her hands busy while her mind screamed for news. Finally she whispered out the words, "Day zero, right?"

"It was so much more than that." Again, he stopped speaking, but this time continued after a deep breath. "Today was her last radiation treatment, too."

"Right. That's a big thing to check off the list."

"Even better than the day they stopped those tent treatments for her RSV. You know what they do in radiation when it's a patient's last treatment? The nurses have a bell they ring. You can hear it in the waiting room, so everyone out there knows that someone just finished up. When your mother came walking out the door, everyone in that entire waiting room clapped. I mean, there were people sitting out there missing all sorts of body parts, most of them hairless, and yet they still rejoiced for one of their own. . . ." Her father's voice choked into silence. The sounds of quiet sobs came from the other end of the phone. It was the second time Paige had ever known him to cry. The first was the day her mother was diagnosed.

Warm tears spilled down Paige's cheeks as she pictured her mother, weakly walking into the waiting room, finished with this step of the process. She knew her mother well enough to know she smiled at them—likely stopped to squeeze a hand or offer a hug, too. How she wished she could have seen it. "How was the transplant itself?"

"Good. They gave her four bags full of stem cells. It's quite a process."

"How'd Mom do?"

"They gave her a bunch of medicine stuff before-

190

hand, so she mostly slept through it. Then they watched her real close for a while, making sure there weren't any signs of rejection. And there weren't. Everything's looking good so far."

Host versus graft disease. Paige understood it well. If they could avoid that, maybe her mother stood a fighting chance.

"Oh, Daddy, I'm so glad. I've been praying like crazy all day."

"You, and about half of Sledge. In fact, I heard the church ladies organized some sort of twenty-four hour prayer chain for your mother for the transplant."

"I know. I was the one to two a.m. shift. And do you remember me telling you about Ora, who has coffee with me every morning, and the way she comes out with all those bizarre references?"

"Yeah."

"Well, she gave me some verses for today. Here I'll read them to you." Paige pulled out the index card she'd made after Ora had fed her this latest reference. "Ready, Dad? It's from Ephesians 4, it says, 'You were taught, with regard to your former way of life, to put off your old self, which is being corrupted by its deceitful desires; to be made new in the attitude of your minds; and to put on the new self, created to be like God in true righteousness and holiness.'" Paige held her breath so she wouldn't giggle while waiting for her father's response.

"Um, nice verse. I guess. And that would apply to your mother how, do you reckon?"

"I'm so glad you asked, because I asked the very same question. Ora says Mom's cancer cells are like the former way of life which we're supposed to put off, and the new stem cells are like the Holy Spirit helping us to put on our new selves." Paige had to admit, after a few moments' consideration, this Ora metaphor resonated with her. "What do you think?"

Paige looked up to see someone standing at the counter. Dawn was still on lunch break, and Clarissa was nowhere to be seen. "Dad, I've got to go. I'll call you tonight. Okay? Love you! Give Mom a hug for me."

They said good-bye and Paige wiped her eyes and then stepped over to help the waiting woman. "May I help you?"

The woman handed her a bottle. "I need a refill, please."

"Have a seat. It'll be just a minute."

Clarissa was sitting at the back desk, writing on a pad of yellow paper. When she saw Paige looking at her she quickly flipped the pad over.

Paige typed the prescription into the computer and didn't think more about it, until Clarissa showed up at her side. "Sorry. Just thought of something that needed to be done immediately. I didn't see her standing there."

"No problem." What was Clarissa working on

that she felt she needed to justify, and why had she flipped it over so quickly when she saw Paige looking? As much as she wanted to chide herself for being paranoid, given what she'd lived through in the past year, she didn't go there.

Clarissa had been acting more and more strange since Tony's call a few days ago. None of it made any sense. Clarissa was the one who had insisted she go to dinner with them, she was the one who had acted like she wanted the two of them to get together, and now she seemed upset that he had called once. Who knew what was going on in her head?

Or on that yellow pad of paper?

"Good afternoon, ladies."

Clarissa looked up to see Tony leaning across the counter. He grinned at Paige. "How are my two favorite pharmacists this fine afternoon?"

"Tony, what are you doing here?" Clarissa knew that every bit of her irritation came through in her voice, but so be it. Tony was crossing the line and he needed to back off now.

He continued to lean across the counter but turned his attention, minus the glowing smile, toward her. "Oh, checking in upstairs again. They've gotten a little behind schedule, and I'll probably be here several times in the next few weeks to help out."

"Well, I'm glad you checked in." She nodded

toward the group of people sitting in the waiting area. "Little busy now. I'll come find you later when we're all caught up. Okay?"

"Sure. Don't want to interfere with the business day, I've heard the boss can be a real bear." Tony winked, then waved his goodbye to Paige. "See ya later."

Something about that wave bugged Clarissa. What was it, besides that it had been directed only at Paige? It was only a stupid hand gesture. Then it hit her, even harder than the initial reaction. It was his left hand—there was no ring on it.

In spite of the fact that Laurie had left him two years ago, in spite of the fact that she'd already remarried and had a child, Tony had never taken his ring off. Clarissa had asked him about it once, and he'd said it felt comfortable, and he wasn't ready to move on just yet.

She looked at Paige, who stood working at the counter like nothing had even happened. It was more than time to put a stop to this.

"Did you tell me you two are going out this weekend?"

Paige couldn't have been more thankful that Rachelle was coming to town. Something about Clarissa's tone warned her that a yes answer might push her beyond the flash point. "No. I've got a friend coming into town tomorrow."

"That's too bad." Clarissa smiled even as she

said the words. The brightness in her eyes, the tone in her voice. It was so hard, so cold. It sent a chill down Paige's spine.

She had never been so glad for the escape that lunchtime offered. At least for the next half hour she could sit outside in peace. She'd had more than enough tension for one day.

"Mind if I join you?" Tony squatted before her so that they were face-to-face.

"I didn't see you come out."

"So I gathered by the way you jumped when I spoke." His grin could light an entire room. "I'm about to go buy lunch at the coffee counter, but I'll come sit out here with you if you'd like some company."

"Sounds great."

"I was hoping you'd think so." He stood upright. "You want anything from inside?"

Paige shook her head, then stopped. "You know, maybe I do. If they still have some scones left from this morning, I'd love one. And a bottled water."

"You got it."

Paige watched the people milling around the square, some smiling and laughing—just a leisurely day out shopping—while others looked stressed, tired, or just downright miserable. She thought of her mother, whose circumstances would be enough to break the most upbeat of people, yet she was still teasing and laughing with her family. It was a deliberate choice; Paige knew that. Her mother had chosen to stay positive, had chosen to rely on her faith—believing God would ultimately do the thing that was best for all of them. She could still hear her mother's voice—"God is not a vending machine that gives us everything we want. He does what is the *best* thing—for all involved."

Paige pulled out the index cards again. She knew what was best for all of them. Her mother being completely rid of this cancer was what was best.

She couldn't shake the rest of her mother's words, no matter how she tried. She didn't want to remember them, didn't want to accept them. "If His plan means I go through all of this, and the cancer—or the treatment—still takes me, then I say that's where I want to be. Right in the middle of His plan."

Paige shook her head. *God, give me that kind of trust.* She closed her eyes and pictured her mother's sweet face. *Give me that kind of trust, but please still heal my mother.*

"Tell me you are not going out with *him* this weekend." Cory's voice came from beside her, but he spoke so loud it carried down the sidewalk.

"Not that it's any of your business, no I am not going out with him this weekend. I have a friend coming in from Atlanta."

Cory stood and looked at her, slowly uncrossed his arms, and dropped onto the bench beside her. "Sorry, that guy just makes me crazy." He looked at Paige and smiled. "And after a couple of lunches you keep turning me down. What do you say? For my sanity's sake, aren't you ready to go out? I know you wouldn't want a fellow human being's mind to be warped because of you."

Paige laughed. She had to admit, Cory's persistence was flattering. And he was fun to be around—most of the time, anyway. "Well, I—"

"Here's your scone." Tony stood before the two of them, balancing paper plates in his left hand, a foam coffee cup in his right hand, and a bottled water under his right arm. He looked at Cory, still sitting so close. "Hi Cory. Didn't know you were going to be out here."

Cory turned toward Paige, his expression too nonchalant to be believable. "Oh, I'm leaving. I just stopped to talk to Paige about something."

"Great. See you later."

Cory took his time in standing, yawning and stretching. He looked at Paige one last time and nodded. "See *you* later."

Tony sat beside Paige and watched Cory until he was inside the lobby, doors closed behind him. He handed Paige her water. "So, I know your friend's coming to town tomorrow and all, but you want to grab a quick bite of dinner tonight?"

The guest room really needed some cleaning before Rachelle got there. And she had already planned to spend the evening at home. Alone. In the quietness of her parents' house. Suddenly, she couldn't stand the thought. "Sure. Sounds great."

"I was hoping you'd think so." He rested his arm across the back of the bench, and Paige leaned a little closer in spite of herself. He squeezed her shoulder. "I need to ask some professional advice."

"Really? What?"

"I think you're addictive and I'm in trouble. Is there any hope for me?"

Paige rested her head on his shoulder and looked up at the sky, pretending to concentrate. "Hmm, let me think back to my pharmacology classes. Let's see, there's . . . no, that wouldn't work, or maybe . . . nah, that's not it, either." She straightened up and smiled at him. "There might be a cure, but I don't think it's in my best interest to help you find it."

"I guess I'm done for, then." He leaned forward and kissed her lightly on the lips. "I must say, I can't think of a better way to go."

chapter **twenty-five**

Saturday night, the first thing Paige saw when she pulled into the driveway was the rearranged furniture on the front porch. She started laughing and couldn't stop. Shell never changed.

She climbed from her car still laughing, eager to find her friend and get to the reason behind this visit. The smell of charcoal wafting through the air caused her to change course and walk toward the backyard.

Rachelle did not exaggerate her ability to grill the best burgers in town. In fact, Rachelle never exaggerated about anything. It was going to be so great to spend time together again. It had been too long.

She remembered the last time she'd smelled those burgers. It had been in Atlanta, the night before everything fell apart.

"Another Sunday night burger feast done right. I may only be able to cook one thing, but I'm pretty good at that if I do say so myself."

Paige laughed. "Yes, you are."

The phone rang and Rachelle picked it up. "Hello."

She held the receiver out to Paige. "For you. It's Helga." Rachelle grinned and stuck out her tongue. "Told you so."

"Hello?"

"Paige, Helga Parker here. I need you to come in a little early tomorrow morning. Can you meet in my office at say, eight o'clock?"

Paige looked at Rachelle, who was practically bouncing up and down. "Sure, I can be there early. What's this about?"

"Best if we don't discuss it on the phone. I'll see you tomorrow morning at eight."

"Okay." Paige had barely set the receiver on the counter before Rachelle had grabbed her by both arms and was dancing around in circles.

"Told you so, told you so. You're getting that promotion, right?"

Paige planted her feet. "I don't know, she sounded so . . . serious."

"Helga always sounds serious. She's just trying not to give away the surprise. This is so great! Let's go get some ice cream to celebrate."

The next morning, Paige rode into work with Rachelle, who continued to chatter with excitement about all that awaited Paige, but somehow the more excited Rachelle got, the more nervous Paige became. Something wasn't right; she sensed it in Helga's voice.

They pulled into the employee parking lot; Rachelle turned off the car and looked toward her. "If you get an executive parking sticker, will you tell them you lost the first one and give the second one to me? I've always wanted to park on the first level."

"Really, Shell, knock it off."

"My, my, aren't we a little grumpy on promotion day? Boy, I hate to think of what you'll be like if you ever make director."

Paige took the elevator to the fifth floor administrative offices, wondering why she wasn't as convinced. She knew that she'd been recommended for the assistant chief position and that everyone expected her to get the job, but still . . . something about Helga's voice last night. It just sounded so . . . hard.

Paige opened the door to the outer office and bestowed her brightest smile on the administrative secretary. "Good morning!"

The woman didn't even look up. "First conference room on the left. They're waiting."

Conference room?

They?

Did Sharitz make that big a deal out of a simple promotion? It must be something big because Siena didn't even trust herself to look at her.

Paige opened the door to the conference room, exerting all her effort to appear calm and professional. Like someone who could be trusted with this new responsibility.

The room was full of people. She had expected only the administrator and perhaps the pharmacy chief. In addition, there was Brian Harper, whom Paige had been dating the last few months, the head nurse, and two other doctors, including Dr. Pilcher, chief of staff.

She looked at Brian and smiled at him. He nodded at her, then looked away.

"You, uh, wanted to see me?"

Helga pointed her toward the empty seat at the end of the long conference table. "Yes, we did."

Paige noticed that Dr. Pilcher had a medical chart on the table in front of him. He was looking at it, then looked back at her. He leaned forward on the table and laced his fingers together. "Have you heard that one of our patients, Jerry

Bartlett, had a serious auto accident last week?"

Paige nodded. Jerry Bartlett was a well-known civic leader in the greater Atlanta area, as well as one of the nicest patients in the entire HMO system. Everyone knew and loved him. "Yes, I heard about that. How is he doing?" This seemed like a strange subject for small talk before a promotion announcement. Paige looked at Brian, but his eyes remained fixed on the chart. She felt her pulse begin to thrum in her ears.

Dr. Pilcher rubbed his forehead, wrinkling the skin on his bald head into shiny little mounds. "Not so well, I'm afraid. And the passengers in the other car have filed a lawsuit."

"I didn't think the people in the other car were hurt." Why were they telling her all this?

"They weren't. But the mother started talking to a lawyer. Their claim is that she can no longer drive with her child in the car without fear, and it's causing undue pain and suffering."

Paige looked around the table. Brian continued to stare at the chart, and Helga sat stone-faced, arms folded across herself. Everyone seemed to be waiting for a response from her. "So, I guess I'm not clear on what that has to do with Sharitz. Are we planning to help Mr. Bartlett defend himself in the lawsuit or something?"

"It appears as though Mr. Bartlett suffered a seizure behind the wheel, and that's what caused the accident. As for helping him defend himself, he *died in our hospital late last night."* He picked up the chart in front of him and set it before Paige. *"Do you recognize the initials beside the pharmacy sticker on the last phenobarbital order?"*

"They're mine."

The rumble of a large motor came from what sounded very close. She turned.

Cory's white truck was pulling into the driveway; he waved from behind the wheel. What was he up to now?

She walked up beside the truck before he had a chance to get out. If he stayed behind the wheel, it wouldn't take as long for him to leave. "Cory, what are you doing here?"

"Well, a good evening to you, too." He climbed out of the cab and shut the door behind him, effectively thwarting Paige's plan. "I do believe you lived in the big city too long if that's the way you're greeting guests. Yep, I think I'm offended. How do you plan to make it up to me?" He grinned and leaned against the truck door.

"Cory, I have comp—"

"I came into town to visit Mom today. She picked some fresh corn for you, to show her appreciation for taking care of all her meds."

"Well, tell her thanks." She looked at his empty hands and wondered why he was still standing there waiting. *Get the produce out of your truck, hand it to me, and get out of here.*

He shifted on his feet. "I was going to bring it by the pharmacy on Monday but decided I'd just bring it by your house, since I'm nearby anyway." His gaze lingered on the blue VW bug parked in the driveway. Rachelle's car. "Thought it would be the neighborly thing to do, and I, for one, still want to be neighborly."

"Well, thanks." Now that he'd verified there was indeed a friend's car present, he could leave happy. Paige looked toward his truck, trying to send a not so subtle hint. Time to bring the corn and move on.

He looked toward the house then back at Rachelle's car, and still he didn't budge. His clothes were neatly pressed, his hair still damp. Obviously he was ready for a big night on the town. So what was he waiting for?

"You're here." Rachelle bounded around the corner of the house in typical fashion, throwing her tiny little frame at Paige with full force. The sparkle of her eyes and the spring in her step seemed to contradict Paige's assumption that this trip was brought on by heartbreak. "Hey there, tall, blond, and handsome. Glad you made it back so fast."

Paige looked at Rachelle, thinking surely she'd heard her wrong. "Made it back?"

"Young Mr. Cory stopped by a while ago. It seems he'd brought some corn to leave on your doorstep and just happened upon me unloading my car."

"Imagine that." Paige looked between the two of them, unsure of whom she should be more suspicious.

"Being the gracious hostess that I am, I invited him to come partake of some of the riches of the earth he'd so kindly bestowed—provided, of course, he make a quick trip to the store to get me some Tabasco. What's up with the lack of hot sauce around here?"

Oh no. She wouldn't. "Partake how?"

"Cory's having dinner with us." Rachelle smiled, but the hard set of her eyes told Paige something else was going on.

Paige opened her eyes wider at Shell, hoping she'd get the message to back off. "Cory probably has other plans for the evening."

Cory reached into his shirt pocket and produced a small bottle of Tabasco, which he handed to Rachelle with a smug smile on his face. "None at all. If you're sure you don't mind."

Rachelle smiled. "Of course we don't." She turned a serious expression on Paige. "Burgers are on the grill, go change out of your work clothes. Cory and I have some talking to do."

Cory smiled down at her. "I'm glad to know there are some big-city girls that still have that sense of southern hospitality that seems to be lacking in so many people these days." He looked over his shoulder and winked at Paige. Without another word, Rachelle took Cory by the arm and led him toward the backyard.

Paige watched them walk off together, totally frustrated by the turn of events. She wanted to talk to Rachelle, alone, find out what was going on. In all the time she'd known her, Paige had never known Shell to do something this air-headed. In fact, she'd never known Shell to be anything but deliberate in everything she did. There must be some reason for all this.

A few minutes later she was back outside in shorts and a polo with an icy smoothie in her hand. Paige took a small sip. As far as Rachelle's health drinks went, this one was not all that bad. "Pretty good."

"Delicious, you mean. Right, Cory?"

"Delicious." Cory set his nearly full glass on the ground beside his chair and leaned forward, elbows on knees. "So, Rachelle, do you think you could mix up one of your special potions that would make your friend go out with me? She keeps giving me the runaround, and it's starting to hurt my pride."

"We'll just have to see what we can do about that, now won't we?" Rachelle cocked her head sideways and grinned at Paige. "But before that, you'll have to meet my grueling approval process, which means for the rest of the evening, you'll be quizzed unmercifully. Let's start with . . . say . . . your life history. Have you ever lived in Nashville?"

Again, Rachelle had put on the light and friendly façade, but Paige knew better. She was digging for something.

The evening went well, though Rachelle never once hinted that something might be amiss. She just kept Paige and Cory laughing with her exploits in Atlanta. Cory flirted and grinned but Rachelle did a good job of keeping him off-balance during the night, and Paige thought he even looked relieved when it was time for him to leave. Paige and Rachelle waved from the front porch, and as Cory drove away in his truck, Paige turned to her friend. "Now, would you mind telling me what that was all about?"

"What, you didn't like the burgers?"

"That's not what I'm talking about and you know it. I'm talking about Cory."

"Oh, him. He's cute. Seems nice. He obviously likes you, and you at least seem to have fun when he's around—although I am picking up a weird little vibe of resistance on your part."

"If I told you that corn won't be harvested here for another couple of months at least, would you begin to get the picture?"

"Do what? Where'd he get the corn, then?"

"I'd guess the grocery store, imported from wherever it is they import from this time of year."

"No wonder it didn't taste that great." Shell looked at the street, in the direction Cory had gone, and shook her head. "I must be going soft. After all that questioning I did, he had me totally convinced he was on the up and up. Now I'll have to rethink everything."

"Rachelle, what's going on? Something's wrong, and it's time you tell me what it is."

Rachelle's face grew serious. "Let's go sit inside."

They went to sit in the tiny living room. Paige perched on her father's old recliner; Rachelle flopped on the sofa—for about three seconds. She popped up and dragged the couch sideways about six inches, then centered the old storage locker that served as a coffee table in front of it. The side table was adjusted accordingly, and she sat down and nodded. "Better. Don't you think?"

It was better. Much better, in fact. "You didn't come all the way here to rearrange my mother's furniture. Now, let's hear it. Did something happen with Mr. Centerfielder?"

"He's a man. A man is a man." Rachelle twisted a lock of her short hair around her index finger. "Actually, I didn't come to talk about what's up with *me*. I came to talk about what's up with *you*."

"What do you mean? I'm doing just fine."

"Yes, *you* are doing fine. But there might be other people who aren't so fine."

"Honestly, Rachelle, you can be so frustrating at times. What other people?"

"Last week Brian came to talk to me. It seems a

strange little man showed up at Sharitz, asking questions. General at first, then slowly narrowing down to you. He's been talking to the bosses and everything."

Oh no. *Please God, no.* "Something about Mr. Bartlett?"

"That was my first thought. So I called David Brown, you know, that lawyer I went out with a few times? And he sent his investigator to investigate the investigator."

Paige couldn't help but laugh. "Rachelle, your former paramours sure do come in handy sometimes."

"Don't I know it?" She began to twist her hair again. "Anyway, it seems the guy who's been checking you out is an investigator from Tennessee. Nashville, to be exact. That's why I kept asking Cory questions about Nashville. When he showed up this afternoon, I figured he was a likely candidate to be mixed up in the middle of this somehow. He claims he's never lived there, but then again, he claims his mother picked corn, so I don't know what to think."

"Nashville?" Paige stared at the pale pink flowers of her mother's throw rug. Who in Nashville would want her investigated? There could be only one possible answer, but that didn't answer the biggest question: *Why?*

"He's still trying to figure out exactly who hired the guy, but I guess that piece of information is a bit harder to get. The old man who got you your new job, he lives in Nashville, right?"

"Yeah, and so does his granddaughter—my boss."

Rachelle flopped back onto the couch, put her left hand behind her head on the armrest, and stretched her legs across its length. "Can you think of a reason that either of them would do this?"

"No. Yes. I don't know." Paige stared at the ceiling, straining to think it all through. "Clarissa is pretty hard to read sometimes, but there's definitely some friction where I'm concerned, and has been from day one. I can't imagine what would make her investigate me—or what might happen if she gets too close to the truth."

"You just need to keep both eyes open. I'll let you know when I find out anything else."

Paige felt the walls of security that had just begun to rebuild around her start to crumble. She made an exaggerated stretch. "I'm really tired. I think I'll turn in."

Rachelle nodded, but the expression on her face said she knew better. Paige needed some time alone to process, and Rachelle would understand this. "See you in the morning."

Both women stood and walked down the long hall; Paige turned right to her bedroom, and Rachelle went left to the guest room. The floors squeaked with every step, a noisy reminder that this place had seen more than its share of life, trouble, and heartache. Would it ever again see happiness?

Long after she climbed into bed, Paige lay staring at the ceiling. Even in the dark, she could make out the shadowed areas caused by the warped plaster. The air-conditioner hummed from the other room, fighting against the heat and humidity. But all it really did was cover the truth. In this one little building, they could pretend it wasn't miserably hot and humid. Ignore what was just outside the window.

Just like the "new life" she was starting. The old one wasn't gone; it was just covered up. All it took was one little flick of the switch, a sudden loss of electricity, and the truth of the situation would once again be obvious. Hot was always hot, warped was always warped.

She felt the pain of loss all over again. She tried to pray, but mostly it came out as, "Why, God? Why?"

chapter **twenty-six**

Dawn drove away from work, glad the day was finally over. What a Monday it had been. The phone had rung constantly, and people were lined up five deep at the counter, every one of them in a grumpy mood. To top it all off, Clarissa had called in sick, leaving only two of them to handle it all.

She turned onto her street, glad to finally be home. A nice cool shower and a mindless TV show were what she needed.

A metallic green Plymouth sat parked in her driveway. *Oh no. Jack's ex.* If the kids were coming over tonight, nobody had bothered to tell her—not that they ever did. She would go put a stop to this right now. This was the day she planned to let everyone know she was through letting others take advantage of her.

No, wait. She remembered Jack this morning, up early, making her coffee, kissing her before he left. He'd been as sweet as he was when she first moved in—like he finally woke up and remembered how much he loved her or something. Things were getting better, she wouldn't let an unexpected kid visit ruin that. Besides, Nicole and Jeremy were lovable kids, most of the time anyway.

A stream of water arced from the side of the house. Nicole's high-pitched squeal and Jeremy's laughter came from the direction of the geyser. Dawn smiled, picturing Jack chasing them with the hose, cooling off on a hot night. Maybe things here were going like she'd always known they would, if she'd just hang in there long enough.

She climbed from the car and moved toward the commotion. A spray of water blasted through the air again. She did not want to turn the corner and get soaked, so she cupped her hands to her mouth and called, "Watch out, coming through," and chanced a peek around the corner.

When Nicole saw her, she ran over and threw her arms around Dawn's leg, still giggling. Her hair hung in wet strings, her blue sundress clung to her—every inch soaked through.

"What are you doing?" Dawn looked toward Jeremy, who was almost equally wet. He turned the spigot at the hose. "Cleaning up."

"Cleaning what up?"

"Ourselves."

"That's not what it looks like."

Jeremy shrugged. "Nic was all sticky, so we came over here to rinse her off a bit."

"And one thing led to another, I see." Dawn looked toward the house, expecting to see Renee coming out any minute now. She never hung around long when she dropped off the kids. "Why was Nicole sticky?"

Nicole licked her lips. "Cotton candy. Mmm. We got some at the fair."

"Wow, y'all drove over to Lawrenceburg today for the fair? That's special." No wonder Renee had brought them by. A day at the fair, the kids pumped up on sugar. Yeah, she'd probably called Jack and made some lame excuse about why he needed to take the kids tonight. "Was your mom off work today?"

"She took off special. Just like Dad."

"Like Dad?"

"Yeah, he took us all. It was so much fun. He bought Jeremy a balloon, and he won stuffed animals for mama and me."

The door to the house remained closed. The kids were soaking wet. How long had they been home? How long had Renee been here?

Dawn shook off the thought. Jack had gotten up early today, fixed her coffee. He loved her. The two of them were probably in there fighting about child support. Still, it was probably time for Renee to get on her way. "Let's get you inside and into some dry clothes."

Jeremy shook his head. "Can't. Daddy said not to."

Dawn took Nicole's hand and started toward the house. "Said not to what?"

"Come inside. He said him and mama were going to take a nap. He said we had to play outside."

Dawn dropped Nicole's hand and turned to look at Jeremy.

A sick anger boiled inside her. She took the front porch steps two at a time. When she pushed on the door handle, it didn't move. Locked.

She jerked open her purse flap and shoved her hand past the torn wallet and the tube of lipstick to find her key ring. The heart-shaped key ring Jack had given her when they first started dating. She jerked it out and shoved the key in the door. In one motion she turned the key, pushed the latch, and flung open the door.

Renee stood in the front room, brushing through wet hair. She was wearing an old shirt of Jack's and not much else. "Oh, hi. Didn't realize it was time for you to be home yet."

I'll bet. "What are you doing here?"

"The kids was just spending a little quality time with their daddy. That's important, you know."

Jack came walking into the room, hair dripping wet, a towel wrapped around his waist. "I've got to fix that water heater. I hate cold showers. I'm about frozen through."

Renee set down the brush. "Funny, it was plenty warm when I was in there. Hot, I'd almost say." She smiled coyly at Jack. "Things cooled after I got out, hmm?"

Jack smiled but didn't answer.

Renee crossed the room to stand beside him. "Well, I'd best be getting home." She rubbed a finger down his bare chest. "Talk to you . . . later." She turned and looked at Dawn, a smirk on her face. "Have a nice evening." The faint sound of suppressed giggles trailed behind her as she walked out the door.

Dawn didn't even wait for it to close. "What was that all about?"

"I spent the day with my family. That's what it was all about."

"Your *family*? Your family? I seem to remember that you are divorced from at least part of that family. Any of that ringing a bell with you?"

215

"It's good for kids to spend some time with both parents. Even if we're not married, they need to see that we still get along."

"Get along is one thing. Locking the kids out of the house and *getting along* is another." She pointed at the couch. "I hope you'll be comfortable here tonight, because you are no longer welcome in my bed."

Jack grabbed her by both shoulders and put his face only inches from hers. His breath was thick with the smell of beer. "This is my house. Mine. Got it? I live here, I own it. That includes the bed. I'll do whatever I want, with whoever I want. Got it?" He pulled her toward the back room.

"Let me go." She knew even as she said the words that he wouldn't. It was hopeless.

chapter **twenty-seven**

Tuesday morning, Paige watched Clarissa make her entrance into the pharmacy. Something about her seemed different today. The bored disinterest that always radiated from her felt forced today. Defiant almost. She walked into the dispensing area, her jaw set.

"There's something I need to tell you, but I don't want any lectures or 'I told you so's.'"

Paige held up the first three fingers of her right hand. "Scouts honor. I'll leave the lectures to the mothers of this world."

Clarissa did not smile. "Yeah, well, I'm sure I'll get plenty of yap from my step-monster." Her eyes glinted hard and flat.

"What's the matter?" The news must have been pretty bad for Clarissa to be this serious about it. Paige dropped onto the stool behind her.

"You remember Ms. Feldhouse? The Zebeta lady?"

"Yes."

"Well, she's filed a lawsuit." Clarissa looked toward the ceiling. "I mean, come on. It wasn't like anything bad happened to her or anything. She's just out to make a little money."

Pictures of Atlanta flashed before Paige's eyes. Things could get worse from here—a lot worse. Clarissa might not see the big picture yet, but she did. "Do they know yet? About Dawn taking the call, I mean?"

Clarissa snorted. "Are you crazy? And I'm not going to tell them."

"So, you plan to lie?"

Clarissa waved her hand once. "Relax. My father's lawyer is going to handle it. He's already started looking into it and said her lawyer is some backwoods loser. We'll settle it fast so there won't be a trial or anything—and insurance will cover it. So, it's an inconvenience." She ran her fingers through the black silk of her hair. "An inconvenience I don't want to deal with, but what can I say? There's a lot I'd rather not deal with."

"Are you sure? It definitely wouldn't go to trial?"

"He'll handle it. We just need to keep our mouths shut about what happened, and it'll all be over in a quick and painless manner."

It might be quick, but for Paige it would not be painless. The memories were already awakening in her mind.

Clarissa reached over and took Paige by the arm. "If someone comes around asking questions, you know what you are *not* going to say, right?"

"I'm not going to lie. You were doing something that you knew was wrong. Something I kept telling you not to do."

Clarissa pulled her hand away. "So much for scout's honor about lectures, hmm?" She looked at her fingernails. "Besides, I'd think someone with your past, more than most people, would understand this situation."

The words slipped like a cold blade between her ribs. She could barely manage to say, "What?"

"Have you forgotten about Mr. Bartlett so soon?"

Paige looked at Clarissa, knowing now without a doubt who had hired the investigator.

"In case you need a reminder, that was the name of the man in Atlanta who had a seizure behind the wheel because he got the wrong strength of his medication. He hit an SUV carrying a mother and her toddler. Ring any bells?" Clarissa crossed her arms and leaned against the counter, victory shining from her eyes.

Breathe. Just breathe. You've got to be strong, your parents need you to be strong. "The things that happened in Atlanta . . . They were . . . That was different."

"You think so? What was so different about it?"

"Those were *mistakes*, made by people who were working according to the law. What you're doing is *negligence* plain and simple."

Clarissa looked at her fingernails. "I doubt my grandfather would see it that way. Don't you?"

"It was different," Paige insisted, trying hard to forget the memories that flooded back.

Paige sat in the committee meeting, looking at Mr. Bartlett's chart, her heart pounding. What was going on here?

"Would you read for us, please, what the order says?" Dr. Pilcher put his finger above the order in question.

The refill had been written on a call-in form, which would then have been paper clipped to the front of the chart, sent for a doctor's signature, then sent to the pharmacy to be filled. After the completion of all those steps, the order was permanently attached to the chart.

"It says Phenobarbital 30 mg BID."

"Yes, 30 mg twice a day. But Jerry Bartlett's regimen is 100 mg twice a day."

Paige looked at the words written before her. "Then why is it written as 30 mg?"

The head nurse spoke up. "It seems that when he called in, he asked for 30. In retrospect, what he meant was a thirty-day supply, since that's what his plan covers."

Paige tried to blink aside the pictures of Jerry Bartlett's wrinkled face, his stooped posture, his withered hands. She could still hear his "Thank you very much, young lady" as she handed him his prescription, see him wink as he took it from her hand. That she had handed him a bag filled with what caused his wreck was unthinkable. She rubbed her fingertips with her thumb, as if to erase the stain.

Dr. Pilcher pressed against his forehead again. "What I want to know, Miss Woodward, is why didn't you catch this?"

"Excuse me?"

"I've spoken extensively with our medical error committee," he said nodding toward the three assembled doctors. Brian did not look at her. "It has been agreed that this should have been stopped by the pharmacy. Would your computer not have flashed a warning that a different dose than normal was being given?"

"Yes, of course. But with a drug like phenobarbital, the doses are often adjusted. I would have seen that and made the assumption that this was being added to his current regimen."

"It sounds a lot like carelessness to me."

Paige cast a glance toward Brian, waiting for

him to speak up. He looked down at his hands and remained silent.

Helga pointed at the chart. "Thankfully, Mr. Bartlett's family has agreed to compensation and complete medical coverage, and they will not file a lawsuit. They just want to make certain that the person responsible for this is held to account."

Dr. Pilcher nodded his head. "This committee is in agreement that you are that person, Miss Woodward."

The room seemed to blink shades of light and dark, as if the injustice of it all was too much for even the walls to take. Paige could hear her own pulse beating in time with the flickering shadows.

"As of right now, you may consider yourself on unpaid leave." Helga's voice carried no hint of remorse. "We will give you a week to think it over. If you choose to resign during that week, it will be recorded as a resignation in Human Resources, thus preserving your reference for another job you might apply for. If you choose not to resign, then we may have no other choice but to let you go."

Paige looked around the room. "But, I only filled the prescription as written. How can you blame me for this?"

"That's all for now."

Paige stood and walked through the front room, her legs barely supporting her. This had to be a dream. A nightmare from which she would soon wake. But never did.

• • •

"You know my grandfather would fire you in a heartbeat if he knew about your past, don't you?"

Paige nodded her head. "Clarissa, I need this job."

"Yes, and I need a lawsuit that is easily settled. If someone comes around asking questions, you keep your mouth shut, and in return, I'll keep my mouth shut to Granddad. Understand?" The hard glimmer in Clarissa's eyes left no doubt that she was completely serious. "Look, accidents happen. I don't judge. I've made mistakes, you've made mistakes. Right?" Clarissa put her hand on Paige's shoulder and squeezed. "Do you understand?"

Paige took a deep breath. "I understand perfectly."

Dawn came back into the pharmacy from the stock room. Clarissa nodded toward her, then turned back to Paige. "Good. Now that we've got that all settled, how was your weekend with your friend?" She said it in the most conversational, friendly tone. It was almost impossible to believe it was the same mouth that had spoken not ten seconds ago.

Paige tried to pull herself back into the here and now. She was in a desperate situation with her parents, and she needed to buck up and get through this. "The weekend with my friend was nice." At least she knew the truth now. Paige pulled up some extra courage from somewhere and forced herself to pretend this was just a casual conversation with a co-worker. "It was good to see her again."

"Good to see Cory, too, huh?" Dawn giggled from the side.

Clarissa cut a sharp glance toward her. "Cory?"

Dawn laughed. "Tell her, Paige."

"Well, I . . ."

"See, he dropped some stuff by Paige's house from his mother, and Paige's friend invited him to stay for dinner. Paige has been trying her best to avoid the guy, and he just keeps showing up."

"I never said that."

"Did too. You told me the whole story just this morning."

"I mean, I never said I was doing my best to avoid him."

"Well, duh, you don't have to tell me that. It's pretty obvious the way you disappear every time he comes around. I bet I've heard him ask you out three times, and you've had an excuse every single time."

"Dawn, why don't you go listen to the refill line? In fact, why don't we all get busy instead of standing here yakking about stuff that makes absolutely no difference to anybody?" Clarissa turned and walked to her desk.

chapter twenty-eight

Wednesday morning, Paige walked the length of the fast-mover section, stopping every now and then to look behind a white plastic bottle, or to pick up and shake a brown one. Yes, they definitely needed to order more furosemide. By the time she finished writing the word on the order list, the ink ran so sporadically that the "ide" was illegible. Time for a new pen.

She looked in the usual coffee cup and found one pencil, three paper clips, a rubber band, and no pens. There had to be some around here somewhere.

Likely Clarissa's desk drawer would have a few. Paige walked back and slid it open.

Three blue pens sat atop printouts of weekend reports; the corner of a yellow legal pad stuck out from the bottom. A yellow pad just like the one she'd seen Clarissa writing on the other day, when she was acting so mysterious.

Paige slid the drawer shut. Whatever it was, it wasn't her business. *Right?*

She stood staring at the drawer, debating. *Maybe one quick peek.*

Paige pulled on the handle and slid the pad out from under the printouts. The first thing that caught her attention was her name at the top of the sheet.

Paige Woodward File
April 1—complaint from Mr. Pauling for slow
*   service*
April 4—Let Dawn take call-in for prednisone
April 8—spent half an hour on the phone, cus-
*   tomers waiting at the counter*

The pad grew heavy in Paige's hand. She couldn't believe this was happening again. This was a page of distorted facts, and one out-and-out lie—Paige never ever let Dawn take a call-in for anything. At least she could prove that one wrong. As for Mr. Pauling's slow service, the doctor hadn't written the strength on the prescription and she'd had to call. How was that her fault? The only truth at all on the page was that she had talked on the phone on April 8th. It was the day her father called about the stem cell transplant, but there were no customers waiting at the window until the very end.

Something cold and pointed seemed to take residence inside her chest. She walked over to the computer and looked up the prescriptions filled on April 4. Sure enough, a prescription for prednisone had been filled that day under Paige's initials. She went to the cabinet and pulled out the hard copy. The paper slipped through her fingers and fell to the floor. Paige collapsed beside it and picked it up again.

The handwriting was not her own, and on closer

inspection she knew it wasn't Clarissa's either. It *could* be Dawn's, she supposed, but since when did Dawn print anything? And since Paige did not authorize Dawn to take this call-in, and Clarissa knew it had happened, it had to be part of a setup.

Why would Clarissa do this? Was Dawn unaware, or part of it?

She needed to start taking measures to defend herself, and right now. She would write out her own account of the Pauling incident, while it was all still fresh in her mind. She'd write out the account of the phone conversation with her father, and write out the truth about the prednisone—or at least the untruth of what was written on the legal pad.

Today was Clarissa's day off, so she couldn't talk to her about it until tomorrow. Maybe in the meantime, she should confront Dawn.

No. Maybe Clarissa had just done this when she was mad, and nothing would come of it. After all, she hadn't entered anything in almost a week. If Paige got Dawn involved now, it would make it hard for things to settle down. Maybe she should just watch. But she wouldn't be caught unawares this time. Never again.

By the time she got off work that night, Paige's head was swimming. As soon as she locked up the pharmacy, she walked around the corner to the neighborhood grocery store in search of some soup. One of the few remaining family-owned groceries, it was small and a bit outdated, but it felt quaint and cozy. Nothing like the gigantic chain store just across town.

She walked to the soup aisle and stood staring at the red and white labels: *Chicken with Stars, Cream of Chicken* . . . there it was: *Chicken Noodle*. She picked up two cans for good measure.

"I hope your boss wasn't too hard on you." Rita Konkel was standing beside her, hands wrapped around the handle of a metal shopping cart.

"Hi, Mrs. Konkel." Paige looked at the cans in her hands. "Hard on me?"

"About your mistake, I mean. I didn't want to get you in trouble, honest. But, boy, I sure am glad I came in to double-check when my pills looked different. It could have been a disaster otherwise, huh? You must feel pretty lucky. Of course, since I'm the one who was about to take the wrong thing, I feel even luckier."

"Wrong thing?" *Bright smile. Calm voice,* she told herself. "Mrs. Konkel, I'm afraid I don't know what you are talking about."

"My arthritis pills. My daughter picked them up for me on Tuesday. They looked different, and I came right in to ask about 'em. Sure enough, you'd given me the wrong stuff."

"*I* gave you?"

"Yeah. The other young lady, Miss Richardson, looked it up. She changed everything out for me,

227

was real nice about it. She told me she'd have a good long talk with you about being more careful in the future. The way she was acting, I was afraid she'd really let you have it."

"She . . ." Paige's mind reeled. She thought about how strange Clarissa had been acting lately. "She left a note. I haven't had the chance to talk to her yet."

"Tell her to go easy on you. I'm sure you'll be more careful next time."

"I'm just sorry you got the wrong thing, Mrs. Konkel. So, are you . . . okay?"

"Just fine, didn't take a single one. Mistakes happen, that's why I always double-check everything."

"Did you find it out before you left the store then?"

"No, doesn't it just figure? This is the one time I had my daughter pick up my stuff. That's why I can't trust other people to do things for me. Like I said, I'm just glad I caught it before I took any."

"Me, too."

Paige looked at the cans in her hands. "I just remembered something I need to do." She set the soup back onto the shelf and ran from the store, back to the pharmacy. Nothing else mattered but finding the truth about what she'd done—or at least what Clarissa had made it appear she'd done.

Once inside the pharmacy, she turned on the computer and paced nervously while waiting for it to boot up. Finally, she got Mrs. Konkel's prescription number and looked it up, then went to the cabinet and found the hard copy.

Naprosyn 500 BID #60

Paige's computer initials were stuck to the paper, along with her customary hand-written initials beside them, the date, and "Used GenXrix brand." She had a vague memory of filling this and then reordering.

Down in the bottom corner was a notation from Clarissa.

Bottle was filled with Anaprox DS instead of Naprosyn. Patient did not take any. I replaced with correct medication.

Anaprox? The mistake would be easy enough to make, because Anaprox, *naproxen sodium,* would be directly beside Naprosyn, *naproxen,* on the shelf.

Paige walked to the shelf and looked. She saw the bottle of GenXrix brand generic Naprosyn, and right beside it, the generic Anaprox from LLZ Pharmaceuticals.

Odd.

Her note clearly stated she'd used the GenXrix brand. Tomorrow, she would talk to Clarissa and find out exactly what happened.

• • •

When Dawn arrived the next morning, Paige made small talk for a few minutes, then leaned back against the counter in what she hoped look like a casual pose. "Do you remember Rita Konkel coming in this week?"

"Like you can ever forget Mrs. Konkel coming in." Dawn rolled her eyes. "I was so happy when her daughter came to pick up her prescription for her. I mean, you know how she is, I always have to stand at the counter for an hour while she counts everything for the bijillionth time. It just figures that the one time she doesn't do all that is the time we mess her stuff up."

"What happened?"

"Mrs. Konkel came back in, just after you'd left for the day, I think. She was all dramatic and carrying on."

"So what was in the bottle?"

"I don't know. Some sort of blue caplets, and hers were supposed to be white caplets. Clarissa spent a lot of time talking to her, then replaced it and sent her on her way."

"I just don't understand it." A disquiet began to jab at her, a thought so jaded she knew it couldn't be true. Still, she had to ask the question. "Before you gave it to her daughter, did Clarissa do anything with the prescription?"

Dawn shook her head and looked at Paige as if she were crazy. "Not that I saw."

And that was the problem. No one would have seen a thing. *Come on, Paige, you know Clarissa wouldn't do something like that.*

Don't you?

Mrs. Konkel and her Naprosyn would have presented the perfect opportunity for a setup, if Clarissa had been looking for such a chance. Mrs. Konkel always double-checked everything, so it was bound to be discovered. And, if by some miracle the switch escaped notice, the difference in the drugs was so small that it wouldn't make that much difference. Still, Clarissa wouldn't do that.

Would she?

When Clarissa arrived at work a little later, Paige approached her casually. "I ran into Rita Konkel at the grocery store last night."

"That's nice."

"She said I misfilled her anti-inflammatory prescription."

"That's right. She brought it back in, and it had Anaprox DS in the bottle that was supposed to have Naprosyn. Didn't I tell you about it?"

"No, you didn't."

"Must have slipped my mind."

Paige felt a chill run the length of her spine. "Clarissa, what is going on?"

"What would make you ask that?"

"Well, for one thing, you 'forgot' to mention to me an apparent misfilled prescription. For another, I wrote the generic manufacturer on the hard copy for Naprosyn, not Anaprox. I put the correct thing in that bottle."

"Listen, say what you will, the wrong thing was in that bottle. There's nothing I can do about that. And as for forgetting to tell you—as I recall you 'forgot' to tell me that you'd gone out with my uncle. People forget things. In fact, I'll bet if the truth is known, you're seeing him this weekend. You are, aren't you?"

"Yes, I am, but it's not the same."

"Of course it is. You didn't mean to hurt me by not mentioning the date, I didn't mean anything bad by not mentioning the mistake—in fact, I thought I'd spare your feelings by just letting it pass. I'm sorry if it upset you. Okay? Let's just put this whole misunderstanding behind us."

"Is that all it is? A misunderstanding?"

"Of course."

That afternoon when Paige returned from lunch, she found Dawn alone in the pharmacy. "Where's Clarissa?"

"She's next door at the travel agent's. I think she's helping her friend plan a honeymoon or something." Dawn pointed to a row of five pre-scriptions. "I left out everything I did while she was gone, so you can double-check."

Paige felt her stomach plummet. She looked at the prescriptions and the bottles beside them, and they did all look correct. But she would not put her initials on them. If Clarissa wanted to run her pharmacy this way, she would have to take responsibility for it, because Paige certainly would not.

chapter **twenty-nine**

"Dusty. Here, boy." From where she sat on her mother's bench, Paige saw Tony's car pull into the driveway—ten minutes early. "Dusty, come on." Where was that dog?

Tony started across the lawn, waving a greeting as he did. "Hello."

Paige jumped to her feet and moved away from the sitting area. This was her mother's special place; it felt sacred almost. Not a place for outsiders. She walked forward and peered between the trees. "Dusty."

"The old boy's out carousing, huh? I knew he still had some spunk left in him." Tony leaned forward and squinted into the thicket. "Young ma-an. Young man."

"You always call him that, but you know, he's actually a senior citizen."

"Youth is all about frame of mind, and I'm telling you, Dusty's a young buck if ever there was one."

Dusty loped out from the trees, his tongue hanging out of his mouth, his eyes bright. He hobbled directly up to Tony, who bent down to pet him. "Listen here, young man, you come from much too nice a family to be out carousing at all hours, worrying us like this. From now on, I expect you to come the first time you're called. You understand?"

Dusty lay down during the middle of the admonishment, his tail thumping against the clover. Tony stood up. "There, I think that's all settled. Let me know if I need to have another talk with him."

Paige felt the sudden urge to throw her arms around Tony's neck and hug him in sheer delight. How long had it been since she'd been with someone who made her feel so good?

But . . . he was Clarissa's uncle. As much as Paige was growing to like him, as much as she believed the feeling was mutual, she couldn't help but wonder what he knew about Clarissa's apparent conniving. The answer to the question sobered her enough to stop her from doing anything foolish.

He wore a black polo shirt that brought out the brown in his eyes—and provided a sharp contrast to the yellow Labrador fur that now clung to it.

"Oops. We better get you inside and use the lint roller on you. That dog sheds enough fur in a day to knit sweaters for a dozen Eskimos, I swear it."

"Now there's an idea for you: Labrador sweaters. Sounds like it would be right up there with cashmere if you ask me."

"I'm sure." When Paige opened the back door,

dog and man followed her inside. She brought the lint roller out of the kitchen drawer and handed it to him. "Mom found Dusty at the animal shelter. He had been abused and abandoned, and when she first brought him home, he was scared to death of people—men in particular. My mom took it upon herself to 'love the fear right out of him.' She kept him with her constantly. If she was working in her flower bed, that's where he was, if she was cooking dinner, he was in the kitchen. Before long, he didn't want to go outside at all unless someone was with him. So, even before the accident, he was more or less a house dog. Dad says he's a poodle in a Labrador's body."

Tony leaned down and scratched Dusty's ears. "Nonsense. You just have to stay inside and protect the women and children. It's purely sacrificial on your part, right, buddy?"

Dusty rolled over to get a belly rub and Paige laughed. "Well, that does *sound* more noble. I'll have to give Mom that piece of ammunition the next time Dad teases her about it." Dusty sneezed and rolled back over, apparently satisfied. "You better watch out or you'll have to use the roller again."

Tony stood up and looked down at his shirt. "All clear." He handed the roller to Paige and went to the sink to wash his hands. "I took the liberty of making a reservation at Frederick's. Does that sound good to you?"

"Wouldn't you rather eat somewhere closer? You drove forty-five minutes to get here, do you really want to go another half-hour south?" She pulled a hand towel from the drawer and held it out to him.

"You're worth it." His fingers brushed against hers as he took the towel.

Paige rubbed her thumb across her fingers, remembering the feel of his touch. She needed to refocus and fast. A stray cup in the sink provided just the distraction. She picked it up, rinsed it carefully, then opened the dishwasher. The top shelf needed a little rearranging. This morning's cereal bowl went to the bottom, the juice glass went to the right, the saucepan's handle got adjusted.

"Is this for your mom's treatment?" He was touching the countdown poster with the index finger of his right hand. Paige hadn't overwhelmed him with the news of her mother's health, but it had come up a few times.

"She has to remain in the Houston area for one hundred days after the transplant, in case of emergency. That's how many days are left until she can come back here."

He whistled low. "Have you heard from her lately?"

Paige nodded. "They check in every couple days. The treatment . . . she's only the ninth person they've tried it on. Five have had fantastic results so far. The other three, not so great. So . . . we'll see."

"I can't wait to meet her."

I can't wait to meet her. There was a hint of a promise in those words. Wasn't there? The potential answers both thrilled and terrified. It was almost too much right now.

"Irene's."

"Irene's?"

"For dinner. I say I'm worth Irene's. You won't have to drive so much, and they have the best southern cooking for miles around."

"Southern cooking?" He offered his elbow. "Sounds great to me."

She put her hand in the crook of his arm, feeling the warmth of his skin. He put his free hand atop hers. "Off we go, then."

While they drove through town, Paige tried to look at this place through Tony's eyes. Compared to the sleek high-rise buildings of downtown Nashville, the old brick storefronts must look bland, boring even. Nothing glamorous to keep his interest here. Of course there wasn't. The comment about meeting her mother had just been polite conversation. Paige could do that, too. "So, how is the job coming along at Shoal Creek?"

"It should wrap up in the next month or so."

"What's the next project on the agenda?"

"Most of the guys from this job will move over to work on the Lawrenceburg square. We're refurbishing the whole thing. Since it's so close to Shoal Creek, most of them will stay in their same apartments, they'll just commute a little. That always makes it nice, when everybody doesn't have to pack up and move again."

Paige nodded. "I'm sure."

When they walked inside Irene's, Paige watched for Tony's reaction as he surveyed the room. The noisy atmosphere, scarred Formica tables, and red vinyl seats were a far cry from Frederick's. He looked toward her, a twinkle in his eyes. "Now *this* is what I call *ambiance.*"

"Listen, city boy, if you're going to hang out with me, you've got to learn to do things the small-town way."

They took a seat in a window booth. "I'm thinking that something's not exactly fair here, country girl. I think it's time for you to come to Nashville and walk my turf for a day."

"I don't know."

"Come on, it's only fair. How about tomorrow?"

"The church ladies would have a fit if I didn't show up for services. They would assume that either something was wrong with Mom or I had fallen into sin. When they found out I was in Nashville visiting a man—well, let's just say, things could get ugly." Paige was laughing as she said it, but there was more than a little truth to her words.

Tony shook his head. "Small towns—oy! Okay, next weekend. You finally have a Saturday off, right? I'll come pick you up."

"I can't ask you to do that."

"You didn't ask me, I offered."

"I can drive. It sounds fun." And it did.

When they got back to Paige's house, Tony walked her to the door. She turned to him. "I had a really nice time."

"So did I." He rubbed his chin and grinned. "Eating hush puppies. In a place that was noisier than a Titans' game." Oh, the charm of that smile, it was a magnet whose pull grew stronger with each passing second. "You're the best thing that's happened to me in a long time."

"I can say the same about you." The words barely came out, but she knew before she said them they were true.

He stepped closer and lifted her chin with his fingers until she looked into his eyes, their faces inches apart. "I'll see you next week. On my turf this time." He leaned forward and kissed her, his arms wrapping around her.

She leaned closer, put her arms around his neck, and felt herself falling into something she knew she could no longer escape.

chapter **thirty**

Late Sunday night, Paige sat in front of the television, still alone, but less lonely than she'd been in a long time. The phone rang. "Hello."

"Hey, Paige. How are you doing?" Rachelle's

voice was so low and so flat, Paige barely recognized it.

"You sound tired. What, has Steve been keeping you out too late?"

"I'm not tired." In all the years Paige had known Shell, she'd never heard this tone.

"What's wrong, then?"

"Unfortunately, I've got some rather dismal news. You remember I told you that David Brown's investigator was investigating your investigator?"

"Yes. You can rest easy, you don't even have to tell me. I already know it was Clarissa who hired him. She already confronted me about what she found out."

A commercial for oxygenated dish soap came from the TV, the air-conditioner hummed from the next room, but no sounds came through the phone line. "Shell? You still there?"

"Oh, Paige, honey . . ."

"Rachelle, it's okay. She knows everything, but she's keeping it to herself." As long as Paige kept her mouth shut, anyway.

"She may know everything, but she isn't the one who hired the investigator."

"If she's not, then who is?"

"Tony Richardson."

"I . . . I . . ." The words died before they could even form in her mind. What could she say? "Are you sure?"

"I made them double-check everything before I broke the news to you. After the way you talked about him during my visit, I didn't want to tell you this. You've been through so much, but I thought you should know."

"Yeah. Thanks. I'll call you in a day or two."

"You know where to find me."

Paige walked over to the window and looked out into the night. She saw the very place where she and Tony had stood just last night. He had been so charming, so unexpected.

And he had been using her all this time.

Why would he do that? How could he do that?

She thought of the way he'd held her just last night, the words he'd said. The words she'd believed. Pain gave way to fury. She wanted answers, and now would be the time to get them. While her anger still cloaked her like a suit of armor. Nothing would hurt her now.

She dialed the number that she'd had stored in her book for weeks now, but never had the courage to use. Tony answered on the third ring.

"I need to talk to you."

"Well, well. It's about time you called me. I've been sitting and waiting all this time." He sounded so upbeat, so happy. She pictured his grin on the other end of the line. Was it all an act?

"Why have you been seeing me?"

"Uh . . . well . . ." He let out a half laugh. "I would think that answer would be obvious. You're beautiful, sweet, and single. I'm handsome, sweet, and single. It's a perfect match. See?"

"I'm not joking."

"Well . . . umm . . ." The silence of indecision lasted only a second. "I'm not joking, either. Well, not the part about you anyway. We all know I'm not *that* sweet, and maybe handsome is an over-statement, but that would go back to your reason for wanting to see me, right? Maybe I'm the one who should be asking you this question."

Time to get to the point. "You've been doing nothing but helping Clarissa try to get rid of me all this time."

"What are you talking about?" The shock in his reply sounded so real. But so had everything he'd said last night. "Clarissa's not trying to get rid of you, and you know I'm not trying to get rid of you. Like I said yesterday, you're the best thing that's happened to me in a long time."

The words had meant so much then. But not now. "I got an interesting call from a friend in Atlanta."

"Atlanta?" The rise in his voice told her this change in direction of the conversation confused him. Good. It would keep him off balance and make it more difficult for him to think up an expla-nation.

"Yes. Atlanta. She told me there was an inves-tigator there, asking all sorts of questions about me. Turns out, this investigator was hired by . . .

you." She stopped speaking and let the silence fall between them like heavy stones.

When he said nothing, she unleashed the next round of ammunition. "Clarissa's been keeping a file of complaints and out-and-out lies about me at work. Why? Why would either of you do this?"

"There obviously is some misunderstanding. Clarissa wouldn't do that."

"All I want is to be a good pharmacist—to make people feel better—to have a job so I can help my parents out during this terrible time in their lives. What would make two people go so far out of their way to hurt someone like me—someone you'd never even met when you started all this."

The seconds ticked past. Paige said nothing. Intended to say nothing. Her father had always taught her to let silence work to her advantage in a case like this. If you remained quiet long enough, the other person would fill the silence.

Finally, Tony sighed. "Okay, I guess I did know at one point there was an investigator, but I'd forgotten all about it. I didn't hire him, and it's not what you think."

"Not what I think? Until a few hours ago, what I *thought* this was, was an early dating relationship. One I enjoyed. One you enjoyed. Obviously, nothing is what I think."

"Paige, listen to me. We talked about hiring that guy before I even met you. I gave his name to

Clarissa, never dreaming she would actually call him. I just wanted to calm her down, she's so certain everyone is out to get her. I haven't thought another thing about it."

Tony went quiet and waited—for what? Was he hoping she would say something here to absolve him of his part in this? Tell him she didn't want to know anymore, that it was all okay?

He groaned. "You know what? I'll tell you the whole truth. That first day I came to Shoal Creek? I was supposed to come in and check you out. You know, evaluate the situation, then leave. Of course, after I met you, my plans changed and I stayed for dinner."

"Yeah, I'll bet. You decided it would be easy to control me if you led me to believe that you were interested in me."

"Wrong. Within two seconds of meeting you, I knew enough to know you weren't after Clarissa's job, but I sure wanted to get to know you. In fact, I'd forgotten we even talked about hiring an investigator until just now. I haven't thought about it since, and Clarissa hasn't mentioned it either. Most likely, she's let the whole idea go, or realized there's nothing but good things to find."

Oh, but there were plenty of things to find, and Clarissa had already found them. "You can take your investigator and your smooth talk and shove it someplace else. I don't believe a word of it."

"Paige, I—" Paige pushed the button on the

244

phone, slammed it onto the table, and was amazed that there were more tears left to spill.

Clarissa sat on her living room floor, paper work spread all around her. A satisfaction came from deep within as she began to believe she was actually going to make this all work—in spite of the obstacles that would have stopped most people from even attempting to move forward. Finally, there was a light somewhere in this whole dark mess.

The phone rang and she planned to let it go to voice mail, until she heard the caller ID voice announce, "Call from Richardson, Tony." She stood and hurried over to the receiver. "Hi, Tony."

"Hey, Sweet Pea." His voice was so quiet she barely heard him.

"You okay? My old uncle working too hard these days, or what?"

"I need to ask a favor."

"Sure. What do you need?"

"I want you to talk to Paige for me."

"Do what?"

"Talk to her. She thinks I hired that investigator guy. Tell her that it was something you did on impulse at the beginning, just trying to cover our bases. Tell her that I haven't been setting her up."

"I'll do no such thing. We didn't just cover our bases, I found out the truth about her. She's not at all the perfect little angel Granddad thinks she is— and apparently you've come to that conclusion yourself, although I'd always thought you were the one person on my side."

"I am on your side. But she's on your side, too. Don't you get it? She's not out for anything other than a job. She's not trying to do anything to hurt you, or Dad, or anyone else for that matter. She's trying to help people, that's all she's trying to do."

"Help people? Ha!"

"When she told me that you were out to get her, I said, 'No way, Clarissa is not like that.' Hearing you talk right now, I wonder if I was wrong."

"I've had it. No one in this family can see the big picture except me. I'm not going to talk about it anymore." Clarissa set the phone back up on the table. They were all so blind.

Dawn waited until after midnight before she left the house. Only now, when darkness cloaked her movement, would pride allow her to do this.

Her back was still sore, so she leaned forward away from the seat, trying to forget the way Jack's fist felt against her skin. At least he'd saved her the humiliation of leaving bruises where they showed. She supposed he'd expect her to be grateful.

She drove across town with the radio off. Noise of any kind would ruin this for her. All of her senses needed to be heightened; she needed to remember every sight, sound, and smell. It would be all she had to carry with her when she drove away.

Once on Reginald Street, she doused the headlights and pulled to the side of the road, just one house away from her parents'. The houses all sat dark—as she'd known they would. Peace and quiet. It had been one of the things she hated most about this place growing up. Now, how she longed for that tranquility.

When she turned off the engine, the car's usual sputtering seemed so much louder tonight. She looked around at the darkened windows, hoping the sound didn't wake the neighborhood. No lights came on. After a moment of holding her breath, she finally relaxed and allowed herself to do what she'd come here for. She looked around. And remembered.

The front porch had begun to sag badly, and the bottom step had fallen through altogether. Her father's rusty old truck sat in the driveway while her mother's petunias still offered the one bit of beauty from the small patch of dirt that fronted the house. And in the distance, the gentle pattering of the creek filled the quiet of the night. How many times had that very sound sung her to sleep through her open bedroom window? The smell of oil and machinery always overpowered even the thickest summer blooms. She took a deep breath and almost cried with the joy of it.

All the years she'd spent here—hating the dull-ness of it all, hating the constant drain of hard work, hating her parents for being poor—what she wouldn't give to have it all back now. She'd given it all up for what she believed was a better life.

She wanted to go knock on the door right this very minute, tell her parents how wrong she'd been, tell especially her mother how sorry she was. But the choice was not hers. Her father had kicked her out, and she couldn't come crawling back now. Her pride was all that she had left—and there was little enough of that.

Memories floated through her mind of her mother's face, celebrating yet another straight-A report card. A heady expression would fall across her face, especially when the teachers started sending notes home about this scholarship or the other. "Oh, to think of you in college. It was a dream that was out of my reach—but for you, sweet girl, everything is possible." Maybe at the time she'd been right. Not anymore. Now nothing seemed possible.

Dawn didn't want to stay with Jack, but how could she get out? He spent her paycheck almost as fast as she brought it home. If she started holding money back, he'd know it, and the retribution would be horrible.

No, she was stuck. She turned on the ignition and drove home, thankful that Jack had recently switched to the night shift. Between that and his newfound "time with his family," it at least kept him out of the house and away from her. Most of the time. And right now she needed even the smallest of victories.

chapter thirty-one

Monday morning, Ora waited as usual beside the door. She followed Paige inside. "Looks like you've got yourself a new index card."

"How do you know that?"

"Easy . . . that one's pink. I've seen lavender ones, yellow ones, and green ones. If you opened a new pack of cards, something must be happening. You needing me to give you another reference?"

"Ora, I'll take anything you've got."

"All righty, what's your verse?"

"I've got two. The first one is Psalm 56:3, 'What time I am afraid, I will trust in thee.'" Paige looked at Ora and smiled. "I didn't even have to write that one on a card, I remembered it from Sunday school."

"Wonders never cease. What's the other one?"

Paige looked at the pink card. "'God is our refuge and strength, an ever-present help in trouble. Therefore we will not fear, though the earth give way and the mountains fall into the heart of the sea.' Psalm 46:1–2."

Ora nodded and rubbed at her chin. "Sounds like you're needing a little reassurance in a tough time, huh? Let me think now. That Psalm 46 is ringing a bell with me, but somehow I think you're stuck on the wrong verses. Did you read verses 4 and 5? I'm thinking that's where it gets to the heart of the matter."

Paige went to the Internet, punched in the appropriate Web address, and waited for it to pull up. "Let's see, here it is: 'There is a river whose streams make glad the city of God, the holy place where the Most High dwells. God is within her, she will not fall; God will help her at break of day.'" She looked at Ora, as usual having no clue how these verses were supposed to apply to her. But by this point she'd learned that there usually was some sort of reasoning behind it—even if it was a bit oblique. "Are you sure this is the chapter you wanted?"

"Course it is. How much more perfect can it get than that?"

"Call me slow, but I don't really see what a river into a city has to do with me."

"*Listen*. That's the problem with kids these days, they want an easy answer, but they don't listen when it's laid out perfectly clear."

"On behalf of my generation, I offer humble apologies. Now, would you maybe help me out a bit here?"

"What does it *say*? It says God's gonna help her at daybreak, right?"

"Yeah."

"If you lived in a city back in those days, and an army was outside the walls, when do you reckon would be the scariest time?"

"When the enemy started shooting arrows?"

"No. It would be in the dead of night, when you couldn't see a thing, but you could hear the clanking of armor as enemy soldiers surrounded your city, and the heavy footsteps of who knows how many. You're not sure what's out there, but it sure sounds like it's going to be bad. It's the time you'd want to get out of the city and quick, right?"

"Yeah, I guess so."

"But see, this is all about staying and standing your ground. Things sound bad now and you've got no idea what terrible things are out there, but God's gonna help at *break of day*. You just got to have enough faith to stand firm all night at the city wall and wait for daybreak."

"What if day never comes?"

"It will. Says so right there in the Scriptures. You stand firm and believe."

Someone knocked at the pharmacy door. Paige looked to see Cory standing there. Ora nodded and smiled, "I was thinking of leaving a little early this morning anyway. I'll leave you and your young man to talk."

"He's not my young man."

"Couldn't prove that by him."

Paige opened the door. "Hi, Cory."

Ora nodded. "Hello there, young man. Did you come to ask Paige to lunch again?"

He grinned. "As a matter of fact I did."

Ora turned to her. "Well, how 'bout it? You want to go to lunch with young Cory again?"

251

Paige had resolved to quit seeing Cory after the weekend with Rachelle. "I don't know, I was kind of thinking—"

"I know, you probably figure you'll be needed on the front lines today, but I figure you're gonna be all stressed out, with your computer issues and all, and by noon you'll be needing a little Cory cheer."

"You'll have to come up with a better excuse than that, because we're not having computer issues."

"Really? Since Jason was here, I figured your system must have crashed big time."

"Who's Jason?"

"The computer guy. You know, the geek who set up the computer system in here? He used to start drooling anytime Clarissa came anywhere near him." He laughed. "It was pretty humorous. She could get him to do anything she wanted—poor kid. He never had a clue."

"Computer guy? Not here, he must have been next door at the travel agent's."

"No. He was in here last night. I came in about nine o'clock to check on something, and Clarissa's car was parked out front, right beside old Jason's. When I came through the lobby, I could see the lights on in the pharmacy."

Paige had worked alone on Saturday, and the computer had been working just fine. Since they were closed on Sunday, and Clarissa lived an hour away, what could possibly have brought her here?

"Must have been some issue with the report end of the software, because the regular dispensing stuff is working fine."

"No worries. I'm still willing to spread some Cory cheer."

"I'm sure you are." *Why not?* It wasn't like Tony was holding her back—not anymore. Still, she would not use Cory to get her over Tony, and she knew she had no interest in Cory. "I think I'd better go it alone."

"Well, all right then. Let me know if you change your mind." He nodded at Ora, then walked up the stairs.

Ora snorted. "Ah, you let him down easy. Nice job. See you later, young 'un."

When Paige went back into the pharmacy, she walked past Clarissa's desk, letting her gaze fall on the top drawer. She noted the neat stack of papers on the right of the desk, the large black stapler just to the left of it. And she wondered what she'd find just inside that drawer. If there was something in there about her, it was her right to know. Right?

She slid the drawer open. Once again, a stack of weekly reports was at the top of the drawer. Paige reached beneath it and carefully removed the legal pad. It appeared as though a couple of top sheets had been removed. The new top page was covered from top to bottom. There was even a second page of writing.

March 15—Mrs. Harris got wrong strength Coumadin. Paige replaced the tablets but lied to the patient. Dawn witnessed.

What? Clarissa had failed to mention that the mistake had been her own. That Paige was just covering for her.

April 12—Paige misfilled Mrs. Konkel's prescription for Naprosyn. Mrs. Konkel caught the mistake herself and brought it in. Clarissa had to replace as well as offer apologies.
March 29—Ms. Feldhouse prescription, misfilled Zetia. Apparently call-in taken by Dawn with Paige's blessing. Current lawsuit.

That was a blatant lie. No way could Clarissa pull that off; the proof was in the computer. Paige went to the keyboard and typed Ms. Feldhouse's name. She couldn't believe what appeared before her on the screen. The initials *PW*. Still easy enough to disprove; the handwritten original prescription had Clarissa's initials. Paige went to the file and removed it.

The printout initials stuck to the hard copy had been changed. It now said *PW*. There were no handwritten initials beside it—a sure sign to anyone who knew her that Paige had not touched this prescription. But what about the people who didn't know her? How could this have happened?

She remembered Cory talking about the computer guy being here after hours last night. The computer guy who'd had a crush on Clarissa—followed her around like a puppy, he'd said.

Paige felt everything slipping away.

Even holding the prescription up to the light, it was very difficult to see the slight tear on the top layer of the paper where the first label had been removed. In fact, someone who wasn't sure of the truth could doubt they were even seeing it. Paige dropped into the chair. She couldn't believe Clarissa had done that. Why? Why would she do it?

Okay, Dawn had been here the day Ms. Feldhouse came in; she remembered that Clarissa had filled it. She could always back Paige up if it became necessary, but what was Clarissa hoping to prove?

She looked at the sticker on the prescription again, and at the date on it. She stood and walked to the calendar. March 29. It was marked on the wall calendar—*Paige off.* She hadn't even been working that day. But she couldn't confront Clarissa without telling her she'd been in her desk. How was she going to do this? There must be a way to get to the bottom of what was happening.

All through the first hour of the day she prayed. *God, I'm at the end here. I've been praying all along, and things are just getting worse. What am*

I supposed to do? I'm trying to stand my ground like Ora says, but when is day going to break? It just keeps getting darker and darker and darker.

After opening, she triple-checked everything she touched because she was so upset, and that was when she could make a mistake for real. When Clarissa came in at ten o'clock, even though it hadn't been an overly busy morning, Paige was running behind. She didn't let it stop her. She waited only until Clarissa came to stand at the counter before she started in. "Clarissa, is there anything you'd like to say to me about my work here?"

"What would make you ask a question like that?"

Paige tried her best to look nonchalant, but she was sure that she was not pulling it off. "Sometimes I feel an undercurrent, like you don't like having me here. If that's the case, I'd like to know what it is that I do wrong that makes you feel that way."

Clarissa didn't look at her. "I don't know what you're talking about."

"I think you do."

"Well, if you understand me so much better than I understand myself, maybe you also understand what it is I supposedly don't like about the way you work. As for me, I've got nothing to say about it."

Paige couldn't let it go. "Then why has the

sticker on Ms. Feldhouse's prescription been changed so that it now has my initials on it?"

"If your initials are on it now, then they always have been. I don't have your code, I couldn't change something like that if I wanted to."

"Well, someone did."

"Like I said, obviously you *are* the one who filled the prescription if your initials are on it."

"Then how are my initials on a prescription for March 29—a day I wasn't even here? A day I was at a retirement luncheon with fifty other people in the city of Sledge?" The lie slipped out before she had a chance to think about it. But she wanted Clarissa to know that she was certain who had done this.

Clarissa did look at her this time, but did not hold her gaze for long. "You sure about that?"

"Quite sure."

"Then I don't know what to tell you. It must have been some sort of glitch with the computer."

"Are you girls going to keep talking all day? I've been waiting for half an hour." A tired-looking woman leaned across the counter. "Sorry if me getting my medicine is taking away from you ladies' social hour, but fact is, I'm sick and I want to go home. Now, will you please stop your talking and get me my stuff?"

chapter thirty-two

Clarissa drove toward Nashville, wondering how Paige had found the changed computer initials. She never should have seen it.

The plan had always been to settle the lawsuit, make it look—to Milton Parrish, at least—like it was Paige's fault, and get on with life. No one the wiser. No one hurt. Once again, her plans had failed.

She punched voice dial on her phone. "Call Tony."

The two of them hadn't spoken since he'd called about Paige and the investigator. Clarissa had planned to wait for him to be the one to cave. But . . . tonight she needed his company enough that she would forgo pride.

"Hello."

"I've had a really bad day. You want to meet for dinner somewhere?"

"I'm kind of in the middle of something right now." Was he really, or was he just angry? "How about I pick you up in a couple of hours and we go for ice cream?"

Clarissa smiled. Tony knew her so well. All she needed after a hard day was a chance to remember her goals and refocus on her dreams. "Ice cream it is."

"I expect you to eat something along the lines of health food before we do this. Got it?"

She laughed. "Broccoli, spinach, and carrots."

"That's what I like to hear."

Later, as they drove across town, he smiled and laughed perhaps a bit too much. Big personality or not, Tony was putting on. It was the same act she'd seen after Laurie left him and moved in with her senior law partner. It could only mean one thing. His heart was broken. Clarissa knew it was her fault. All she had to do was talk to Paige, tell her the investigator was her idea, and she and Tony could work it out.

And Tony would love Paige more again.

"Here we are. Oh look, they saved a spot for us." Tony slid his car into an empty spot right out front.

At nine o'clock at night, the street was busy with up-and-coming twenty- and thirty-somethings dressed in trendy clothes, driving trendier cars. Several new "it" dinner spots had opened in the area, as well as a couple of dance clubs and a gym. Clarissa looked at the door to what was now a warehouse and smiled at the thought of having her own store here, soon.

Tony held the door open to the ice cream shop. She curtsied as she walked past. "Thank you, kind sir."

"Hi, Clarissa." The girl working behind the counter of the ice cream shop smiled and waved to her. She had braces on her teeth and a long blond ponytail running down her back.

"Hi." Clarissa tried not to show her complete ignorance, but who was this kid? "How have you been?"

"Oh, great. I graduate this year. I'm heading to University of Tennessee in the fall. Gram is so excited."

Gram? Clarissa felt her jaw drop. "Are you Brenna? Brenna James?"

The girl smiled. "Of course. Who did you think I was?"

"Tell you the truth, I was trying to figure it out. You've grown up a lot since I saw you last."

"Huh, huh." Tony nudged Clarissa with his arm. "Are we forgetting our manners?"

"Oh, Brenna, did you ever know my uncle Tony? He's my dad's brother."

She shook her head. "Don't think we've ever met. Nice to meet you."

Clarissa turned to him. "Brenna's grandmother Judy was Grandma's morning walking buddy. Brenna and I used to tag along."

"Tag along is not quite the word I'd use—get dragged along is more like it."

"There's definitely some truth to that. So how is your gram Judy these days?"

"Good. She's still walking five days a week, playing bridge, the usual." Another customer walked into the store, and her expression sobered. "So, what would you like?"

"A scoop of chocolate on a sugar cone, please."

Tony coughed the word *boring* into his hand. "After you're done scooping that mundane order, I'd like a scoop of razzle dazzle fruit frazzle."

Clarissa looked at him. "Razzle dazzle fruit frazzle?"

He shrugged. "I'm in touch with my youthful side tonight."

Brenna handed the cone to Clarissa and started scooping Tony's order. "So, I see your dad around here a lot. I guess he and his wife are planning to put a yoga studio next door or something?"

Clarissa almost dropped her cone. "What?"

"They had someone over there taking measurements last week, and Carrie, that's the lady I work for, she got all excited. She said they're going to put in a gigantic yoga studio, with a spa and the works."

Clarissa took a bite out of her cone. "I . . . hadn't heard that."

Later, Clarissa sat alone in her condo, thinking over the events of the night. She could still see the sadness on Tony's face. She could picture Becky measuring for a yoga studio. And there was one person to blame for all of it.

Paige.

She thought about the painstaking way she'd gone about changing the initials on Ms. Feldhouse's prescription. What if Paige decided to go to Clarissa's grandfather and tell him about that,

that the lawsuit wasn't her fault? It would ruin everything. The only reason that Milton Parrish would even consider not counting this as a mark against Clarissa would be if he didn't consider it her fault at all. If Paige started talking, she could ruin that.

Maybe she should call her grandfather, just lay a little groundwork that Paige was in denial or something. It would help if things got out of hand. She picked up the phone, and as soon as her grandfather answered, she started weaving her defense.

"So, you're telling me that she made the mistake, but you feel that she might try to blame it on you?"

"I don't know. Her initials are in the computer and everything, but she just seems to be in denial. I'm afraid she might try to stir up something."

"Somehow, this doesn't seem like the Paige I know. She is very careful. Are you quite sure there's no truth to her idea that you somehow were involved in the mistake?"

Why did he never believe her? "Yes, I'm sure."

"Maybe I'll come down there and take a look at what's going on." He paused for a moment. "You know, maybe you're just not ready for a store in Nashville yet. It seems to me there are a lot of problems in your small-town pharmacy."

Something flashed inside of Clarissa. She was not going to take this, not for one more second. "Okay, there are some other things that you ought to know. Some things that I've known for a while, but I haven't told you because I knew it would hurt you. But I think it's time you knew the whole truth about Paige. Starting with her job in Atlanta."

chapter **thirty-three**

Paige went in to work the next morning ready to talk to Ora. She wanted to hear her thoughts on what was happening here, and what Paige should be doing about it.

Not there.

Oh yeah, it seemed like she'd said something about a doctor's appointment this morning. Well, she'd just have to wait until tomorrow to tell her about it. What verse would Ora pull out of her repertoire for this one? Paige smiled at the thought, certain there would be something.

She heard a rap at the door and looked toward the front. Lee Richardson stood silhouetted in the doorframe. "Hello there, Lee. Haven't seen you in a while."

He followed her inside but did not return the greeting—in fact, he didn't even smile. "We need to talk." His voice was as gruff as Paige had ever heard it.

"Okay. Let's go back to the waiting area, where we can sit."

He nodded and followed her, his boots clacking on the tile floor the only sound.

Paige perched in one of the padded chairs and motioned to the one beside her. She sat straight and did her best impersonation of a Miss America contestant smiling inanely when there was absolutely no reason to be smiling. "So, what did you want to talk about?"

"A few things have been brought to my attention." He looked her straight in the eye, a steely hardness to his gaze she'd never seen before. This was Lee Richardson the businessman, the one who'd built and run one of the largest contractors in the South. "I had no idea about the incidents in Atlanta when I hired you, or I would never have hired you in the first place."

"Lee, I—"

He held up his hand. "I'm not blaming you. I never asked, there are obviously reasons that you wouldn't want to volunteer that information. It was my own fault and I accept that." His face began to harden again. "What I cannot accept, however, is the apparent continuation of your carelessness that has carried over here."

Paige heard herself gasp before she'd realized that she'd done it. "It's not true."

"I really thought I saw something in you, something different. You seemed to take so much time with your patients at the clinic, seemed to be so careful. I guess my instincts are dulling a bit with my increasing age, but I never would have believed it of you."

"I've done nothing. Clarissa is setting me up."

Lee stood then. "I can abide a lot of things, but a liar is not one of them. I know all about the mistakes you've made here. I know you lied directly to a patient about another mistake. My wife died because of negligence. I will not turn a blind eye to what you're doing here and risk allowing someone else to face that same kind of agony. You may consider yourself terminated as of this very minute. Pack up anything from here that's a personal item and clear out."

Paige stood up and pointed a shaky finger toward the dispensing counter. "Every mistake that's been made in this pharmacy since I've been here has been Clarissa's. Wait, that's not completely true. A couple have been Dawn's when Clarissa was supposed to be supervising her, but was out at the coffee shop or in the back room on the phone instead. Not one thing that I've dispensed has come back wrong. I triple-check everything because of what happened to me in Atlanta."

"What is it with you people that you always have to cast the blame on someone else, even when it obviously rests on you? I won't listen to any more. Get your things and get out."

"Lee, I *need* this job. My family needs me to have this job."

"We need someone to work here without a track record of negligence like you have—someone who won't come in here and lie to me about my own granddaughter. I've got half a mind to take you to court and get the first half of that signing bonus back, since you signed under less than honest conditions. If you say one more word, so help me, I will."

Paige opened her mouth and took a breath. She stared at the hard anger in his eyes and knew he meant every word. She couldn't say anything. It was over.

She nodded, reached down for her purse, and walked back into the dispensing area to retrieve her coffee maker, then walked to the door with as much dignity as she could muster. She remembered the keys in her pocket, turned and handed them to Lee without a word, and walked out.

Once outside the store, she ran through the coffee shop, currently full of customers, then down the sidewalk toward her car. She saw Clarissa's red convertible pulling into the lot—a couple of hours earlier than usual. Obviously she'd known that her grandfather was going to do this today. Obviously she was the one who had told him about the mistakes. *But why?*

Time to find out. She took purposeful steps toward the car, each one jarring her as it hit the pavement with such force.

"Why? Why did you do it?"

Clarissa bent down to pull her purse and lab coat from the car. "Do what?"

"Come on, Clarissa, you know exactly what I'm

talking about. Why would you lie to your grandfather like that about me? What have I ever done to you that would make you do that?"

"You've got some nerve calling me a liar. What you need to do is look in the mirror. You lied to my grandfather to get this job, and you hadn't been here a week before you lied to a patient."

"I lied to a patient to cover for you, because I wanted to protect you. And when have I ever lied to your grandfather?"

"Whether or not you stated a lie, the fact that you did not tell my grandfather the whole truth was a lie in and of itself and you know it. As for me, I'm sure if you think about it, you'll figure that one out." She threw her purse over her shoulder. "Now, if you'll excuse me, I've got to get to work. I've got a pharmacy to run." She sashayed toward the square as if she didn't have a care in the world.

Paige watched her go, saw the extra spring in Clarissa's step. The way her hair bounced with each movement. How could anyone be so apparently happy about wrecking another person's life? It just didn't make sense. None of it made sense. Where was God in all this?

She somehow managed to cover the distance to her car, open the door, and put the key in the ignition. How was it that in spite of incredible, mind-numbing pain, the body could continue to move in a way that looked perfectly normal from the outside, while inside everything was falling apart? She drove away from the lot, having no idea where she was going.

When Clarissa got to the Theater Shops, she ordered a mocha—full caffeine, full fat. Kathy raised an eyebrow from behind the counter. "My, my, walking on the wild side today?"

"You only live once." Clarissa laughed like she didn't have a care in the world and went in search of her grandfather.

She found him upstairs. His face was paler than she could ever remember seeing it. She realized that this had been hard on him, and for just a moment, she felt a pang of guilt at the suffering she'd caused him. Well, maybe none of this would have happened if he'd have felt a little guilt about the way he'd jerked her around all her life.

He walked across the room. "Let's go downstairs and talk." His voice sounded husky.

"Sure." She took a sip of the mocha and noticed it wasn't quite as satisfying as she'd expected when she ordered it.

They walked into the pharmacy and locked the door behind them. He went to sit at the back desk and scrubbed his hands across his face.

"I take it that she didn't take the news so well."

"I've fired more than my share of people in my life, but for some reason, this one just gets to me.

I've always prided myself on being such a good judge of character. The things that she did, it just doesn't seem possible that she is the same person who was so conscientious at the homeless clinic, using her own money to buy grocery cards for her customers."

Clarissa took another sip of the mocha, then set it on the counter. Definitely not satisfying.

"Well, I'm sure she'll find another job somewhere and she will have learned from all this. She'll be more careful from here on out."

"No. I plan to report all this to the State Board of Pharmacy. We got her out of here, but I don't want her doing the same kind of dangerous practices somewhere else. It's people who do things like this who need to be kept out of pharmacies altogether. I plan to do my part to make sure she never practices pharmacy again."

Clarissa flinched. This was not part of the bargain. Getting Paige out of the pharmacy, off the payroll, and away from Inspector Powell was one thing. Reporting her to the board was another. She couldn't tell her grandfather that, though. Time for plan B.

"You know what, Granddad, you're right. You've been saying that you want to really see me step up and take some responsibility, and that's what I'm going to do. When the board inspector was here a few weeks ago, he left his card. I'll call him this morning and report all this. I'm the pharmacist in charge; it should come from me anyway. You don't think another thing about it."

He nodded his head grimly. "Okay."

"Promise you'll let me handle it?"

"Frankly, I'm more than happy to let you handle this one." He stood. "I'm going back upstairs."

Paige has no idea just how grateful she should be right now.

"Okay. Will I see you for lunch?"

He stopped and turned. "I'm not really in much of a lunch mood. In fact, I think I'll head back to Nashville early. I just don't feel like being around here right now, with all that's happened."

You're not the only one. "Well okay, let me know if you change your mind."

Clarissa looked around at the empty place, knowing that Paige wouldn't be coming back. The regret hit her with surprising force. Still, Paige had brought this on herself. She would get another job and be fine. A few months from now, she would have forgotten any of this ever happened, and Clarissa would get her dream, as well. It would work out for all of them. This was just a bump in the road, that's all.

Dawn came dragging in twenty minutes late, her hair a mess, her face pale. She sat down and listened to the refill line without saying a single word, then walked to the printer and pulled off the labels. "Where's Paige?"

"She's not working here anymore."

"Huh?"

Clarissa drew her shoulders up tall. "My grand-father fired her this morning."

"You're kidding. Why?"

"There were some things going on, things you don't need to worry about. Anyway, it's all taken care of now." Clarissa studied her face. "What's up with you? You look tired. Jack have you out dancing until the wee hours of the morning?"

"Hardly." Dawn's voice sounded choked, like she was about to cry.

Clarissa felt sorry for her, but honestly what did Dawn expect when she chose that idiot for a boyfriend? If that's the kind of man she chose to spend her time with, she was going to have problems, and it was no one's fault but her own. When you made bad choices in your life, you had to pay the price. That was the truth of it.

chapter **thirty-four**

Paige drove to her parents' home but didn't pull into the driveway. How could she think of going into her mother's house, knowing that she'd just lost the means to help her fight against cancer? The next payment would come due next week, and while they might make that one, those following would be almost impossible. She needed to keep moving; she needed to talk to someone.

Of course, the pat answer would be to pray and

tell it all to God. That solution rang hollow. She'd been reading and claiming His Word, and He still allowed this to happen. No, this time she needed someone who could actually tell her what to do, give her some direction. Give her the strength she needed to break this news to her parents.

Rachelle was the obvious answer, but she didn't want to do this over the phone. It was now that she realized she didn't have a single friend here. Not one. Except . . .

Ora.

That crotchety lady had become the dearest person in her life right now, and it took a crisis like this to make her realize it. She remembered Ora saying something about living on the corner across from the junior high. Maybe she would just drive by and see if anything looked like it might belong to Ora. She was definitely not in any shape to start ringing odd doorbells.

When she got back to the city of Shoal Creek, she took care to take side roads and avoid downtown. The last thing she wanted to do was have Clarissa see her crawling back into town.

The ancient brick building of the junior high came into view up ahead. The old place looked like it needed a bulldozer; not a single part of it appeared worth saving. Paige understood how it felt.

What would Ora say about Paige showing up on her doorstep crying about some problem like this?

She'd probably have some obscure verse that wouldn't make sense at first but would ring true after Paige spent a little time thinking about it. And Paige longed for anything to ring true for her right now.

She looked at the corner of Lafayette and Granger. On the left stood a small brick house, aluminum awning, and a front porch with wooden posts that had seen their better days. The other corner held a little yellow house covered in vinyl siding, flowers in the window box. Which one would Ora most likely live in? Paige had no idea what kind of car Ora drove, so looking in the driveway didn't help.

She slowed to almost a stop, trying to decide which, if either, house she should try, when she saw Ora come around the corner of the brick house, dressed in dirty jeans, spade in hand. Paige whipped her car into the driveway, thankful that she'd seen her.

Ora looked up from beneath the brim of a pink visor covered in Hawaiian flowers and waved. She wore bright orange gardening gloves with a big Tennessee T on them. She set her spade on the steps to the front porch and walked over to Paige's car. "Morning there, young 'un. Where you been?" She put her hands on her hips and sized Paige up. "You're looking like you just found boll weevils in your last forty acres."

"I don't know who else to talk to."

"Hmm. Well, it's not over flattering to be the last choice, but since I'm the only choice I guess that makes me first, too. Come inside, let's get a cold drink and talk about what's bothering you."

"Thanks."

Ora stopped at the doormat to wipe the dirt off her clogs, then removed them before entering the house.

The wood floors were slightly uneven and creaked with every step, but they were waxed to a perfect shine. The wallpaper had probably been in style thirty years ago, but something about the place felt homey and comfortable. Inside the kitchen, green linoleum flooring contrasted with faded yellow countertops.

Ora went to the refrigerator and removed a giant pitcher. She put ice in two glasses and poured tea into both, handing one to Paige.

"Now sit down at the table here and let's start from the beginning. What's going on?"

"I got . . . fired today."

"Fired?" Just the sound of the word made Paige flinch. It felt sharp and hard, like broken glass. "So that's where you were. I went in there just a bit ago with a prescription from my doctor's visit. I asked for you, and the redhead acted kind of funny and said you weren't there today. I thought maybe you were just playing hooky or something. What happened?"

"So many things, I hardly know where to start."

"Try the beginning."

When had it all started? The first day at work really. "From the beginning, Clarissa has made it clear she didn't want me there, I've never really understood why."

"Did you ever ask her?"

"Not in so many words."

"Kids." Ora shook her head. "No wonder there are so many problems. No one ever talks to each other anymore. So today she just up and fired you?"

"She didn't. It was her grandfather who hired me in the first place and he's the one who fired me. He drove all the way from Nashville this morning just to tell me to leave."

"Did he say why?"

"Clarissa's been using some questionable practices at the pharmacy, some mistakes have been made, a lady filed a lawsuit."

"You make any of the mistakes?"

"No."

"I may be a little dense here, but I'm still not getting how that gets you fired."

"She's blaming it all on me. She told her grandfather everything that happened in Shoal Creek was my mistake, not hers."

"Can't you prove who filled the prescriptions?"

"You can look at whose computer initials are on them. Apparently, she's learned how to change the code though, because one of the prescriptions mysteriously changed initials. It was for a date when I wasn't even at work. When the lady first came in to report the mistake, Clarissa's initials were in the computer, I think even Dawn saw that. There was another that was misfilled, but I think I filled it correctly, then for some reason she changed it to make me look bad."

"Why didn't you tell Mr. Richardson what you just told me?"

"I tried to, but he doesn't believe me over his own granddaughter."

"Maybe you should have Dawn call him. If she did see that first one, he'd have to take her word. Right?"

"I found a file Clarissa's been keeping on me. It details all sorts of stuff about me—from patient complaints to one of her mistakes that I covered up for her."

"You covered up one of her mistakes?"

"Well . . . yeah. It was when I first started working there. The lady hadn't taken any of the pills yet, so no harm was done. "

"Why would you have done something wrong to cover for her? Girl, you been learning anything from those verses you been carrying around?"

"What about 'love others as yourself'? I was going out of my way to help Clarissa. Doesn't that count for anything?"

"Maybe you need to 'trust in the Lord with all your heart and lean not on your own understanding,' hmm? I don't see anything in there about helping God out by lying."

"I . . ." Paige rested her forehead on her right palm. "I wasn't trying to help God out by lying, I was just . . . just . . ."

Ora reached over and patted her arm. "You're not the only one who's failed when the pressure was on. Everyone's done it—I've done it more times than I care to remember. But what you've got to do now is look back over all this and see where you do carry some blame, lay it all out there. Face up to the truth and determine that you're going to trust Him no matter what comes."

Paige stood up. "I don't think I can do that anymore." She walked out the door and to her car, started the engine, and drove toward home.

There was more truth than she cared to admit in her statement to Ora. She couldn't trust anymore. She'd prayed and trusted, and claimed verses and trusted, and God had let her down. Over and over again. Daybreak never came.

It was midafternoon before Paige worked up the nerve to call her parents. There was no easy way to do this; might as well get it over with.

"Your mother's not here, she's down the hall having a meeting."

"A meeting?"

"You know how she is. There's a woman a couple of doors down—not nearly as sick as your mother if you ask me—and she's always carrying on about how terrible things are. Leave it to Doris to start spending time with her, trying to cheer her up, talking about hope. Soon enough, word gets out on the hallway that she's some sort of positive-thinking guru or something. Now she's got three other women she meets with every night—every night that they're able, anyway. Some sort of Bible study going on."

"How can she do it, Dad? She's so sick, her world seems to be falling apart, and she's still out there trying to help other people as if her own problems don't even matter."

"Got me."

"I'm actually glad she's not there right now, because I have something to tell you."

"Secret, huh?"

"Dad . . ." Sobs choked back any further words. Her entire body convulsed with the pain of having to tell her father this news. What would happen now? She knew they counted on her monthly rent checks to help them get by, and where would she get that money now? It wasn't like there were tons of openings in the rural area of Shoal Creek.

"Paige, what's going on?"

"I . . . got fired today."

"Oh, Paige." His voice was firm, calm. Understanding. He'd always been. "What happened?"

She started from day one and told him everything about the mistakes, and the list, and the setups. Somehow, she couldn't bring herself to tell him that she'd lied to cover for Clarissa, and it really didn't matter at this point, anyway. "Dad, I'm so sorry. I know I've let you down again. Don't worry though, I'll get a job fast." Of course, they both knew better. It had been almost impossible to find a job after the Atlanta debacle. Add the Shoal Creek mess, and she would be lucky to ever work in pharmacy again. And the hospital payments weren't just going to vanish.

"Of course you will. We'll just have to trust that something will come up soon."

Trust. It was something that Paige didn't know how to do anymore.

Paige looked at the clock. It was just after five p.m. An hour before closing time. She wondered what Clarissa had told Dawn about the firing. She pictured Clarissa going happily along her way today, smiling, laughing with her friends on the phone. She'd finally won. But why? It still made absolutely no sense.

Clarissa didn't even need this job. She had probably never worried about not being able to make a car payment, much less keeping her parents out of bankruptcy.

For all her talk about hard work, she'd been given everything by her grandfather. Minute after minute, Paige thought about the situation. And the more she thought about Clarissa's life of privilege, the angrier she grew. There was no way she could just walk away and let the spoiled brat win without a fight. Paige jumped into her car and drove back to Shoal Creek. She would wait for Dawn, talk to her, see if she would be willing to back her up. Then she'd confront Clarissa directly before going over her head to her grandfather.

She pulled into the lot with fifteen minutes to spare. Dawn's old brown Skylark sat in the far corner, and Paige pulled into the spot beside it. Clarissa's car was far enough away that she would be able to have this conversation out of the earshot of Clarissa, whose presence would likely intimidate Dawn.

The day was close to eighty degrees and the humidity soared even higher. Less than two minutes after turning off her engine, the air became thick to breathe and she could feel the beads of sweat forming on her forehead. She turned on the ignition and let the air-conditioner run until the car once again reached a comfortable temperature, then turned it off. Within a minute she needed to turn it on again to repeat the process. By the time she had repeated it six more times, Dawn finally came walking out into the parking lot. She looked tired and worn down. Paige opened her car door and stood up when Dawn drew near.

Dawn stopped. "Paige. What are you doing here?"

"I came to ask you for help."

"I don't know what I can do."

"Clarissa told her grandfather that I am the one who misfilled Ms. Feldhouse's prescription. Clarissa has changed the computer printout so it looks like that is what happened, but you know better. You were there the day the prescription came in, right? You saw it, you had to. Will you tell Lee Richardson the truth?"

Dawn looked in the direction of the sidewalk, as if to make certain Clarissa hadn't yet followed. "Why would he believe me over Clarissa?"

"If both of us tell him, maybe he will listen. Dawn, I *need* this job. If I could go somewhere else, believe me I would, but at this point, this place is my only hope. I need you to help me."

"I need this job, too. I would be easy to replace if Clarissa got mad at me. Do you have any idea how many people are out of work in this county right now?"

"How can you even consider not helping me? What's to stop her from lying about you next?" Dawn froze for a split second, and Paige knew without turning that Clarissa had entered the parking lot.

"Paige, I like you. I'd like to help you, but there's nothing I can do." She got into her car and drove off.

chapter thirty-five

Without her hours at the pharmacy to fill her days, time slowed nearly to a stop. Days passed, each spent trying to correct the horrible mess that had become her life, but Paige had never felt more cut off from the world. By the end of week two, she barely went outside except to take Dusty for a walk. And that's what waited for her today, too. Printing out résumés and a walk.

Paige waited for the printer to finish its task. The cream-colored paper looked so professional sitting there in the tray, the typing fastidious, the credentials impeccable, until you looked deeper. No matter how nice the surface of this résumé appeared, the truth behind it was too ugly for any future employer to consider. With two weeks of silence and rejections, she'd more than proven that. She tossed the papers across the room and watched them spiral through the air before coming to rest on the tan carpet.

Being a pharmacist was apparently no longer an option. All those years of pharmacy school, of studying to all hours and cramming for board exams, had been rendered meaningless. Nothing remained except the student loans she still needed to repay.

She went into the garage and removed the blue mesh leash from its usual hook. "Dusty, here boy." Dusty hobbled over, his tail wagging.

Maybe she could convince him to walk the half mile down to the pond today. He usually made it only to the wooded lot behind their house, but Paige felt trapped, claustrophobic. She pulled the leash in the direction of the road, but Dusty tugged back in the direction of his favorite trees. She tugged a little harder. "Come on, we need a little adventure, some excitement."

Dusty stopped walking and lay down. He looked up at her, big brown eyes pleading his case.

Paige knelt before him. "Don't you want to do something different today?"

Dusty licked her hand and put his head on the ground.

"Okay, okay. I give. To the trees we go." She started walking toward the trees and he immediately pushed up to his feet and ran ahead of her, tugging at the leash. She stopped him. "Sit." She removed the leash from his collar. "I guess we don't need this if we're not leaving the yard, huh?"

Once free, Dusty hobbled into the trees and disappeared into his favorite spot, the sound of crunching twigs following in his wake. Life was so simple when you were a dog. Even a disabled dog. You lived your life with the people who loved you, you did what you were supposed to do, and they did what they were supposed to do, and everyone was happy. Simple. Uncomplicated. So unlike the life of a human.

Paige sat on the bench and longed to have her

mother beside her. And healthy. She needed to talk to someone, to share the burden of all these doubts. But her mother needed *her* strength now. Problem was, Paige didn't possess any.

Maybe she'd drop by and see Ora again. Yeah, that's what she'd do. After she was done walking Dusty, she'd drive over.

The engine roar of a truck sounded close by on the street—they must be doing work at the neighbor's house again. But then came the slam of a vehicle door, followed by the doorbell. Dusty started barking.

She called for Dusty to come inside, and as she moved through the house her heart began to hammer wildly.

The truck she'd heard—it was Lee Richardson, she knew it was Lee Richardson. Maybe Dawn had persuaded Clarissa to tell the truth; maybe her conscience had gotten the better of her. Whatever the reason, she was about to open the door to hope.

She pulled the door open, a smile already forming. "Hello—" The words died on her lips when she saw the plumber Sam Jackson standing on the front porch. "What are you doing here?"

"Came by to pick up the truck. Your father said you had the keys and a spare."

"Pick up the truck?"

"Yeah, you know. Drive it home. Your father and I made a deal last night. Didn't he tell you I was coming?"

Paige stared at him, too stunned to think of a response. Finally she said, "It'll take me a minute to round up the keys, why don't you go on out there. I'll meet you outside in a minute."

He tipped his dirty baseball cap at her. "Alrighty."

Paige closed the door and ran to her cell to call her father, who answered on the second ring.

"Dad, are you selling to Sam Jackson?"

"He's there, I guess? I was going to call you about that this afternoon, and things got a little hectic around here. Sorry I forgot to warn you. Do you know where the keys are, hanging inside the cabinet in the garage?"

"Yes, I know where the keys are hidden, but why are you selling to him?"

"Honey, you know we're tight on money. We were just barely squeaking by as it was, and it just adds to your pressure if you've got us to provide for. If I sell all my things then we'll have enough to get us through for the next few months."

"But what about after that? How will you go back to work if you don't have a truck and your tools anymore?"

"Sweetie, we don't have a lot of other choices at this point."

Paige felt the tears flow down her cheeks as she walked out to the garage and opened the cabinet that held his keys. It was neat and tidy, just like everything he owned. To turn these keys over to

the unkempt man who stood in the driveway—
how could she do it?

She put her hand on the keys. She could feel the
cold of the metal against her fingertips, smell the
hint of oil and glue that came from inside the cupboards. Her father's cupboards, where her father's
keys should belong.

Before she walked out the door, she wiped hard
at her eyes. No way would she let Sam Jackson see
her crying. No way would she give him any hint of
the defeat that her father was suffering in this
transaction.

She pushed open the door, held her chin high,
and concentrated on keeping her shoulders back,
her expression pleasant. "Here you are, Mr.
Jackson. I hope things work out well for you."

He grinned and touched the dirty ball cap again.
"Much obliged." He nodded toward his dirty truck
parked on the street in front of the house. "I'll have
my girlfriend drive me by later on tonight and get
my other truck."

Paige nodded. "Fine."

He opened the door to her father's truck, sat in
the driver's seat, and turned the key. He closed the
door, rolled down the window, and said, "Tell your
father it was a pleasure doing business with him."

"I'll tell him." *Not likely.* This was one episode
of her life Paige never planned to think about or
mention ever again.

Her father's truck disappeared down the street,

past the filthy truck of its new owner. Paige knew that it was more than a little symbolic of what had been happening in her life lately.

Paige rang the doorbell again, still no answer. It would figure that she would drive all the way over here when no one was home. *Maybe she's in the backyard doing a little gardening.* Paige walked around the corner. "Ora?"

"You looking for Ora?" A man in a white T-shirt and plaid shorts was cleaning out the gutters of the house next door. He tossed some leaves into the trash can beneath his ladder but kept his eyes focused on Paige.

"Yes, do you know where she is?"

"Last I heard, she was at Crockett Hospital. They may have already taken her to Nashville by now, I don't know."

"Hospital?"

"Yeah, the ambulance was here not more than an hour ago."

"What happened?"

"Don't know for sure. Think it was a heart attack."

Paige sank to the porch steps. "Was she . . . is she . . . okay?"

"Don't know that *okay* is the word I'd use, but if you know Ora, you likely know she's too stubborn to die."

"Yes, she is. Thank you so much." Paige raced

back to her car and drove to Crockett Hospital. She parked in the closest spot, then ran toward the building.

The automatic doors of the emergency room swished open. The coolness of the air-conditioned inside collided with the sticky heat from outside in a battle of wills that could only be won by moving forward or turning back. Paige walked to the counter.

"Ora Vaerge. Is she here?"

The receptionist looked up, her face blank. "Who?"

"They just brought her here in the ambulance. This afternoon."

"Oh, the heart attack lady. Yeah, they're trying to get her stabilized. They've called for the helicopter to take her up to Nashville."

"Can I see her?"

"You family?"

"Not blood family."

"That's all we look at here, hon. Blood. Nothing else matters."

"It matters to me. Please, she doesn't have anyone else in this area. I've got to see her."

The *thwack, thwack* of helicopter blades began to resonate through the hospital. The receptionist looked at her. "There's your friend's ride now."

Paige hurried out the door and watched from the sidewalk as a team rushed a stretcher into the waiting chopper. The group in their blue scrubs and lab coats blocked her from getting more than a glimpse of white sheet and black safety straps. In a matter of seconds, the helicopter was airborne and her friend was gone. Maybe forever.

Paige could contain it no longer and started to weep. Silent, unstoppable tears. *Please don't leave me, Ora. Please don't leave me.*

"You all right, miss?"

Paige looked through her tears to see an older man in a tan suit. "Do you need me to get someone out here to help you?"

Paige shook her head. "No, I'm fine."

"That's funny, you don't look so fine." The man carried a small book in his left hand but extended the right one for Paige to shake. "I'm Joel Bennett."

Paige wiped the tears off her hands before she shook. "I've heard your name somewhere."

He smiled and nodded. "I'm the pastor of the church downtown. I didn't catch your name."

"It's Paige. Paige Woodward."

"Nice to meet you, Paige. Now, tell me, what can I do to help you?"

"Nothing. I'm fine, really. It's only that they just flew a friend of mine to Nashville. Heart attack."

"Well, if they bothered to put her on the helicopter, that means she's still alive and fighting. That's better than the alternative, isn't it?"

Paige nodded. "I suppose so." She hated to cry in front of people. She looked toward the parking lot. "Well, I better get going."

"Are you sure there's nothing I can do to help you?"

There's nothing anyone can do. "No, I'll be all right."

"Okay, then, if you're sure. I'll be sure to say a prayer for that friend of yours. See you later, Paige Woodward." He smiled and walked away.

Paige put one foot in front of the other by sheer willpower. She got in her car, determined to drive to Nashville and see her friend. "Ora, please don't die."

Joel Bennett was right. At least Ora was still alive. Still fighting.

chapter **thirty-six**

Clarissa looked at the pile of paper work that waited for her twenty minutes from now when they closed. It had definitely caught up to her in these past couple of weeks. Having Paige here had made her life easier in a lot of ways, but an easier life was not the main goal. Her goal was to power through this job, in this place that she hated, and be running her very own Parrish Apothecary by this time next year. With Paige off the payroll, that just might happen.

She wondered where Paige had found a job. She almost envied her—she was out of this place, at least. Probably working back in Nashville, happy to be out of dullsville.

Clarissa thought back to her times in pharmacy school, working in the pharmacology lab, all the potential of the world right at her fingertips. Now she stood at the counter and argued with people about whether or not their insurance covered generic or brand-name tranquilizers. Why didn't she feel all-knowing and self-sufficient like she'd always thought pharmacists did?

Dawn walked over and whispered, "Isn't that the inspector guy who just walked in?"

Clarissa looked up, and sure enough Gary Powell was heading her way. It surprised her that he hadn't come sooner, since Paige had likely called him after she got fired a couple of weeks ago. No matter, Clarissa had seen to it that her interests were covered. She was prepared to deal with this head-on. She walked down to meet him at the counter. "What brings you back our way so soon?" She smiled and leaned casually on the counter even though she could feel her palms starting to sweat.

His lips screwed up into what could have been a smile, but maybe it was a grimace. "I was hoping you'd pull up one prescription in particular for me to look at."

"Of course, come on back." Clarissa almost forgot herself and went straight to the Feldhouse prescription, but at the last second she looked up at him. "What is it you want to see?" She rested her fingers on the keyboard and waited.

"Do you have a patient at this pharmacy named Ora Vaerge?"

"The name doesn't sound familiar. Let me check the computer." She typed some commands into the keyboard. "How do you spell that last name?"

"V A E R G E."

"Oh yes, here she is. What do you need to know?"

"Do you have a prescription for Topamax on file for her?"

Clarissa looked at the information that filled the computer screen. "Yes. It looks like she got a new prescription for Topamax a couple of weeks ago."

"Can you tell me if she'd ever gotten that particular medication here before?"

When Clarissa scanned down the list, her heart froze in her chest. "No. It appears this was the first time."

The man nodded knowingly. "That's what I thought. Before that, she had been getting Toprol XL, is that correct?"

Clarissa's stomach flopped. "Yes." She swallowed and looked at the initials on the screen. CR. She had no memory of this particular prescription, but then she'd filled several hundred since then. She couldn't remember all of them.

"Can you tell me, Miss Richardson, was this prescription called in or written by the doctor?"

"Let me get the file." Clarissa slowly began to thumb through the prescriptions. *Please be written, please be written.*

She got to the appropriate number and pulled it from the file. When her fingers first closed around the piece of paper, she almost cried with relief when she realized that it was written on printed blanks from the doctor's office. It would be the doctor's fault, not hers. "It was written by the doctor . . ." The words died on her lips. The writing was scratchy and not easily read. But, it was clear enough for her to know what had been written.

$Top_{rol}X_l$ 25 1qd

She handed the piece of paper to the inspector, who looked at it and nodded. "Miss Richardson, do you understand the potential problems that would be suffered by a patient on Toprol XL who suddenly stopped taking her medication—or in this case started taking Topamax instead?"

Clarissa's throat went dry. "I, uh, I . . ." She fought for words, any words. "The names are so similar."

"Too similar, unfortunately. This is not the first time I've seen this mix-up." He looked at his watch. "I've got to make a phone call. I'll be right back."

After he walked away, Dawn came to stand beside Clarissa. "Isn't Toprol some kind of heart medicine?"

"Yes."

"I think I heard someone say that Mrs. Vaerge had a heart attack."

"A heart attack?" Clarissa's tongue stuck to the roof of her mouth. "Did you hear how she is doing?"

"Don't know. I think they airlifted her to Mercy Hospital yesterday afternoon."

Clarissa looked at the light fixtures in the wall, the tiny rows of supplies she so carefully designed, and realized, whether or not she wanted to, she was about to lose it all.

Dawn broke out in a cold sweat. She could still remember the paisley top Mrs. Vaerge had been wearing the day she came in, remembered Mrs. Vaerge asking for Paige—but Paige hadn't been there because she'd just been fired. She remembered squinting at the writing, the large "X" at the end finally helping her to see it as Topamax. She remembered counting, pouring, handing the bag to Mrs. Vaerge—all while Clarissa was taking a quick lunch break.

She had left everything on the counter for Clarissa to double-check when she came back. Did Clarissa check it?

Clarissa said, "I think it's important that we let Gary Powell know that sometimes Paige and I worked under each other's initials in the computer, that this might very well have been her mistake."

"What do you mean?"

"You know, like I would log on, and Paige would come in and fill prescriptions before she realized that she wasn't under her own code. The computer trail doesn't necessarily truly show who filled the prescription."

"That is a lie and you know it. I remember this prescription, because I remember Mrs. Vaerge coming in here and asking for Paige the very day your grandfather fired her."

"I'm just saying, it seems as though Paige might have worked for an hour or two before my grandfather fired her that day. Maybe she did fill this. I'm not blaming her, saying that she did it, I'm just saying there's no way to know for sure."

"I know. Like I said, I remember this one. As I recall, you were in the coffee shop at the time. Maybe it's time to tell the truth. For once."

"I think you're forgetting about who it was that found you languishing in a part-time job. Who entrusted you with the work in here. I mean, if we don't let Paige share at least the possibility of some of the blame, a lot more will fall on *you*. You don't want that, do you?"

"Maybe I was given responsibility I shouldn't have had."

Clarissa rolled her eyes. "This mistake you made could just as easily have been made by a pharmacist. The doctor's handwriting was atrocious, the drug names are too similar. The inspector himself said this is not the first time he's seen this mistake." Clarissa flipped her hair and looked toward the front of the pharmacy as if to verify that the inspector wasn't back. "It's the FDA's fault for approving such similar names, that's whose fault it is. Since they're not going to take the rap for this, all I'm asking is that we share a little of the weight with Paige. This store has been doing pretty well financially. I was planning to give out bonuses sometime before the holidays. Probably a few thousand dollars. I'm sure you don't want to do anything that would jeopardize my ability to do that, now do you?"

Dawn stared at the woman talking to her, seeing her more clearly than she ever had. The depths she'd sink to to get her way. But, then again, she thought of her own life with Jack—trapped and hopeless. Unless . . .

With a few thousand dollars free and clear—money that Jack didn't even know about—she could get her own place. Leave him for good. Finally she could be free. But could she trust the spoiled little rich girl to keep her word?

If Clarissa wanted to play this game, she was going to do it right. "Well, it's just that I'm having some financial problems now, and Christmas is a long way away." Dawn looked her full in the face, allowing the dare to shine through her eyes.

Clarissa arched a single eyebrow and tilted her head. "My, my. Aren't you the crass little thing?"

Dawn shrugged. "Promises don't mean much to me, but three thousand dollars would mean a lot."

Gary Powell came back into the store, dropping his cell phone into his coat pocket as he walked.

Clarissa whispered under her breath. "Okay. Three thousand. But you have to tell him exactly what I told you to say if he asks any questions."

Dawn looked her straight in the eye. "I want my money by the end of the week."

"Okay." Clarissa started to walk away.

Before she got out of hearing distance, Dawn whispered, "Cash."

Clarissa did not respond in any apparent way, but the slight dip of her chin told Dawn that she'd been heard loud and clear.

Gary Powell walked up to Clarissa. "I know it's your closing time. I've just got a few questions, then I'll be back tomorrow morning." He didn't look any happier about this than Clarissa did.

"But why?" Clarissa's voice squeaked, and she coughed in what Dawn knew was an effort to cover it up. "You said yourself it's an easy mistake to make."

He nodded. "Since your pharmacy is currently undergoing legal action because of another dispensing error, we're going to be a little extra vigilant this time."

chapter **thirty-seven**

For the third day in a row, Paige made the trip to Nashville to see what she could learn about Ora. For the past two days, she'd gotten nothing but suspicious stares and warnings that information would only be passed on to family. Today, however, the nurses and doctors seemed surprised by her devotion. And obviously they knew no one else was looking after Ora, so when Paige saw Dr. Prince come through the double doors of the Cardiac Care Unit, she rushed to beat him to the elevator. "Dr. Prince, how is Ora Vaerge?"

He looked at her over the top of his glasses. "You don't give up easily, do you, young lady?"

"I'm sorry, but please, I have to know something."

He pressed the button for the elevator and turned to her. "I told you yesterday, for confidentiality reasons, I'm not allowed to give specific information."

Paige looked again at the posted sign on the door. *Visiting hours 10–10:15, 2–2:15, 4–4:15, immediate family only.* Paige tried one more time. "I'm the closest thing to family she has anywhere near, and she's the closest thing to family I have anywhere near. If you won't discuss her case with me, at least let me see her during visiting hours."

He folded his arms across his chest and looked hard at Paige.

She did not allow herself to look away, even when she felt the sting of tears in her eyes. "Please."

He uncrossed his arms. "She's not responding to external stimulus. Her heart has stabilized, but she was hypoxic for so long . . . I don't know if she'll ever regain consciousness." The elevator doors slid open. He walked inside, then turned and blocked the doors open. "Go home, get some sleep. Tomorrow afternoon, if she's still stable, I'll arrange for you to come in during family visitation."

"Thank you." She choked back tears as the elevator doors closed. Would Ora still be stable tomorrow afternoon? Would she even be alive?

One day. Dawn knew Clarissa was nervous about the lawsuit, but she didn't realize how nervous until she saw the white envelope in her purse as she left from work. One day later and she had three thousand dollars. Three thousand!

Freedom was just a few days away for her. She would spend the weekend looking for somewhere to live, a place she could afford, and with whatever was left she could maybe buy a piece of furniture or two.

She drove past a small apartment complex on the way home, and her heart raced with the knowledge that she would soon have her own place. Where no one took her paycheck or showed up drunk and mean. Or failed to show up altogether. It would be great to be on her own.

But somehow her joy didn't soar like she had expected it would.

Paige could not possibly have filled that prescription for Mrs. Vaerge, but Clarissa had assured her it wouldn't hurt Paige if they said maybe she did. All they were doing was casting a little doubt. Paige would never even know it. Maybe she didn't deserve to have these lies told about her, but hey, she wasn't the only one who'd been stomped on by this crummy little world. Dawn didn't deserve her current situation, either. Life was stinking unfair sometimes.

She stopped at a four-way intersection. Loud voices filtered through the windows she had to keep open because her air-conditioning didn't work.

"I'm eighteen, I don't have to listen to you anymore." Dawn saw a girl wearing a frayed denim skirt and black tank top. Gigantic loop earrings bouncing against her neck as she yelled.

"As long as you live in my house, you'll follow my rules." The man wore a white T-shirt and shorts, grass-stained and wrinkled. He looked tired. She remembered her father looking the same way.

Before she could think about what she was doing, she pulled her car to the side of the road and walked toward the pair with more determination than she'd felt in a long time. She stopped just short of the front porch, arms stiff at her side. "You should listen to him."

The daughter and father both turned at once. The girl crossed her arms and glared at Dawn. "What do you know about it?"

"I know that freedom looks great when you see it in the distance, from the security of your home. Let me tell you, in real life, freedom stinks." She turned around, went back to the car, and pulled away from the curb. When she looked in her rearview mirror, the duo was still standing on the porch, both looking at her, mouths open.

This new release of power felt great. She knew she hadn't made one bit of difference in the life of that girl or her father, but she'd made a stand that took courage. She actually possessed courage!

Maybe she could apply that at work. Maybe she wouldn't lie. Not for Clarissa. Not about Paige. She would tell Clarissa to keep her dirty money, because now she had the courage to tell the truth even if it did cost her. Yeah, that's what she'd do.

She picked up the cell phone in her purse and dialed Paige's number. "It's me."

"Dawn?"

"Yeah, I have something I need to tell you." Dawn felt her throat constrict around the words.

"Okay."

"A board inspector has been at the pharmacy the last couple of days. That friend of yours, Mrs. Vaerge, do you remember her?"

"Yeah, I remember her. In fact, I'm just on my way home from visiting her at Mercy. She had a heart attack." Paige trailed the word off at the end. "What about her?"

"From what I've been able to piece together, it

301

seems that when the medics responded to her 9-1-1 call, they bagged up all her meds and took them to the hospital. It helps them to know what the patients are taking. Anyway, one of the bottles was Topamax."

"Topamax? I never knew she had migraines. The only thing I've ever filled for her was Toprol XL." There was a long pause at the other end of the line. "Oh, no!"

"It was filled the day you were fired, so she can't blame it on you this time, but I think she's still going to try."

"Did the inspector see the prescription? Did it have Clarissa's initials on it?"

"Yeah, he saw it and made a copy of it."

"Dawn, you've got to tell him the truth. About everything."

The truth about everything could land her in a whole heap of trouble. She knew that, but maybe Paige was right. Maybe it was time to come clean.

Dawn turned onto her street, looked down the block, and saw Renee's green car in the driveway. The kids were out playing in the front yard; neither Jack nor Renee was anywhere to be seen.

Not again.

She pulled to the curb before the kids saw her and tried to decide what to do. There really was nowhere else for her. Even if her parents did for-give her—and that was a big if—she knew her father well enough to know that he would never let her move back home. This was all she had. There was no other choice. Unless . . .

Unless she took Clarissa's money.

"I've got to go." Dawn hung up the phone, regretting her impulsive decision to make the call.

chapter **thirty-eight**

Paige rode the elevator to the fourth floor, her heart pounding. How could she even think of coming here, knowing a mistake from her pharmacy had caused this? That she, as much as anyone, was to blame?

When she reached the waiting room for the Cardiac Care Unit, she went to the visitors' desk. A gray-haired woman in a green volunteer jacket smiled up at her. "May I help you?"

"Can you tell me . . . Mrs. Vaerge, is she still . . . in this unit?"

The woman scanned a printout on her clipboard. "Let's see, Vaerge." Her finger ran the length of the paper before it stopped. "Oh, yes, there she is. Yes, she's still here."

Paige exhaled a sigh of relief. One more day and Ora was still living. Still holding on. But would she ever wake up again? "Do you know, has Dr. Prince been in to see her recently?"

"Not since I got here a couple of hours ago." She looked at the round white clock on the wall. "He usually comes in around noon, so my guess is that he'll be here soon."

"Thank you." Paige took the seat across from the elevator. To distract herself she picked up a *National Geographic* from the end table and skimmed through an article on volcanoes. She turned page after page but saw little of the photos inside.

How could this have happened? Why Ora of all people?

Paige thought about the woman who had met her at the door on most mornings. The coffee-making tips. The mixed-up, yet often useful verses.

The elevator doors opened and Paige was on her feet before the occupants even emerged. Dr. Prince stepped off, deep in conversation with a man in blue surgical scrubs. The two of them disappeared behind the double doors of the unit, seemingly unaware of anyone else around them.

Paige got up and began to pace. On one end of the room, she walked toward the framed print of a lighthouse, then turned and went back toward the couch. Over and over. Lighthouse to couch, couch to lighthouse.

None of the other occupants of the room seemed to pay this any attention at all. Perhaps they understood the restless feeling, or perhaps they were just too exhausted by their own concerns to care.

Finally, the doors opened and Dr. Prince reemerged. Paige rushed over to meet him. "Dr. Prince?"

"There's not a lot of change, I'm afraid. The nurses have reported minimal response to stimuli. I will add your name to the approved visitor list, but I want strict adherence to posted visiting hours."

"Yes. Definitely."

Paige looked at the clock on the wall. Two o'clock. "May I go in now?"

"Yes. She's in the last room." He pointed down the hall to her right.

"Thank you." Paige pushed through the doors before he could think to change his mind.

She walked to the last doorway, and when she first looked inside, she thought she was in the wrong place. This woman wasn't Ora; she was much too old. The deep lines in her face, the pale cast to her skin—they belonged to someone else.

Paige knelt beside the bed and took Ora's cold hand in her own. "Oh, Ora. I'm so sorry."

Warm tears dropped onto their intermingled hands. "This is all my fault."

She looked at the helpless woman lying so still and found herself asking questions she didn't want an answer to. Was the pain excruciating when the heart attack began? Did she gasp for breath, wondering if she'd even be able to make the phone call to 9-1-1? And did it ever, in the midst of her great pain, occur to her that Paige's own negligence was the very thing that had caused this?

"Ora, I love you. Please get better. This is all my

fault, and I'll do anything I can to make it up to you, if you'll just wake up. Okay?"

The wax hand moved in her own. Or had she just imagined it?

"Ora? Ora? Can you hear me?"

The hand squeezed hers, and the left side of Ora's mouth twitched.

Paige pushed the nurse call button, but before a response even came she was screaming for help down the hall. "She's awake. She's awake. Mrs. Vaerge is awake."

Paige drove toward home, wishing so much that she would find her mother's comforting presence when she got there. Someone who could tell her that a hand squeeze was just the first step toward a full recovery, in spite of the reserved reactions of the nurses. Ora just might wake up and be all right again someday. Right?

Paige picked up the phone as soon as she walked in the door. Maybe just by hearing her parents' voices, she would feel their strength.

"Hello." Her father's voice sounded so flat—dead almost.

"Daddy, are you okay?"

"I'm fine, but unfortunately your mother doesn't seem to be. She spiked a fever, and her blood work came back suspicious for . . . let's see . . . got it written right here. CMV."

Paige's hand went numb on the phone. "But they

gave her antiviral medication to keep that from happening. She got the treatment like she was supposed to, this shouldn't happen."

"You're the one who works in the medical field, I reckon you know better than me that things don't always work out like they're supposed to."

Yes, Paige understood that more than she had ever hoped to. "What are they doing about it?"

"Oh, the usual. More IVs, more tests. I'm having to wear the banana suit and mask every time I go into her room. There's a guy from the breathing department in there now, checking out her lungs."

Paige knew that CMV could cause major problems post-transplant, and she also knew that pneumonia was one of the biggest concerns of CMV. "Dad, is she having trouble breathing?"

"She's had the cough since before they treated her for that other thing, you know, the RSV. I'd say it's maybe gotten worse in the last day or so." He paused for a minute. "The guy from respiratory wants to talk to me. I'll call you later if I hear anything new, one way or the other."

"Thanks, Dad." Paige hung up the phone and ran to the computer. CMV was something she knew a little about, but now was the time to broaden her knowledge base. She scanned the headings under Google and clicked on a link. The article filled the screen with a long list of problems CMV could cause post-transplant, starting with pneumonia. It was the very end of the list that stopped Paige's heart from beating.

Post-transplant marrow failure.

Marrow failure? *No. Please God, no.* He wouldn't allow them to go through all this for nothing. Would He?

The Internet wasn't always accurate, especially when it came to medical things. Paige closed the article and returned to the Google search page, looking for something a bit more comforting. Number ten on the list of links said *Fatal CMV pneumonia following transplant.*

Paige turned the computer off.

chapter **thirty-nine**

Clarissa stared out the window of her condominium. The golf course below looked so green, manicured, perfect. In the fading light of a spring evening, a group of twenty-something men putted four little white balls into the hole and hurried over to the last tee, trying to get their game in before darkness enveloped them.

The darkness was closing in on her, too.

If only she could get through all this, open up the store in the Lancaster Building, everything would be all right. She knew that she wouldn't hate retail so much if she worked in Nashville instead of Shoal Creek. Not having to deal with all the insurance, the crowds, and just being able to provide top-notch service to the people who wanted it would be so much better. Yes, that wouldn't be nearly as miserable as normal retail.

Then she thought about Mrs. Vaerge.

A person had almost died because of a bad decision Clarissa had made. Even if Mrs. Vaerge recovered fully, even if her bills were being taken care of, the thought of what might have happened was staggering.

Her doorbell rang. She wasn't expecting anyone, but it wasn't unlike her friends to drop by.

"Hey." Tony's eyes drooped at the corners in a way Clarissa hadn't seen before.

It had been several weeks since they'd last talked—not since they went out for ice cream. Surely he wasn't still moping about Paige. "What's wrong?"

"How do you know something's wrong?"

"Like you don't have the most readable face in the western hemisphere. Come on in and tell your darling niece all about it."

He followed her inside. "You busy?"

"Never too busy for you. What's up?" She motioned him toward a seat at her dinette.

He dropped into it. "I got a visit from Jeff Sweeney today."

"Really? Why would he come see you?"

Tony studied her face while she spoke as if he expected some sort of clue to emerge. "I had him checking out a few things that just didn't add up."

"Like what?"

"All that stuff in Atlanta, something didn't seem right to me. I asked him what he thought about it. I believe his exact words were, 'I smell a PR rat.' What he found confirmed that. Paige took the fall for blame that could have been spread in a lot more directions."

Clarissa shrugged. "I'm sorry to hear that."

"Are you?" He leaned his chin into his hand and continued to watch her evenly.

"Why wouldn't I be?"

"Did you set her up?"

"Hello. That happened a long time before I'd ever even set eyes on the girl. How exactly do you think I set her up?"

"You know that's not what I'm talking about. I'm talking about in Shoal Creek."

"What do her mistakes in Shoal Creek have to do with the situation in Atlanta?"

He leaned farther across the table. "Did you set her up?"

"Of course not."

He sat back in his chair and folded his arms. "I knew you wouldn't do something like that. I told him there was *no way* that the sweetheart of a niece I've known all my life would do something like that. I said, 'She's been the one who was getting stomped on most of her life. She would never do that to another person. Especially another person who was working and saving every penny to help pay her mother's medical costs."

"Medical costs?"

"Come on, Clarissa, tell me you knew that her mother has cancer."

"All she's ever told me about her family is that her parents are on a trip to Texas for a few months, so she's house-sitting."

"Her mother's in Houston getting a stem cell transplant. According to Jeff Sweeney, her parents' credit is maxed out, and Paige was apparently helping to support them financially. You can't tell me you didn't know any of that."

"I . . . didn't . . ." Clarissa thought of the times she'd talked about shopping, and how Paige had always said something to the effect of, "I'm trying to save my money right now." Never once had she mentioned anything about sending money to a sick mother. Never once in all that time. "No, I didn't know. She never talked about it."

Tony shook his head almost imperceptibly. "I'm sure you realize that she's having trouble finding another job because of all this. In fact, what you probably don't realize is that her father had to sell his truck and plumbing supplies. That'll make it kind of hard for him to return to work when he gets back into town, wouldn't you say?"

Clarissa looked at Tony and recoiled. The look in his eyes was one she recognized well; she'd seen it often enough in her stepmother. Disgust. Just another family member disappointed in her. His accusation awoke in her the only thing that could defend her now. Anger. "Well, she shouldn't have made mistakes, then."

If Tony had even blinked during this conversation, Clarissa hadn't seen it. He nodded very slowly. "I'm glad to know your conscience is clear."

"Sparkling." Clarissa folded her arms and propped her feet in the chair across the table.

"Then I guess I don't have anything else to talk to you about. Have a good evening." He stood and walked to the door. He opened it, then turned. "Sleep well."

Paige was driving down the busy freeway. Cars whizzing past. A beautiful young girl with huge blue eyes was waving to her from the middle seat of her mother's SUV. No, wait, she wasn't waving, she was screaming.

Paige sat up in the bed, gasping for breath. The dream never seemed to go away, or lessen in intensity. In fact, it seemed to be getting worse.

She got up and walked to the kitchen for a drink of water. The digital clock on the oven displayed 4:30 a.m. in brilliant neon blue. Paige sat down at the oak table and took a sip of water. She couldn't go back to bed and face the possibility of another dream, so she went to the den and picked up the remote, but never pushed the button.

"God, will you please tell Mr. Bartlett it wasn't my fault? I want him to know that."

A twang of something ran through her, and it felt a lot like guilt. She shook her head. "Well, it wasn't. The nurse wrote it, the doctor signed it. I filled it just like it was written." The feeling did not subside, in spite of her logic. But it was true. She did not carry the blame.

She remembered the nightmares she'd had so many times, of Mr. Bartlett's seizure behind the wheel. "You know what, I'm not backing down here. The blame is at least fifty percent the nurse's who wrote it down wrong, and the other fifty percent was the doctor's who signed it."

Her words were true. Why didn't they give her any relief?

"Okay, maybe three percent of the blame is mine. But that is three out of one hundred. Get it? Not my fault!"

Three percent.

Three percent blame in a man's death.

The thought battered her with a force that knocked the breath from her lungs. How was she supposed to live with that?

Until this very moment she'd insulated herself with the knowledge that she carried the lesser blame. But any blame was too much. A man lay in a grave in Atlanta, and if she had taken extra precaution, he'd still be with his family today. Maybe watching his granddaughter's ballet recital, or his grandson's little league game.

Paige leaned her head back against the sofa cushions and thought about the wreck. What must Mr. Bartlett have felt when his limbs started to jerk as he drove down the interstate? Did he see the toddler in the other car, try his very best to control his arms one last time so that he avoided hitting her? Maybe he was a hero, and they would never know. Because he hadn't lived to tell them.

Then a thought occurred that rocked her even more. What percentage blame was hers for Ora's heart attack? If she had told the truth to the board inspector that very first day, would this still have happened? Was her cover-up even now putting more people in danger?

She went to her wallet and found the business card she'd put there over a month ago. She knew the office was closed, but if she didn't make this call now, she might change her mind. She punched in the appropriate numbers on her cell phone and held her breath until it clicked over to voice mail.

"This is Paige Woodward. I'd like to make an appointment to see Gary Powell. It's about my time at Richardson Apothecary," she said and left a call-back number. This was something that she had to do if she was ever going to sleep with a clear conscience again.

chapter forty

"What would make you lie to cover up a mistake of a co-worker, if you weren't even involved in the mistake?"

Paige forced herself to meet Gary Powell's gaze directly. "Because I've seen firsthand how someone can twist a mistake around and destroy someone else's life."

"I understand where you're coming from, but there *was* a death in Atlanta."

"Mr. Bartlett's situation was a tragedy—" Paige tried to blink away her memories of the sweet older man "—and I've come to accept the fact that I do share in the blame for it. But he is not the reason I have trouble finding a job, he's not even the reason I got fired in the first place. Basically, my life was ruined because of the mother's lawsuit. The mother who was driving a Mercedes SUV that was paid for by a previous lawsuit. The mother who didn't have a scratch on her or her child. Getting rid of me was the best way the HMO could protect themselves."

"I see."

Ora's words ran through her mind again and hit her with all the force of conviction. "You know, that's actually not the truth, either. The truth is, I lied because I didn't have enough faith."

"Faith?"

"I didn't trust God to handle the situation if I told the truth. I suppose I tried to help Him a little, in the form of a lie." She looked Gary Powell in the face. "No surprise that didn't work out, huh?"

He folded his arms across his chest. "If you've given it that kind of thought, I don't expect you'll be doing it again in the near future."

"I don't know that I'll have the chance."

"You understand that this is not the same story I'm hearing from your two co-workers."

"Yes, sir, I know. And I don't expect that my telling you all this will change anything for the better for me. But, if the two of them are going to continue to work together, then someone needs to know what is going on so that someone else doesn't get hurt."

"You realize until this last error, your initials were on all the prescriptions that were misfilled."

"Yes, I believe that Clarissa went in and changed computer records. I always hand-initial everything I touch—a habit I picked up in the Sharitz days. You could go look through the old files from the Nashville Clinic and confirm that, and I was the only pharmacist who was working there. One of the mistakes—Ms. Feldhouse's—was made on a day that I wasn't even at work."

Gary Powell opened a folder on his desk and removed a sheet of paper—a copy of the prescription. "So, you're telling me that on March 29 you weren't even at the pharmacy?"

"Yes, sir, that's what I'm telling you." Paige pulled her shoulders upright and concentrated on keeping her chin lifted. She knew how this sounded, what Gary Powell must think, but it was the truth.

"Can you prove where you were?"

"No."

He nodded slowly. "I'll take what you've said under consideration. Thanks for coming in."

"You're welcome." Paige walked down the hallway, realizing that she'd accomplished absolutely nothing. Regardless, she'd finally done what she should have done all along.

Houston was only a day's drive away, but on the phone that night it might as well have been a million miles. Her father had never sounded more scared, more alone.

"How's Mom?"

"Still pretty sick. The doctors say her lungs are staying clear, but her fever's been steady. She's on the knife's edge, Paige." There was a rustling on the other line. "She's awake now and wants to say hello."

"Hi, sweetie."

"Oh, Mom. How are you feeling?"

"I think—" there was a slight wheezing sound as she took a breath—"I'm getting better."

She didn't sound better, but if she could pretend, so could Paige. "Good. You stay strong and keep fighting this thing."

Paige's father came back on the line. "The doctor said that this CMV might or might not materialize, 'cause the blood work's kind of iffy. All we can do is wait it out." He paused for a moment. "There's nothing I hate worse than waiting, but in this case, I guess it beats the alternative. How are things with you?"

Dusty began a low-throated growl at the front window. Paige walked over to look out, and what she saw made her gasp. "I think I need to get off the phone."

"What's wrong?"

"A car just pulled up, and I'm pretty sure it's Dawn's."

chapter **forty-one**

Dawn pulled over to the curb and looked at the address she'd written on the piece of paper. This must be the place. From first glance, it even looked like the kind of home where she'd expect Paige to live. A nice brick one-story on a couple of neatly trimmed acres, with nothing but trees for neighbors in the back. It all looked so nurturing, so welcoming.

Well, she wouldn't be welcomed, she knew that. Desperation may have caused her to drive here, but common sense wouldn't let her get out of the car. No way. She closed her eyes and took a deep breath.

A knock on the passenger side window jarred her. She turned to see Paige standing by the door, leaning forward, looking at her. "Dawn?"

Dawn started the car without rolling down the window. This was a mistake, and it was time to get out of here.

Before she had a chance to pull away from the curb, Paige jerked open the car door and jumped into the passenger seat. "What happened?"

Dawn didn't have to wonder why Paige asked the question. She touched her puffy lower lip. "I'm sorry. I shouldn't have come here. This is not your problem. If you'll get out, I'll be on my way."

"Not until you tell me what happened."

"Why would you even care?"

"I care because you're obviously hurt. You're also obviously pretty desperate if you're showing up here. Now, what happened, and how can I help?"

"Jack happened, and there's nothing you can do." Dawn turned to look at Paige then. "Does it make you feel better to know that the person who could have helped you but didn't is getting what's coming to her?"

"Dawn, *this*"—Paige touched a sore spot on Dawn's cheek—"was not 'coming to you.' Regardless of what you did or didn't say, no one deserves this. Now, pull your car into my driveway, and let's go inside and talk."

"Just get out, okay? I made a mistake in coming here."

"I'm not going anywhere."

Dawn whipped around to her then. "All right. You want it, you'll get it. You see these bruises? Jack put them there. You want to know why? He found the money I've been hiding so that I can get away from him. It was a lot of money. Three thousand dollars to be exact. You want to know where I got it? You're going to really love this part of the story, because I got it from Clarissa. She gave it to me to keep quiet about what's really been going on in the pharmacy."

Paige covered her mouth with her hand. "You what?"

"You heard me. Now you found out what you wanted to know. Get out."

"But . . . Jack hurt you. You can't go back there."

Her anger spent, Dawn felt herself deflate. It was all she could do to keep her head up. "You're right. Even if I wanted to. His ex-wife moved in today."

"Wow." Paige leaned forward as if her stomach suddenly hurt. She rubbed her temples with the thumb and middle finger of her left hand. "I guess I'm not the only one with trouble around here."

"You can say that again."

Paige reached over, pulled on the handle, and turned to climb from the car. She stood halfway, then dropped back into her seat, her head shaking slowly from side to side. "You know, this is my parents' house. They're out of town for a couple

320

more months, and I'm staying here all alone. You're welcome to the guest room."

Dawn looked at her, waiting for the laughter. "Yeah, right. I'll just bet."

"No, I mean it."

"Why would you do that?"

"Because I'm standing my ground and waiting for daybreak."

"Huh?"

She shook her head. "Let's just say I'm doing it because it's the right thing to do. And it doesn't seem to me like you have a lot of other choices."

She was right about that. "You're just doing this because you want me to back up your story to the inspector guy."

Paige shook her head. "It doesn't matter anymore. It's impossible for me to ever get a job in pharmacy again, so that part doesn't matter, and I told him everything I know, so my hands are clean. Whether or not anybody ever believes me is not my problem."

"You can't get another job, really? What will you do?"

Paige sighed. "I don't know. Once my parents get back, I'm going to try looking for a job in another part of the state, maybe. For now, I start work as a cashier at Long's Hardware next week—I've got to do something to pay some bills."

"Maybe I could just stay for the night. Until I find another place."

"You're welcome for as long as you need to stay. Do you need me to go with you to get your stuff?"

"Nah, what little I got is in this car."

"Well, pull this car into the driveway and come on in. I'll show you to your room."

Clarissa straightened her lab coat, smiled at the volunteer manning the desk, and pushed through the double doors to the CCU. She'd done part of her post-graduate internship in this hospital; she knew her way around. As long as she looked like she knew what she was doing, no one was likely to stop her. Of course, the ID badge helped, too. She just hoped that no one looked close enough to notice it was expired.

She rounded the corner into Ora's room, prepared to face her mistakes head on. Her frustrations with Paige and her grandfather and *everything* had turned her into a person she didn't even want to look at in the mirror. But that had to change. She had to be an adult and accept what had happened. Until she saw the woman in the bed. Then it was all she could do to hold her ground.

Breathe, breathe, stay calm, and breathe. Clarissa took a step closer and looked hard, trying to find something about the woman that was familiar. Her skin was so pale it almost had a bluish cast, her body still. There was a little mole on the left side of her chin that offered the only hint of flesh color at all.

In this moment, the situation reached full reality in Clarissa's mind. A woman's life was at stake—and probably ruined even if she did live, because of something Clarissa had done. She dropped into the seat beside the bed and gasped for air. She had done this to someone. Another real, live, breathing person. Not just an insurance number or prescription record.

"Can I help you?" A heavyset brunette nurse stood at the doorway to the cubicle.

Clarissa looked at her. "I . . . no . . ." She stood and walked toward the double doors of the unit. "Nobody can."

chapter **forty-two**

Paige watched Dawn pull out of the driveway on her way to work, then walked outside and sat at her mother's favorite bench on the edge of the property. "Forgive me. I know I haven't been trusting You. I mean, I'm not going to sit here and lie to You. You know everything anyway, but it doesn't seem like You've come through for me much lately. Why should I expect this time to be any different?"

A squirrel ran across the grass, picked up a piece of a twig, and sat up, holding it in his paws. He leaned forward and nibbled a little, then dropped the twig and moved on. Paige understood how he felt. How are you supposed to know what to ignore and what to pick up?

"Okay, I thought I was praying in faith all along, but obviously I need some help. Ora was right, I wouldn't have done something that was obviously wrong to 'help You out' if I'd really had faith in the first place. I guess this is one of those times that I need You to 'help my unbelief,' because let's just be honest, I don't have any belief left." The truth of the words sickened her, but she was done playing games—especially with God.

She looked through the oak leaves above her to the traces of blue beyond them. The vastness of the sky was blue, but the leaves right in front of her kept her from seeing it—just like her problems were keeping her from seeing the entirety of God, she supposed.

There is a river whose streams make glad the city of God, the holy place where the Most High dwells. God is within her, she will not fall; God will help her at break of day.

The verse echoed deep within her as she focused on the largest spot of blue she could find. "I'm going to stay at my post and trust You. But I've got to tell You, I sure hope daybreak is coming soon."

"Come on, Dusty, let's go back up to the house." He stood and followed her. "Why don't we do a little deep cleaning today, boy? What do you think—should we start with the kitchen?"

Dusty walked into the house and into the front room, where he took his usual spot at the bay window. "I guess I can't count on you for help, eh, boy?"

Paige opened the bottom drawer and removed the cast-iron skillets that had seen more years on this earth than she had. How many chicken drumsticks had been fried in these? Paige could almost hear her mother's slightly off-key humming that always accompanied her cooking. The memory made her both smile and ache.

Dusty began to bark with a fury from the front room. Paige slowly pushed to her feet, reluctant to leave the bittersweet connection.

She went to the window and peered out at the driveway. Dawn was climbing out of her car.

Oh, no.

Dawn walked into the house, looking rather less upset than Paige would have supposed for someone who had just been fired.

"What happened?"

"Clarissa called in sick. The pharmacy will be closed today."

Clarissa exited the elevator and started down the long corridor, hearing the clack of her sandals against the floor. This had to be the hardest walk she'd ever taken. She drew a deep breath when she reached suite 301 and pushed through the door.

The receptionist looked up from the keyboard, her chin tilting down so she could look over her half-glasses. "May I help you?"

"I'm Clarissa Richardson. I called yesterday to meet with Gary Powell." The calmness in her own voice surprised her.

"I'll let him know you're here. Have a seat."

How much did the receptionist know? The woman treated her politely, but Clarissa felt condemned. Thoughts of yesterday's visit to the hospital still ached, and this had been the only thing she could think of to try and soothe that pain. Clarissa stared aimlessly out the window. Such a beautiful day and she barely saw any of it.

"Miss Richardson? Mr. Powell is ready for you. Third office on the right."

Clarissa walked across the heavy-duty blue carpet past two doors, then stopped at the third. She could turn now, run out of here, and never come back. Maybe find a little place on the coast and get a job in a tennis shop, where a ten-minute coffee break couldn't hurt somebody.

She suddenly found herself standing inside the office, although she had no memory of making the decision or taking the necessary steps. Yet somehow, here she was.

"Please sit down." He motioned toward a cheap leather chair.

Slowly she lowered herself into it, although every instinct told her not to. She needed to be ready to bolt.

He looked at her with sympathy in his eyes. Or

was it condescension? "Thank you for coming in today."

Somewhere down the hall a door closed softly and murmuring voices drew near, passed by, and fell silent. Clarissa squeezed her fingers tight together, watching the tips turn white.

Gary Powell cleared his throat. "I'm hearing some different versions of the story out of Shoal Creek. Do you have anything new to add to what you've already told me?"

Clarissa studied the manufactured grain on the surface of the desk. Dark black swirls against a dark brown background. She supposed it was meant to look like mahogany, but it didn't. It looked like a cheap imitation. She had always hated fakes.

"There are a few more things you need to know. Something I guarantee you neither Paige nor Dawn has had the guts to tell you."

And so she began.

chapter **forty-three**

Paige straightened from cleaning the bathroom vanity and turned toward the sounds of Dusty barking. The sound of a car door closing followed, and then footsteps. Dawn back again today? Apparently Clarissa was really sick.

Paige went to the front door with a wad of paper towels still in her hand. She took a step onto the porch before she realized that it wasn't Dawn's car in the driveway. In fact, it wasn't a car at all. It was a white truck, the words *Richardson Construction* in red letters on the side.

Her feet stuck where they landed. She wobbled in place for a split second, then turned and retreated, closing and locking the door behind her. She leaned against the door with all her strength, as if expecting a battering ram to begin whacking at the other side at any moment.

Instead, a gentle knock sounded. "Paige, I know you're in there. Open the door." Lee Richardson spoke with the voice of a man accustomed to complete and immediate obedience.

Paige pictured herself walking across the room, escaping out the back door, not turning around until she heard the sound of the truck leaving her driveway. But she couldn't do it. She had run from Atlanta, she had run from the current situation, and she was done running. She flung open the door. "What are you doing here?"

"I need to talk to you."

She held onto the door. "Talk."

"Can I come in?"

Anger surged through Paige and her eyes must have blazed, because he just held up his hands and said, "Here is fine." Then he pointed inside to the portrait of Paige's parents that could be seen on the buffet opposite the door. "You never told me about your mother."

"There wasn't any reason to." Paige could almost hear the conversation around the Richardson family dinner table. While Tony reported his investigator's findings, Clarissa spewed her lies and Lee sat there remorseful for ever hiring such a person. "Look, I'm in the middle of something here. Please say what you need to say so that I can get back to it." She knew her voice sounded harsh, but why shouldn't it?

"I was wrong."

"Yeah, I know, you made a mistake when you hired me, you told me that the day you fired me. If there's nothing new to add, your truck's right there."

He took a tremendous breath, then held it for a moment while studying his hands. After he finally exhaled he said, "Have I ever told you what happened to my wife?"

"No." Paige heard the hardness of her voice and caught herself. "Never the full story."

"She had this terrible headache. She had always been prone to migraines, so I didn't think much of it when she first started complaining, but she insisted that this one was different. Finally, I came home from work and drove her to the emergency room, figuring they would give her a shot of something or other and send her home.

"Well, they put her back in a room, and the next thing I know, she's . . ." He shook his head and flattened his palms against the doorjamb. "I'm sure you learned all about aneurysms in pharmacy school."

"A little."

"Best I can figure, it was like a balloon in the blood vessel that went to her brain. The thing popped before the doctor even came to look at her. She died immediately."

"I'm sorry, Lee."

"I've always blamed the doctors for it. We waited in the waiting room for twenty minutes before she was called back, she'd been back another five without being seen by a doctor when it happened. If they would've moved a little faster, done their jobs better . . ."

He looked at her. "They told me it wouldn't have mattered. The location in her brain would have made it impossible to save her, even if a surgeon had been standing right there. But I've never believed that. I've always thought it was a failure of the medical system." He locked his fingers together and rubbed his thumb across the knuckle of his index finger. "I guess it's people like me who made what happened to you possible."

"You have no idea what happened to me."

"I know everything."

"Clarissa's version of everything?"

"Well, yes actually. She came to me last night and told me the whole truth—including the way she'd been setting you up."

Paige started, but tried not to show her surprise. "Yeah, well, now you know."

Lee held out an envelope. "Here. This is the rest of your signing bonus. At least I can give you that much."

Paige looked at the envelope and thought how much easier it could make her life right now. But it would make Lee Richardson's conscience easy, too. His actions had led to Paige's father selling his beloved work truck, and there should be no relief for that. She took a step back and began closing the door. "What's done is done. I don't want your pity, Lee."

He looked her square in the face. "You're being stubborn."

"Be careful on your drive home." She motioned toward the driveway with her right hand, then shut the door. Before it clicked into place she was sure she heard him say, "I really am sorry."

And in the empty silence of her parents' home, Paige could only reply, "Yeah, so am I."

The nurse smiled at Paige as she walked into the unit. "We've got a surprise for you today."

Paige walked into Ora's room to find her sitting up in bed. A tray sat before her, containing a bowl full of broth and a cup of red Jell-O that was missing a tiny crescent bite.

"Hello, young 'un." The readout behind Ora's bed continued to show a steady cardiac rhythm;

her monitors glowed and hummed with acceptable oxygen saturation, pulse rate, and respiratory rate. It all looked good, in spite of the grayish cast to Ora's skin.

"You're awake!" Paige ran to the bed and hugged her friend as best she could around all the tubing and cords that hung by her bed.

"Reckon I am." Her voice was weak, but her eyes were clear and focused.

Paige grasped the handrail on the bed and looked at the woman who should not be in this place. Wouldn't be here now, if Paige had done what was right. She couldn't even force a smile.

"Take a deep breath, child. Your face looks like you've just seen a specter from the nether world." She picked up the pink plastic cup on her tray and took a sip of water through the bent straw. "Far as I know, I'm still in the earthly regions."

"Oh, Ora. This is all my fault." Paige collapsed into a chair at the side of the bed.

"I've suspected as much." Ora coughed once and took two deep breaths. "If it weren't for you, I wouldn't be an old woman, with an old woman's heart." Her pale lips turned up at the corners. Her eyes twinkled with laughter, even if her body was still too weak to back it up.

This gesture heaped hot coals on Paige's already burning conscience. "It's not a joke. Ora, your prescription was misfilled. That's what caused your heart attack. You were taking the wrong thing for several days."

Ora's expression did not change. Perhaps she had already been told the truth by a nurse or doctor, perhaps she didn't quite understand, or perhaps she was just too sick to care.

"I've known for a while that Clarissa and Dawn were not following procedures. I talked to Clarissa about it, but I should have reported her."

Ora squeezed her hand and her eyes began to flutter shut. "I've never been one to abide tattle-tales, myself." A strand of gray hair fell across her cheek.

Paige smoothed it away from her face. "I'm so sorry." There was nothing more to say.

Ora slept for a couple of moments, then coughed and opened her eyes. "You know, the whole mistake thing. It don't make sense to me because I don't remember my pills looking different." She pointed toward the little closet in her room. "Bring me my purse."

Paige went and found the carpetbag tote in the bottom of the closet and brought it back to her friend.

Ora rummaged through it for a few seconds saying, "I declare, things just get harder and harder to find in this thing. I'd get something smaller, but then it wouldn't hold all my stuff. Let's see . . . here it is." Ora pulled out a plastic strip with seven dividers, the letters S M T W T F S on each of the little lids. Her pill dispenser.

"Let's see here," she said, opening the lid marked F, "isn't this what I've been taking all along?"

Paige looked at the white tablet, scored down the middle. She turned it over in her palm and looked at the markings, A / MO. The correct marking for the correct medication. "Ora, this is your Toprol XL. Are you sure you haven't taken any light yellow pills during all this time?"

"Positive. I always use up my old bottle before I start a new one. So me being in here isn't your fault or the redhead's or even that careless other one. The fault is mine . . . for living so long my heart wants to take a nap on me."

Paige thought about all the implications of this new information. The prescription had still been misfilled, there could be no doubt about that, but if none had been taken. . . . "I need to go make a phone call. I'll be back to see you tomorrow. Okay?"

"I'm not headed to any rummage sales, young 'un."

"Right." Paige rushed outside the hospital, waiting only until she reached the parking lot to dial Gary Powell's phone number. "Mr. Powell, have you counted the pills in the bottle of the Topamax from Mrs. Vaerge's home? I think she might not have taken any." Paige recounted the conversation as best she could, answering his questions along the way.

"Well," he said, "that does put a new spin on things. Let me look into all this and see what we find."

chapter **forty-four**

Clarissa climbed from her convertible and walked toward the front door. She rang the doorbell, hoping maybe no one was home.

Paige opened the door. "Oh."

"Hi."

A dog barked somewhere nearby, the kind of happy yip that suggested a game of fetch or tug-of-war. Female laughter mixed with the sound. "Good boy, Dusty." It was Dawn's voice, coming from the backyard from the sound of it.

"We never really talked like we should have." Clarissa looked Paige full in the face. "You, for instance, never told me the reason your parents were in Texas."

Paige shrugged. "It never came up, really."

"It also never came up that Milton Parrish and my grandfather had given me one year to turn a profit in the Shoal Creek store. If I passed that test, then I would be allowed to pursue the dream I'd had all along. I could open a Parrish Apothecary in the Lancaster Building in Nashville. It also never came up that my fourth stepmother has been planning to take the building for herself—in spite of the fact that it's my grandmother's memories that live there. The drain of your salary at my store was helping to make that possible."

Paige's face softened just a little. "That explains

335

a lot. If I'd only known . . . well, I don't know what I would have done differently. Fact was, I needed the job, whether you wanted me there or not."

"Yeah, if I had known, maybe . . . well, I don't know. I guess it doesn't matter much now. I want you to know I was wrong—dead wrong. I never meant for it to go that far." She took a deep breath and continued. "You know what I've discovered?"

"What?"

"I hate retail."

"You may have just discovered that, but I've known it about you all along."

Clarissa smiled. "I guess I'm a little slow on the uptake sometimes." She took a deep breath. Now came the hard part, the part where Paige was likely to send her packing. "I'm here to ask you to take your job back."

"You want me to work with you again? After all that's happened?"

"Not for long. I'm applying to grad schools. Research has always been what I've wanted to do. I thought that changed when I got a chance to follow in my grandmother's footsteps, but you know what, it didn't. Just because I loved my grandmother more than anyone else in the world doesn't mean I was meant to walk the same path she walked."

"I guess not."

"Yeah, well, all that to say, I'll only be working there long enough to teach you how to do all the paper work and for you to hire a replacement for me. I went to see Gary Powell and told him everything."

"What's going to happen?"

"There are all sorts of hearings and legal wrangling in my future. We'll likely settle with Ms. Feldhouse, but as for what'll happen now with Mrs. Vaerge? Who knows? I'll likely eventually have my license suspended—at least for a while."

"You don't know!" Paige shouted, and Clarissa nearly jumped. "I was at the hospital yesterday and Ora is improving enough to talk and respond. And she never took any of the pills you'd given her. Whatever might have been done wrong"—Paige put her hand on Clarissa's shoulder and looked her directly in the eye—"Clarissa, you did not cause her heart attack."

"What?" Clarissa stared back into Paige's eyes, unable to believe the sincerity she saw there. Could this really be true?

"Are you . . . sure?" The dam of emotions that she'd held so tightly through all of this—all of her life for that matter—burst. Deep, guttural sobs sounded, and she knew they were coming from her, but she couldn't stop them.

"I'm sure. I called Gary Powell when we realized what had happened, or rather what had not happened."

Clarissa leaned her forehead against the brick façade of the house and fought with all that was in her to regain control. Part of her wanted to feel as happy as Paige looked, but the greater part found little comfort in the news. Sure, she wasn't to blame for the heart attack, but that offered only cold comfort. It wasn't the error itself after all, but the way she'd lost sight of everything that mattered.

"I'm glad she's better," she said. "I'll have to swing by." She blinked hard. "You know the worst part of it? I tried to honor my grandmother, and instead I've shamed my whole family." She forced herself to straighten her shoulders. "But my grandfather and I have decided to take the Lancaster Building and open a nonprofit. My grandmother was a big proponent of women's education, so it will be something that provides educational opportunities for women who wouldn't have them otherwise."

"Sounds like that is something she'd be proud of, then."

"Yeah, so . . . anyway. About that job?"

"What would your grandfather think about your offer?"

"I've already talked to him. He's all for it. So is Milton Parrish."

"Let me think about it."

"Sure." Clarissa turned to leave but knew she could not go until she'd said it all. "One more thing you need to know. The investigator . . . that was all me. Tony gave me the guy's name, but he didn't hire him and he wasn't using you. You made him really happy—until you broke his heart, that is."

"I did not break his heart. His heart was never in it."

"Believe me, I know Tony better than anyone else in this world. When I say you broke his heart, that's exactly what I mean."

When she drove away, she could see Paige still standing at the door, tears glinting in her eyes.

Paige sat on her mother's bench, Clarissa's words turning over and over in her head. Her old job back. What was she supposed to do with that?

In truth, she really didn't have a lot of other choices, but for some reason she hadn't been able to say yes right away. She needed a day or two to mull it over. Maybe it was pride. Actually, there was no maybe about it, it was pride pure and simple.

She thought of Clarissa's breakdown when she found out that she wasn't responsible for Ora's heart attack. How the guilt must have haunted her for the last few days.

What she couldn't bring herself to think about were Clarissa's words about Tony. *Broke his heart. Right.* She couldn't allow herself to believe something that would only get her hurt. Again. Besides, he himself had admitted that he originally came to Shoal Creek with the hidden motive of assessing her as a threat to Clarissa. What kind of person would do that?

She reached down and scratched Dusty's left ear. "Yeah, Dusty, what kind of person would do that?" He looked up at her with his soulful brown eyes, and in that moment she knew the answer.

A person who loved his niece and wanted to protect her.

Hadn't she been just as quick to judge—more so, even—when she found out about the investigator? At least Tony had given her the benefit of the doubt long enough to apparently change his mind.

Maybe Clarissa was just trying to be nice. Tony couldn't possibly have a broken heart over her. Could he? And what could she do about it now, anyway? He'd never want to talk to her again, and she certainly didn't want to call him and have him slam the phone down in her ear. What kind of person would set herself up for that?

"Come on, Dusty, let's go inside."

They walked across the lawn and a thought began to buzz through her mind, like a fly that would not go away no matter how hard you swatted at it. *Was that what Clarissa had expected when she'd come here today?*

Likely, she'd expected Paige to slam the door in her face. If she was willing to drive this far, expecting rejection, couldn't Paige at least pick up the phone?

She wasn't sure of the answer.

chapter forty-five

Clarissa walked into the one place she never thought she'd come again. Back to Mercy Hospital. Energized by her visit to Paige, she realized this was the one thing she still needed to do before she could even think of moving on with her life. Now that Mrs. Vaerge was awake, it was time to come and apologize—take whatever the woman might throw at her, because they both knew that Clarissa deserved it.

She didn't bother with the fake ID badge this morning. She would just walk in during visiting hours like she belonged there. She wouldn't stay long.

A glance at her watch told her visitation would start in a couple of minutes. She got into the elevator, her heart pounding in an entirely new way. What would she say to this woman? "I'm sorry we gave you the wrong thing, but I sure am glad you didn't take any, so your heart attack is not my fault"? Come to think of it, if she didn't take any, why did Clarissa need to talk to her at all?

She didn't know the answer to that; she only knew that she *needed* to. And after the last few months of turmoil and disquiet, she was ready to do whatever it took to start over. To become someone new. Someone more like the person she knew her grandmother would've wanted her to be.

Clarissa got off the elevator just in time to see the nurse open the door from the unit to the visiting area. "Okay, everyone. Time for a quick visit."

Clarissa filed in behind a man about her own age and went straight to Mrs. Vaerge's bed, thankful that no one had questioned her right to be there. Mrs. Vaerge was lying back against the pillows, holding her forehead with her right hand as if she had a headache. She let the hand drop as soon as she saw Clarissa. "Hello there, young lady. Didn't expect to see you here."

Clarissa walked inside the divided area, but just barely. She wanted to make a quick escape. "I don't suppose you did. I didn't expect to see myself here."

The older woman nodded to a chair beside the bed. "Take a seat."

"Uh, no thanks. I don't want to keep you long. I just wanted to come by and say how sorry I am that all this happened."

"I had a heart attack. End of story. Wadn't your fault, no reason for you to be sorry about it."

"Maybe it wasn't my fault, but it easily could have been. If you hadn't had a heart attack last week, you likely would have had one in the next few weeks. Because of the mistake that I let happen. And it wasn't just a mistake. It was something I was doing that was plain old wrong and I knew it."

"You're a lucky young lady, then. You made a mistake, found out about it, and no harm came of it. Now you got a chance to do it over." She rubbed her hand across her forehead again and took a deep breath. "Can I ask you one thing?"

"Sure."

"Will you tell Paige something for me?"

"I'd be happy to, but wouldn't you rather tell her yourself? I'm sure she'll be in to see you in the next day or two."

"This is something for both of you, and it's best shared together."

The woman had offered forgiveness. Who was Clarissa to argue the little points? "What shall I tell her?"

"Romans thirteen, twelve."

"Excuse me?"

"Romans thirteen, twelve. You ask Paige, she'll explain it to you."

"Okay." Clarissa looked over her shoulder at the stack of monitors that lined the nurses' station. "Well, I better go."

"On your way out, would you ask the nurse to come in here?"

"Sure." Clarissa walked out of the small enclosure and across to the desk. "Excuse me, Mrs. Vaerge asked for a nurse."

A pretty redhead looked up from the chart she was writing in. "Okay, I'll be right there."

Clarissa walked out of the unit, hoping that maybe tonight she could get a good night's sleep— for the first time in a long time.

She entered the elevator with a group of three medical interns. As they moved downward, a sense of relief washed over her with each floor they descended. The interns talked quietly about potential nephritis in a patient they were following, when suddenly all three of their pagers buzzed simultaneously.

Clarissa had worked around the hospital enough to know a facility-wide page when she heard one. There was a code blue somewhere.

The only female in the group, a petite blonde, looked down at the readout. "I guess we're going back up. CCU, bed 10."

Clarissa's heart fell faster than the elevator. CCU bed 10 was Ora Vaerge.

chapter **forty-six**

Paige was watering her mother's roses when she saw the white truck pull into her driveway. Dusty stirred beside her, swiveled around, and was quickly on his feet and running toward the house, barking full volume. Paige ran after him. "Dusty. Dusty." She turned off the water then went after the dog, who now stood a couple of feet in front of Lee Richardson and another man that Paige vaguely recognized. "Dusty, down boy." She grabbed the dog's collar and he immediately lay down on the grass, but a low growling sound still came from his throat.

"You look like you're busy." The man smiled pleasantly.

"No rain. The flowers need water."

He extended his hand, "I'm Milton Parrish, we met a while back."

The man who owned the small chain of boutique pharmacies that Clarissa was hoping to open. "Yes, I remember."

"I understand Miss Richardson came to see you, and I wanted to speak with you about that job offer."

"Okay."

"I wanted to be certain that we're clear on the details. Lee has agreed to sell me his interest in the store, so I will become full owner, and you would be manager. As such, your salary will be slightly increased, and you'll be paid back wages for the time lost due to this unfortunate incident."

"But I don't want—"

"Not negotiable. The fact is, you were an employee in a store I owned at least a partial share in, and I will set things right—at least, insofar as I am able."

Lee Richardson looked at her evenly, but she could see the twinkle in his eyes. Every bit as stubborn as she, he would consider this the victory that had eluded him with his previous visit.

Paige crossed her arms and looked him full in the face. "I'd want to keep Dawn on as tech."

He smiled outright. "Not a problem."

"Oh, and by the way," Milton Parrish said, "we'll be changing the name of the store. Since Mr. Richardson is selling his share, and I've already got a line of Parrish Apothecaries, if you'd like to suggest a new name, we could definitely discuss it."

"All right, I'll give that some thought."

"So, does that mean you've made your decision?"

Paige extended her hand. "Mr. Parrish, you've got yourself a new manager."

"Glad to hear it." Lee Richardson nodded. "Let me know if there is anything I can do to help you."

Paige smiled at him. "I think I'm going to be just fine."

Just moments after Milton Parrish and Lee Richardson had gone, Clarissa's car pulled into the driveway. Paige waved from the backyard and walked forward, surprised by yet another visit from Clarissa. What would she have to say this time?

Clarissa got out of her car, her hair burnished by the setting sun. She walked around the car, then leaned back against it, as if she needed the support.

Paige hurried forward. "Clarissa, are you all right?"

Clarissa shook her head, letting her hair fall across her down-turned face. "She's gone."

"Who's gone?"

Clarissa looked up, her eyes full of tears. "Mrs. Vaerge."

"Gone where?" Paige did not think she wanted to know the answer.

"I went to see her. To tell her how sorry I was about the mix-up, even if she didn't . . ." Clarissa looked away and shook her head. "She was so gracious about it. So understanding."

"Where's she gone?"

"She kept rubbing her forehead, and as I was leaving, she asked me to send the nurse in. They called a code blue while I was still on the elevator." In the fading light of the day, the final rays of the sun bounced off the tears on Clarissa's cheeks. "They tried everything, they couldn't bring her back."

The strength left Paige's legs and she felt the sharp sting as her knees hit the asphalt of the driveway. "No. No. She was getting better. We talked yesterday. Maybe you've got the wrong person."

"Paige, I was there. I stood by her bed just moments before." Clarissa reached down and pulled Paige to her feet. "You need to go sit."

Paige nodded weakly. "Do you want to come inside?"

The expression on Clarissa's face said that she very much did not want to, but she answered, "Just for a minute."

Paige held the door open and Clarissa entered,

eyes flickering over the simple furniture, the modest decorations. They lingered on a photo of Paige's parents. Clarissa closed her eyes for a moment and then took a seat. "She had a message she wanted me to give you."

"A message?"

"Actually, she said it was for both of us. 'Romans thirteen, twelve.' That's a Bible verse, right? She said you'd know what it meant."

"I do," Paige said. "She liked to give me Bible verses she thought could help me." She could barely get the sentence out without choking up a bit. How was it that words were still coming from her mouth? Her whole being wanted to shut down, to embrace the numbness that followed Clarissa's announcement. She stumbled down the hall and somehow made it to her room. She walked over to the nightstand and picked up the worn burgundy leather Bible that sat there, unable to believe she was about to read Ora's final verse of wisdom. She walked back to the living room. "Romans thirteen, verse twelve?"

"Yes, that's what she said."

Paige's hands shook with grief as she turned the last page. "Here it is. 'The night is nearly over; the day is almost here. So let us put aside the deeds of darkness and put on the armor of light.' "

Paige's eyes teared instantly. How could day be nearly here with Ora gone? But the woman was right; Paige felt it. If losing her job had been the blackest night, then these last few days were certainly the coming of dawn. Paige shook her head to herself, amazed that Ora was still speaking to her. Then she heard a surprising noise and looked up.

Across from her, Clarissa was crying, as well. Slow, round drops pooling in her eyes. "Someone new," Paige heard Clarissa say to herself. Clarissa looked at Paige. "It's about starting over and fresh chances, isn't it?"

Paige nodded.

Clarissa stood, embarrassment evident on her face. She quickly headed for the door, but before stepping outside turned to Paige. "I've got to get back. But when you say your prayers tonight, will you tell God I could use a little help?"

"Why don't you ask Him yourself?"

Clarissa nodded, thinking it over. "I just might do that."

Paige spent the next few hours buried in regret, thinking about all the things she wished she could go back and change. Things she could have done differently.

Then she thought of Ora and her verse. Maybe it was time to stop focusing on regrets. It was time to think about the things she still could change—or at least the things she could at least try to set right.

She picked up the phone. Her fingers were shaking by the time she'd punched the last number, but she refused to give in and hang up. "It's me. I, uh, called to say I'm sorry."

For a moment she heard only silence on the other line. And then simply his voice.

"What for?"

"Being too fast to condemn. Clarissa told me the truth, the same truth you tried to tell me, and I wouldn't listen. I'm sorry."

This time the silence went for so long that Paige began to wonder if he'd hung up on her. When Tony finally spoke, his voice had a raw edge to it. "You want to prove that by having dinner Saturday night?"

"I. . . I . . . so much has happened."

"I know. We'll take it slow and get our footing back."

"Why would you even want to do that?"

"That day I first met you, I spent half the night afterward walking through waist-high weeds looking for wildflowers—all the while praying I wouldn't step on a cottonmouth or a copperhead. I knew then you were special. Nothing that's happened since then has changed my mind."

"You? You're the one who brought those flowers?"

"Guilty."

She couldn't believe it. Everyone had been so certain they were from Cory that Paige had come to believe it herself. Tony had been the one all along. "Why didn't you ever tell me?"

"I thought a little mystery was more romantic."

What could she say to that?

"Well, okay then. Saturday sounds good." She realized then just how much she meant it.

"I was hoping you'd say that."

Maybe Ora was right. Maybe the night was nearly over.

chapter **forty-seven**

Two Months Later

"I wish Dawn could be here for this. Nobody grills baby back ribs like your father," Paige's mother said, and Paige watched as she took a small bite. For her second day home, her mom was doing wonderfully. She was still so thin, so frail. But healthy—for now, at least. And today Paige would finally get to take her parents to see her pride and joy. Her mom looked across the picnic table as Paige's father polished off another rib. "Maybe you should save her some."

He grinned a messy smile. "There's plenty. From the look on her face when she left a while ago, she wished she was staying, too. I hope her daddy's not too hard on her—maybe I should go over and talk to him."

Paige nudged her father with her elbow. "What would you say?"

"You know, don't be too hard on your girl, she's

learned her lesson the hard way. Now's a good time to lighten up." He reached down to pet Dusty. "What are you begging about? You know we never feed you from the table."

Tony choked and coughed. "Oops. Sorry, sir, guess that's my fault."

Paige's father looked over at him. "Say what?"

"Well, the young man has such large brown eyes, and when he looks at me, I just can't take it. I'd give him the steak off my plate if he looked at me long enough."

"Well then, I just got one thing to say to you. You're toast."

Tony smiled at him. "Toast?"

"Cooked. Burnt, if you want to know the whole truth. If Dusty's theatrics make you cave so quick . . . Paige has always been able to melt me with her big ol' blue eyes—she had me wearing a tiara and fake jewels when she was little, sitting through jazz concerts when she got older."

Tony clasped her hand under the table. "There's a problem I think I'd like to spend the next sixty years figuring out."

Paige squeezed his hand. "Only sixty?"

"Yeah, I figure by the time I'm ninety, you'll be getting old. I'll be looking for someone younger then."

Paige swatted at him with her free hand. "Thanks a lot."

"Yep, you're burnt toast all right."

• • •

Paige felt her heart would surely burst as she finally led her parents through the lobby to the door of the pharmacy. "What do you think so far?"

Her mother's smile was still weak, but it lit the room. "It's everything I imagined it to be." She leaned on her husband's arm for support as she looked up at the sign. "You couldn't have chosen a more perfect name, could you?"

Since it was closed on Sundays, Paige had to unlock the door and hold it open. "Welcome to Daybreak Apothecary. Please, come in, look around, make yourself at home."

"Oh, Norman, look at this." Her mother's voice floated across the store.

Paige went back to start a pot of coffee. Today, she would share it with her parents and Tony and drink it in Ora's honor.

"Oh, honey, this is just beautiful." Her mother came to sit in the waiting area. "It's exactly what I always dreamed of for you."

"It's more than I ever dreamed for myself." Paige thought about the truth in that statement. This might have been a fantasy, but she had never allowed herself to dream beyond the HMO job in Atlanta.

It occurred to her then that it had taken every single one of the bad things that had happened to cause her to land here, exactly where she wanted to be, doing exactly what she wanted to do. There was so much truth in what Ora had said. At the time that seems darkest, when the city is surrounded and all apparently lost, the only thing to do is stand your ground and have faith for the break of day.

The next morning, Paige left a bit before everyone else to make a quick detour. She'd made this trip at least once a week and walked to Ora's grave under a beautiful spreading elm. Like each previous time, she stood and marveled once again at the inscription Ora had requested on her tombstone. *Who knows but that you have come here for such a time as this? Esther 4:14.*

"Ora, I still don't know what you had in mind when you selected that verse, but I believe God sent you to me for just this time." She looked at the sky. "Thank You. Thank You for sharing her with me."

The sun broke over the horizon as Paige reached her car and drove away.

acknowledgments

Father in heaven—thank You for once again blessing me with this dream.

Lee, Melanie and Caroline—this was a long and bumpy ride. Thanks for buckling up and hanging on with me. I love you all soooo much!

Mom—you're the best book promoter, and all-around cheerleader, I've ever seen.

Lori Baur—once again, you amaze me with your marketing savvy.

Brother Bill and Barbara Betts—Doris Woodward's struggles are closely based on Brother Bill's own journey and Barbara's amazing journaling and steadfastness through it all.

Dave Long and the Bethany editing team—thanks for the mountains of effort you put into this book.

It's been over ten years since I last worked in a pharmacy, so I was constantly badgering my pharmacist friends for info: Leslie Litton, Jaci Sharitz, Kristi Harb. Also Kim Tucker, tech and photographer extraordinaire. Special thanks to Leslie for forwarding some questions to Rick Karsten, senior agent. Rick, thanks for your great and patient answers.

Michael Berrier and Shawn Grady—thanks for spending the last year and half helping me work through this book.

The Winklings—John Olson, Jenn Doucette, James Rubart, and Katie Vorreiter, for your unwavering support.

Last but not least—special thanks to Dusty Cushman, for "agreeing" to make a cameo appearance in this book, bad leg and all.

questions for conversation

1. Are there times when it is appropriate, correct even, to do the "wrong thing for the right reason"? Do you think Paige's actions ever fell into this category?

2. Do you think that lawsuits in our current medical system encourage cover-ups of mistakes? Should Paige have told Lee about her past when he offered to hire her?

3. Paige finally acknowledged that she carried "3 percent" of the blame. Do you think she carried more or less? Have you ever carried more than your share of blame for something? How did you deal with it?

4. How is family important in the novel? How has family helped or hindered your own life and faith choices?

5. Clarissa has a noble goal and she pursues it regardless of who is hurt in the process. Paige also has a noble goal, yet goes after it in a much gentler way. Do you think the difference is upbringing, personality, or spiritual beliefs?

6. In times of crisis, has a specific Bible verse or other wisdom ever been of comfort to you? How did you discover it and what did it come to mean to you?

7. Have you ever prayed, claimed, believed, yet did not receive what you asked for? Did it challenge or deepen your faith? Have you ever prayed, claimed, believed and received? How did it affect your faith?

8. During a dark moment in your life, what did you do or how did you manage to make it to your "daybreak"?

9. Have you lived or worked with a person like Clarissa's grandfather who pushes, sometimes too hard, for results? Did this motivate you? Frustrate you?